STAR TREK
LOG FOUR

Alan Dean Foster

Based on the Popular Animated Series Created by
Gene Roddenberry

BALLANTINE BOOKS • NEW YORK

For Joann ... of course

SBN 345-24435-4-125

First Printing: March, 1975

Cover art supplied by Filmation Associates

Printed in the United States of America

BALLANTINE BOOKS
A Division of Random House, Inc.
201 East 50th Street, New York, N.Y. 10022
Simultaneously published by
Ballantine Books, Ltd., Toronto, Canada

CONTENTS

PART I

The Terratin Incident   1

PART II

Time Trap   97

PART III

More Tribbles, More Troubles   167

STAR TREK LOG FOUR

Log of the Starship *Enterprise*

Stardates 5525.3–5526.2 Inclusive

James T. Kirk, Capt., USSC, FS, ret.

Commanding

transcribed by
Alan Dean Foster

At the Galactic Historical Archives
on S. Monicus I
stardated 6111.3

For the Curator: JLR

PART I

THE
TERRATIN INCIDENT

(Adapted from a script by Paul Schneider)

I

The view Kirk was studying at the moment differed little from the one normally projected on the main screen up on the *Enterprise*'s bridge. Except the brilliant specks immersed in the sea of shifting black were a uniform white instead of the varigated spectrum of a normal universe. True, the floating motes did vary in brightness and intensity, as did the pale swirls of chalcedony-colored nebulae that formed a backdrop for the white spheres. But it remained a universe singularly devoid of color.

Kirk made a movement with his right hand and a cascade of new stars permeated the void. Contemplating the result, he smiled.

Perhaps the theologians were right after all and there was some idle omnipotent force Out There that treated the real universe with the same studied indifference he was now lavishing on this private one. He moved his hand holding the instrument once more, and the tiny circular cosmos became a maelstrom of white particles and cream-colored cloud-shapes.

"Come on, Arex, play something for us."

Kirk recognized the voice of Sub-lieutenant M'turr and glanced up from his dreams.

M'turr stood off in the far corner of the Officers' Lounge. She and several of the other younger officers

3

had cornered Arex and were gently pleading with him.

The Edoan navigator, like most of his kind, preferred his own company to that of others. This was the outgrowth of a natural shyness and strong sense of modesty, not of any feeling of awkwardness around other beings.

Ordinarily, the crew respected Arex's desire to keep to himself. Kirk wondered what would have prompted them to intrude on the navigator in an off-duty moment of privacy. Curiosity astir, he moved closer to the group; and when one of the belligerant officers moved aside, the reason for the sudden assault on the Edoan's privacy became obvious.

Arex had his sessica with him, and the rest of the crew around him were exhorting him to play. They were not being especially courteous, but Kirk found it hard to be angry.

Arex usually played in the isolation of his cabin. The fact that he had brought his sessica out with him was a hint that he was half-willing to offer one of his infrequent concerts. His sense of humility, however, required that he be suitably harangued until he couldn't escape without playing.

Arex owned several of the slim, flutelike instruments, keeping each one in its own special case. Certain sessicas were used for different songs, others only on special occasions or days of the week.

Sipping his coffee, Kirk studied the one the Edoan was half-consciously fingering now. It was made of some light, ivory-colored wood that shone like fine Meerschaum. Delicately inscribed designs flowed like crevices in the bark of a tree along the instrument's sides and baffles—Edoan trees and mammals and flowers—the work of some master craftsman.

"Do play us something," Ensign Yang implored.

"Anything at all—even improvisation," another urged.

"Really, my friends, I. . . ," Arex started to protest, but his companions didn't give him time to finish.

"We've got you trapped, Lieutenant," an ensign

wearing the insignia of the Quartermaster Department insisted with mock warning, "and we're not letting you go until we hear at least a one-movement Edoan cycle." The threat was echoed enthusiastically by the rest.

"Well . . ." Arex spotted Kirk hovering in the background and appealed to him. "Captain Kirk, can you not explain to my friends that I have to be in a certain outgoing frame of mind in order to be able to play for others?"

"I would, Lieutenant," Kirk said slowly, "except I'd like to listen myself." He thought a moment, then suggested, "Why not tell them the story about the Edoan contortionist who operated on Earth for nine months as an incredibly successful pickpocket until the police discovered he had a third arm?"

Arex hesitated, but once Kirk had mentioned the subject, there was no way the others were going to let the navigator go without hearing the story. So he told it, letting the absurd, amusing tale unravel in his lilting, sing-song tones. Then he seemed as embarrassed as pleased by the resultant laughter.

His nervousness abated—besides, he had run out of excuses—he shifted the sessica in his hands and moistened the curved mouthpiece. Residual chuckles faded into respectful silence, and a respectful hush absorbed the assembly. The Edoan blew a couple of experimental notes, adjusted several openings in the body of the instrument, then paused. He appeared to be looking at something in the distance. Even his voice changed, growing slightly rougher, charged with something out of his past.

"This song," he told them, "is in the form of an ode, in tripartite mode, and is called 'The Farmer and the Road.' "

A recording enthusiast in the group, who seemed to know several Edoan folk ballads, murmured appreciatively.

Arex set the mouthpiece firmly to lips and his boney, rather homely face assumed an expression at once sad and noble. He played.

Despite the inescapable alienness of the song, there was no atonality or sharpness about it. What stood out immediately was an ineffable sense of longing coupled with some mild, admonishing irony. The sessica produced long, deep tones of winsome mournfulness, rather like those of an oboe, but having much greater range in the upper registers.

Arex played easily, almost indifferently. At times he seemed to be falling asleep, then he would suddenly waken in a burst of rapid, calling notes. The delicate fingers shifted in triple patterns that grew ever more complex as he piled variation on variation on top of the basic melodic line.

Like the others, Kirk stood entranced and just listened.

Arex played for many minutes. When the last bit of honeyed sound slipped from the multiple mouths of the sessica, no one broke the mood with rude applause. But there were satisfied smiles all around.

"You liked it, then?" the Edoan asked hesitantly, when no one spoke. Ann Sepopoa of Engineering nodded softly, once, for all the listeners and asked, "More?" Arex made a gesture of agreement, obviously pleased. Another moment of thought, then: " 'The Song of the Orchard-Master and the Twelve Polor Trees,' to be sung to children as they rest on their knees, provided they each see fit to ask, please?"

Supple fingers commenced rapid tattoo on the wood and Arex's head began to weave from side to side on his thin neck. The new tune was the emotional opposite of the one that had gone before. Lively, catching, expressing an interspecies joy which soon had the little group clapping in time, awkwardly at first but with increasing confidence in the peculiar skipping rhythm.

Kirk put cup to lips and became aware that he had ignored his coffee completely during the previous playing. It was cold now. Well, no problem. Coffee was an especially efficient recycler. He moved off and poured it into the proper disposal, drew a fresh cup nearby. Adding more cream and sugar, he stirred idly, listening to the music.

"Plays grandly, doesn't he, sir?" Kirk looked around. "Hello, Scotty. Yes."

"Interestin' fellow, our Arex," Scott went on. "I'd like to know more about him, Cap'n, but . . . well, you know. It's not that he's standoffish, but he dinna have the sort of personality that encourages intimate questions."

"You know how shy the Edoans are, Scotty."

"Aye, Cap'n." He nodded in the direction of the concert. "It's just that to me, Arex seems more so than most. I'll give him this, though—passive he may be, but he's the best damn navigator in the fleet."

"Not everyone's naturally as nos . . . curious as you, Scotty."

They moved to a table. Scott drew a drink of his own, Darjeeling tea, with a touch of nutmeg. He also picked up a hot muffin with loganberry jam before sitting down next to Kirk.

"You wouldn't be implyin' that Arex is normal and that I'm hyper, Cap'n?"

"We all know how ridiculous an assumption that would be, Mr. Scott."

"Aye," Scott nodded vigorously, "and if sometimes I do seem to. . . ." He noticed Kirk's slight smile, responded with one of his own. "All right, so I'm not as restrained as Arex but then, who is, Cap'n? Except Spock, of course."

Kirk nodded agreement, but found himself drifting away from the conversation. Back to the music. The wild piping had turned positively rambunctious. He considered the generally held opinions the crew had regarding Arex. Shy. Introverted. Quiet. Restrained and relaxed and inoffensive. Scott and the rest of them would have been interested to know that Arex had not won his commission as Lieutenant by passing a number of exams, but in the field—during a skirmish with the ever-present Klingons testing the Federation borders.

When all the officers aboard a small Federation cruiser were killed, Ensign Arex took command. Retreat, concealment, and then a re-engagement with the much larger, far more powerful Klingon ship. The Klingon ship was damaged and taken as a prize—charged with violating neutral space.

Arex was entitled to wear three separate decorations for bravery, under his Starfleet citation for conspicuous valor. Kirk had seen the medals once. Arex kept them in a plain bag at the bottom of his personal-effects drawer in his cabin. He kept them at all only because he was required to wear such things to formal Starfleet functions, events that he shunned with dedication. Had Kirk told anyone else on board about the medals, the navigator would have been embarrassed beyond recovery.

So though Kirk thought it was unnecessary modesty on Arex's part, he kept the secret and told no one, not even Scott.

Everyone had to admit that it was this unassuming posture which enabled the Edoans to coexist alongside belligerent races like the Klingons and Romulans and Kzinti while remaining in loose alliance with the Federation. The isolation of their home world also helped. Edos was located in the Triangulum Cluster at the very edge of the spiral arm and was a jumping-off point for scientific expeditions studying the great energy barrier at the galaxy's rim. The planet was not in the path of expansion of any of the would-be galactic empires.

A very long-lived people, the Edoans were able to adopt a relaxed outlook on life. Their civilization revolved around home and family rather than around intersystem politics. Natural neutrals, their loose alliance with the Federation was a matter of convenience only.

One of Kirk's fondest wishes was some day to meet Arex's parents. He always wondered if the remarkable things rumored about them were true. . . .

A harsh buzz, doubly so in contrast to the sweetness

of the sessica's song, broke his thoughts. One of the lounge speakers blared.

"Commander Scott, please contact Engineering. Commander Scott, please contact Engineering."

"Now what?" the chief engineer rumbled. He took a quick bite out of the half-devoured muffin, washed it down with a hurried draught of tea. A quick touch of a button in the table and a small intraship communicator appeared in front of him. He pressed for Engineering, was rewarded with picture and sound.

"What is it, Gabler?"

The voice of the second engineer reported back from distant regions of the ship.

"Commander? It's those extra radiation shields again. They're still not responding properly to external adjustment."

"Are they goin' over into the danger zone?" Scott asked.

"No, sir, but there's some peculiar fluctuations I don't recognize. They may be harmless enough, but I wanted to know if you want us to try and set something else up to compensate."

Scott took a deep breath.

"All right, Mr. Gabler. You did the right thing in tellin' me. I'm comin' down." He flipped off the communicator, and the little screen submerged once more.

"Excuse me, Cap'n, but we've been takin' all kinds of strange stuff from outside lately, and some of it's gettin' through the ship's shields. I've had secondary shields rigged to protect the anti-matter nacelle, just in case, but they seem to be givin' us trouble, too."

"Sensible," Kirk concurred. "In the region of particulate debris from an unmeasured nova you can't tell what sort of radiations you're likely to run through. Better not take any chances with engine shielding."

"Aye, Cap'n." Scott downed the rest of the muffin in one gulp, following it with a sip of tea. He dumped cup and plate into the table disposal.

"Besides," he muttered around the mouthful, "we're gettin' close in now."

"All right, Scotty." Kirk rose. "I'm going, too." He glanced back over a shoulder. "Anyway the concert seems to be coming to a close. I recognize that crescendo. Arex is winding himself up for a finish." The two men started for the elevators together—Kirk to go to the bridge, Scott back to Engineering.

"It's been a fairly standard scientific run so far," he continued. "I don't expect we'll run into any difficulties, Scotty."

The chief engineer looked hopeful. "And so far I tend to agree with you, Cap'n, except I seem to have heard that sentiment expressed on too many occasions before. . . ."

The door to the bridge slid open, and Kirk stepped into a realm of constant but controlled activity. As long as he had been Captain of the *Enterprise,* as long as he would be, he would never fail to feel that slight tingle of excitement as he stepped into the control center of the great starship—into the control center of one of the most elaborate and powerful constructs ever built—and realized once more that its simplest movements had to be duly authorized by him, by James T. Kirk.

Little Jimmy Kirk, whose secondary-school physics instructor had assured him he would never get past second year University, let alone into Starfleet Academy. He smiled and wondered, as he took his seat in the command chair, what had ever happened to that counselor.

If the bureaucracy ran true to form, he reflected, the man was now probably a top economic advisor in the High Counsel. Kirk's musings took on more immediacy as he shifted thoughts to consider the brief discussion with engineer Scott.

He heard a brief hum behind him, and seconds later Arex strolled past to take up his position at the navigation console—minus sessica. The bridge of the *Enterprise* was now at full strength. Overstrength, he reflected, when Dr. McCoy suddenly appeared beside him. The good doctor held a portable life-systems pickup aimed at him.

"I wish you wouldn't stick that thing in my face all the time, Bones." McCoy assumed a put-upon expression.

"Just the usual health checks, Jim. Considering our position, I think it's a good idea. Why does this bother you? We're taking more radiation from outside than the 'Lizer puts out."

"I know that, Bones, but the damn thing still makes me nervous."

McCoy chuckled, carefully passing the detector over Kirk's form.

"Why Jim, you sound like the natives who refuse to have their pictures taken because they think the camera's going to capture their souls."

"Don't lecture me when I'm being obtusely dogmatic, Bones." Kirk managed a grin. "I'm really worrying about the chat I just had with Scotty. We *have* been picking up some heavy, unusual radiation recently and he's concerned about its affecting the engines in some impossibly unpredictable way."

McCoy nodded knowingly. "That's just like Scotty, Jim. He worries twice as much when there's no evidence for it. A good, solid crisis hardly bothers him at all, because he knows what the problem is. It's the nonexistent difficulties that he *really* agonizes over!" He sighed.

"I wonder what his wife must go through when he's home. I can picture it, I can picture it. Can't you see him rolling over in his sleep and muttering something like, 'Darlin', your drive components need an overhaul and lube in the bearings.'" Kirk smiled in spite of himself, looked over to where Spock stood at his science station.

"Speaking of radiations again, Mr. Spock, let's take a look at our immediate environment."

"Very well, Captain." Spock touched a switch. The main viewscreen immediately came to life. Murmurs of appreciation were heard from those on the bridge. The Arachnae nebula had been painted by one cataclysmic, searing stroke from a pallette filled with ruptured atoms and annihilated energy. A star had gone supernova and become a glistening memory. In so dying it had raised in its place one of those strange nebulae that constitute the most spectacular headstones in the universe.

A sprawling, fiery mass of radiant gases and particles streaked across the screen—millions of kilometers of color, mostly electric white, tinged throughout with iridescent shades of crimson, azure and purple. The arms of fire were vaguely spiderish in shape and design, hence the name.

Kirk took time to study the fluorescent panorama, overwhelmed for the thousandth time by the infinite beauty and endless spool of glory the universe unwound. Returning to prosaics, he thumbed the recorder switch set into an arm of the command chair.

And spoke easily. "Captain's Log, Star Date 5525.3. We are approaching the remains of the supernova Arachnae." He paused a moment, studying the scene ahead, then continued: "Initial close-in visual observation correlates with advance telescopic probe-pictures.

"We are moving deeper into the nebular region at standard observation speed. Location survey will commence, as requested, with extensive measurements of expansion rate and radiation levels." Another pause, then: "Certain new types of radiation have already been detected. At present they exist in minute amounts and constitute no danger to either ship or mission. Engineer Scott is taking precautions."

Kirk clicked off the log recorder. That was that. A few days traveling through the region under study with the ship's automatic and manual monitoring systems operating at full capacity, and then they would be on to the next scientific station. Everything pointed to an uneventful yet interesting cruise.

No wonder Scotty was nervous.

"Mr. Spock," he said casually, "what do you think of Mr. Scott's unusual radiations?"

"They have been measured and recorded, and the results are now being analyzed by the computer, Captain. Some of the shorter wavelengths are indeed peculiar. But we have been receiving them now for several hours and have no hint of any debilitating effects. I cannot yet view them as a threat—Mr. Scott's precautionary actions notwithstanding."

"Have we any indication that this radiation might increase as we move deeper into the nebula?"

Spock, having turned back to the computer readout at his console, spoke while studying it. "On the contrary, Captain, there are signs that certain wavelengths are peaking now and, if anything, they should decrease in strength. Arachnae is entering a cycle of very strong emissions, but we should be long gone before any strong bursts reach this area." He hesitated.

"There *are* occasional brief bursts of a wave-form that does exhibit extraordinary characteristics. Extraordinary because they appear to be totally out of synchronization with the normal pulsations of the nebular center. These do seem to be growing stronger. But they are still too faint and of too brief duration for intensive analysis."

"Keep on it, then, Mr. Spock. That's the most interesting discovery we've made so far. Any chance the source might be other than natural?"

"Again, Captain, it is too early to form any definite conclusions. But I am working on it."

Kirk nudged another switch. "Stewart?"

"Here, Captain," came the voice of the head of the *Enterprise*'s Astronomical Mapping Section.

"What have we got on the rate of expansion?"

"Preliminary reports only," the voice replied evenly. "We're just now starting to receive information in bulk. Thus far the rate appears consistent with what we know of other nova and supernova remnants, though it seems to be high. A good deal higher than the Crab Nebula, for example. Too early to say if it's anything remarkable."

"Very good, Mr. Stewart. Let me know if anything unusual crops up."

"Aye, Captain."

Kirk switched off, considered possible details as yet unfinished and turned back towards Uhura. "Lieutenant, inform Star Base twenty-three that we are now officially on station and commencing reconnaissance."

"Yes, sir." She turned full attention to her console, edged a little to one side and gave McCoy an irritated look. "Please, Doctor, can't you keep that thing out of my face while I'm working?"

"It's the only way I can effectively monitor the condition of your exquisite eyes, Lieutenant," McCoy replied, juggling the medical recorder and trying to keep it in line with the communications officer's face. She continued to move around at the console, but no more objections were offered—for all of two minutes.

"As you and others have repeatedly told me, Doctor, they're in perfect condition. Now, if you'll let me complete this call, you can then point that thing at me all you want."

McCoy moved away, shaking his head with an expression of exaggerated disgust. "I wear myself out trying to make sure everyone on this ship stays in perfect health and what are my rewards? Indifference, obstruction, lack of cooperation . . ."

"It is not that, Doctor," Spock suggested helpfully, "but rather that the desire to insure our health sometimes appears to be overridden by an exaggerated sense of what I would call the mothering instinct."

McCoy stopped short, looked up quickly from the recorder's readouts.

"Mother instinct?"

"Your constant solicitude sometimes laps over into an empathic condition of such a degree that it can only be properly defined as such," the first officer continued blandly. "If you will objectively analyze some of your actions, you will clearly see that. . . ."

"Now just a minute. Just a doggone minute," McCoy began hotly. "If anyone's going to do any analyzing of reactions here, it's. . . ."

Uhura broke in, "Excuse me a minute, Doctor." All three officers turned to face her. "Captain, I'm getting some strange interference on the subspace radio, everything in the upper registers."

"Any trouble in getting through to Starbase?"

She shook her head, a puzzled expression on her face. "No, Captain. I'm sure they got the message, albeit a little fuzzily. But this interference is . . . patterned. If it's a signal, I don't recognize it. It doesn't conform to any *known* pattern, though, distress or otherwise."

"Can you pinpoint the source."

"Just another moment, I think. . . ."

There was a long pause while the communications officer worked busily at her console. Occasionally she would trade questions and answers with Sulu or Arex.

"There's a record of a star, with a single planet, in the region the interference appears to be coming from, Captain. Drone records on the system are slight or nonexistent, but . . ." She looked thoroughly confused.

"There's no mention of the area producing any kind of radio emissions. Nothing beyond the normal electromagnetic discharge of the star itself, and it shouldn't produce anything up in these wavelengths. Nothing about them in either the drone records or," she glanced away for a moment to scan another readout, "or in standard radio-telescope surveys of that area."

"Step up amplification and put it on the speakers," Kirk ordered. "Let's hear them. Maybe it'll strike a response in someone else."

Uhura shrugged, looked dubious, but turned back to her instruments and made the adjustments. A minute later the bridge was inundated with a sound like a million electrified shrimp all chattering at once. Normal star chatter, it seemed.

But at ordered intervals they heard a definite, harsh, though modulated screech that pierced the standard static with a regularity that fairly screamed *Intelligence!*

Uhura was right when she said it corresponded to no known broadcast signal—at least, not that of any civilization Kirk was familiar with. Nor anyone else, for that matter. While they listened and wondered, Spock worked at the computer. Great insights were not forthcoming.

"Signals appear random," he said, watching the flow of figures and words across the readout. "There are a number of possibilities. We may be receiving only disjointed parts of a more complete message and that may be why the pulsations make no sense."

"Could it be a radio mirage?" Kirk ventured. "There's certainly enough energy flowing for light-years around to transfer an awfully distant one."

"An interesting possibility that cannot be ruled out, Captain."

"Radio mirage?" McCoy looked properly blank.

"They've been known only for a century or so, Bones," Kirk explained. "They happen when a broadcasting civilization shoots signals in the direction of a highly active electromagnetic energy source, which then boosts and bounces them all over the cosmos, though usually badly distorted. Primitive radio-telescopes on Earth were picking them up for years without ever knowing what they really were.

"And the high cycle of activity Arachnae is entering would be particularly conducive to such," he finished. "It's as good a guess as to what these unknown pulses are as any."

"Correction," Spock put in laconically. "There is one identifiable word detectable in the pattern." Kirk quieted, leaned forward slightly and listened intently. After another minute of trying to sort something recognizable out of the blare of noise, he shook his head.

"I still don't recognize anything, Mr. Spock."

"That is because it is in Interset code, Captain. If you grant the fact that someone may still be using it."

"Interset," Uhura repeated. "A standard deep-space communications code—but one that has been out of use for nearly two centuries. A contradiction within a puzzle. I'm not conversant with *all* the old codes, Mr. Spock. What's the one word . . . help, hello . . . what?"

"It would seem to be in phonetic English, Captain; but the word itself has no meaning. It may be an archaic term. When decoded, the signal spells the word *T-e-r-r-a-t-i-n* . . . Terratin."

Kirk considered a moment. "Try your directional receivers, cued to the code frequency being utilized, Lieutenant. See if we can't pick up more of that message."

Uhura promptly returned to work at her instruments. But before she could make any readjustments the tiny screech which constituted the single burst of interpretable energy had faded abruptly from the speakers. Only normal star hiss was heard on the bridge. She tried the directional pickups anyway, in hopes of regaining that one elusive attempt at communication—if it was that—but with no luck.

"No use, sir. It's gone completely." More adjustments, then a long pause while she studied various readouts. "I just broadcast multiple queries in the old Interset code for further information. No response at all to our signals."

Kirk turned his attention back to the science station. "Spock, anything on that code word yet?"

"No, Captain," the first officer replied, still staring into his hooded viewer. "The computers show no ancient interpretation of the word. Nor do exhaustive scans of all variants of Interset code give any clue to what it might mean."

"Was it a random broadcast, Mr. Spock? A radio freak, perhaps?"

"No, sir. That signal was repeated at least twice, on a patently non-natural frequency . . . and possibly more often. It is difficult to be precise considering the amount of background interference."

Kirk paused thoughtfully, the other officers watching him, waiting. The only noise on the bridge now was the muted hum of instrumentation, the steady babble of interstellar static over the speakers.

"Two times . . . one too many for semantic coincidence. It has to be of human origin, then. Mr. Sulu," Kirk said crisply, swiveling back to face the helm navigation console, "lay in a course for. . . ," he hesitated until the name of the obscure star came to him, ". . . Cephenes."

"Aye, sir," Sulu acknowledged, bending over his controls.

That decision caused McCoy to lower his health scanner and walk over to stare uncertainly at Kirk.

"Jim, you don't mean you're going to abandon the survey mission to check out some coincidence of stellar electronics that might or might not be part of a two-centuries dead code? At the outside, the most it might be is the dying gasp of some forgotten deep-space drone probe. Meaningless stuff. Ships run across that kind of junk all the time."

"Maybe meaningless at the moment, Bones. But there's no record of anyone having come across any old Federation artifacts anywhere near this region. It's well away from the historical exploration routes. And I'd sure like to see any 'old dead probe' that can put out a traceable signal this far from Cephenes. Must have been *some* probe. No, it doesn't make sense. There are other possibilities, too, that we haven't fully considered."

"Such as?" McCoy challenged.

"An intelligence someplace that somehow picked up the Interset code and is trying to contact us." He gave a soft shrug. "There are a host of possibilities."

"We've no indication that the signal—if it was a signal—was even directed at us."

"True enough." The Captain nodded. "I admit it's a long shot, Bones. But if there's even a chance of it being anything more, we're bound to check it out ... even if that means deviating from our planned course. I'm rather surprised at you. Where's your spirit of adventure, Bones?"

"On top of a three-centimeter microscope slide. That's far enough off course for me, Jim."

Kirk glanced to his right. "Mr. Spock, continue intensive research on the word 'Terratin.' Check pre-Interset codes, too. There's always the chance the word may be a carry-over from an earlier, more primitive version of the code."

"I've been doing so, sir," Spock replied. "No signifi-

cant historical references have been revealed as yet. I
suspect that if any do exist they are certainly pre-Federation."

Kirk looked disappointed. McCoy merely turned
away, muttering under his breath. "Waste of time if
you ask me." Hefting the health recorder, he moved
toward the helm. "Sulu, you're next."

"I'm in perfect health, Doctor."

"That's what they all say," McCoy countered, "until
they show up in Sick Bay complaining of internal
pains, vomiting, headache and irregularity and want to
know why I didn't spot something two weeks in advance of symptoms."

"Precautionary checkups are an excellent idea, Lieutenant Sulu," came sudden advice from Spock's station.
"It is illogical to object to the doctor's informal
checks."

"Well, thank you, Spock," said McCoy, surprised
and pleased at support from a totally unexpected quarter.

"Although," the first officer continued mildly, "I see
no reason why they could not be performed with considerably less frequency than at present."

"I'll keep that in mind, Spock," McCoy said, "because you're next. . . ."

II

Actually, McCoy's concern for the mission was exaggerated. They were not too far from Cephenes, so they
could examine the source of the mysterious signal and
return to the scientific mapping of the huge nebula with
little time lost.

Cephenes' lone planet proved to be a world of constant upheaval. Considerably drier and somewhat smaller than Earth, it resembled a convulsed Mars. The atmosphere was in continual motion, as unstable and violent as the surface.

Sulu set a low orbit and the bridge complement stared at the screen as one external viewer after another provided varying closeups of the planet below. Telescopic subviews revealed shimmering flares of crimson and yellow, occasionally blending into violent orange eruptions as volcanoes belched forth the globe's insides at sporadic intervals.

"Cephenes One . . . and only," Sulu reported formally.

"Doesn't look very hospitable," McCoy observed prosaically.

"Mr. Spock, any information on conditions below?" Kirk asked.

"Our only data are from that single early drone probe to this region, Captain, and it passed through the system very fast. Clearly there was nothing to trigger its automatics for a longer stay. We have no record of anything beyond the lower life-forms existing on the surface. Nor, indeed, mention of anything beyond a few basic statistics."

On the viewscreen an enormous orange-red flare temporarily obliterated the view.

"Two items of interest, though. The atmosphere is high in rare gases, but breathable—and surface conditions are indicated as being approximately normal."

Kirk studied the screen. Another gigantic flare tinged distant clouds with hellfire. "Normal, hmmm? So either the probe's instrumentation was at fault, or else these eruptions are a fairly recent phenomenon." He looked at once satisfied and disappointed.

"That probably accounts for our strange 'signal.' Natural source after all. Volcanic eruptions can produce great bursts of short-lived electromagnetic discharge. I still think it's a mighty peculiar coincidence, but it's possible. Still, we're here. We might as well run a more thorough survey. Keep scanners on and recording, Mr. Sulu?"

"Yes, sir. Anything in particular you'd like to see on the screen?"

"There doesn't seem to be anything particular. No...," he watched the changing images of tectonic belligerence. "I see nothing we haven't observed on a half-dozen similar worlds before. We'll run an equatorial survey. If our 'signal' doesn't repeat itself—and I'm not optimistic—we'll return to our planned mission." He glanced back at McCoy.

"You were right, Bones. There's nothing to waste our time on, here."

Actually, this was not entirely so. But at that point Kirk had seen no reason to think otherwise. Had he utilized the starship's high-resolution scopes on a certain area, however, he might have seen something interesting. A particularly protected, barren-looking valley, for example, dominated by towering crags of black and dirty gray, some of which were more ragged than others. Thick streams of viscous molten rock poured down their slopes. Occasionally a crisped-over river would crack, and harsh yellow light would flood the jumbled cliffs and crevasses.

A valley of utter desolation, then, no different from dozens the *Enterprise* had already passed over ...

From an area to the north of a portion of rugged basalt, a beam of intense light suddenly leaped across the valley floor. Instead of a shard of broken, twisted stone, it struck a hemispheric, concave dish studded with curvilinear projections.

The dish was camouflaged, hidden, but the polished metal was clearly the work of something other than nature. Seconds, and then the twisted protuberances began to glow brightly. Slight motion and the dish readjusted itself. From the omphalos a powerful beam probed the ash-laden sky.

Simultaneously, the dish generated another beam, a twin of the one still locked on from across the valley. It disappeared into the distance. Kilometers away, another sky beam replied immediately. Another, and yet again as a webwork of light sprang up across the valley.

Soon the blasted landscape was a bouquet of cloud-piercing beams, all entwined in the atmosphere in a mysterious, purposeful pattern—a photonic macramé.

All the while, the lava fountains played on in more substantial counterpoint to the sudden eruption of light.

Kirk relaxed and turned, bored, from the viewscreen. He had orbited over plutonic landscapes before, over hell-worlds far more spectacular than the one below. He had toured with an Academy class through the Nix Olympica thermal power station on Mars. No, there was nothing here to hold them. The survey would take but a few minutes more.

"Let me know when we've completed initial orbit, Mr. Sulu. A single circuit should be enough."

"Aye, sir." Sulu studied instrument readouts, announced moments later: "Coming up on primary termination, sir."

Involved in winding up their scan, no one noticed the unusual frown that came slowly over Spock's face. Nor the even more unusual gesture that followed. He squinted. His attention was focused on a small readout set just above the main computer screen at the science station.

A gently weaving line there had abruptly produced a violent visual hiccup which sent the line shooting off the top of the screen. Spock jabbed a switch and the moving line froze instantly. Another dial was gently turned and the monitoring gauge ran the readout backwards.

Undeniably, something had given the scanner involved a severe jolt. A powerful jab, as if something had kicked into it from below.

He allowed the dial to snap all the way back. Once again the screen showed a pattern of standard wave disturbances, the easy flowing line. Spock touched another control and a still picture of the violent distortion appeared on the main screen. Isolated, but just possibly. . . .

"Captain, I have registered a prodigious wave-disturbance. An electronic impulse of some sort has just passed through the ship."

All hint of relaxation or lassitude gone, Kirk sat up straight in his chair. "Type and source?"

"Unidentified, unknown," the science officer replied tersely, still studying the readout. "It was a single brief burst, very sharp. If the source is still active, it's extremely faint and diffuse. Too much so to pinpoint while we continue orbit." He looked away from the viewer.

"I suggest we synchronize orbit with the surface at the impulse reception point, Captain, until the effects can be analyzed. Though there is no evidence of damage." He exchanged glances with his fellow officers.

"Bridge reports?"

Sulu made a quick check of the helm monitors. "All instruments functioning. Ship's condition is normal. All status lights green. No damage calls from any sections."

"Warning sensors stable," Uhura said, and Arex added, "External scans detect nothing abnormal, sir."

Kirk drummed fingers on the arm of his chair. It was a definitive rhythm which Sulu had been trying to identify ever since he had joined the *Enterprise*. Some day he would get it.

"You're sure it passed through the ship, Mr. Spock?"

Spock appeared mildly miffed. "Absolutely, Captain. A rapid burst of an unknown type of energy. It is the apparent generative power behind it which impels my concern."

Kirk grunted, hit a switch on the chair arm. "Bridge to Engineering." A wait, then, "Scotty, we just took an energy impulse of unknown type. How are your engines?"

"A moment, Cap'n." A longer wait while everyone on the bridge visualized Scott hurriedly checking half a hundred lights and gauges. The chief engineer's voice came over the bridge as he worked the intercom multiple.

"Davis?" he asked, talking to an unseen subordinate.

"Chief?"

"Any problems?"

"Problems, Chief? What kind of problems?"

"Thanks, Davis . . . . that's what I wanted to know." Back on the main com, now. "Purrin' like kittens, Cap'n. Why, what's going on?"

"Probably nothing, Scotty, but keep a close eye on your telltales just the same."

Scott sounded confused, but willing. "Will do, sir."

Kirk tried a final possibility. After the inanimate machinery, there was one other component that required checking.

"Bridge to Sick Bay. Bones?"

"Here, Jim."

"We've just taken an unidentified energy impulse. Any effect on the lab animals or crew?"

"No sudden sicknesses, if that's what you mean, Jim. Just a second and we'll check the lab animals. Christine?" He looked around for his assistant.

"Doctor?" She responded from her station.

"Time to check the guineas."

Leaving her station, Nurse Chapel followed McCoy into one of the interconnecting lab rooms. This particular chamber boasted a double thick door. It was designed for holding both alien and domestic life-forms, from beings the size of a horse down to new viral strains. The present population was starship standard, small, and quietly spectacular.

To doctor and nurse, however, the flashy experimental animals were everyday acquaintances. McCoy went first to the modest aquarium.

Nothing could look more ordinary. Small stones, waving water plants and even a few decorative bits of coral offered naught to tease the eye. One had to look much closer to see that the sole occupant was most definitely not ordinary.

Rather like a cross between the tropical trumpet and

angelfish of the warm Terran ocean, the single fish was beautiful enough. What turned it from beauteous to breath-taking was the extraordinary ring of rainbow light that encircled it completely from top to bottom, floating centimeters away from the body proper.

No one had yet figured out how the halo fish produced its remarkable Saturnian ring. Its brilliance shaded the phosphorescence of Terran deep-sea dwellers into dullness.

The importance of the tiny swimmer derived not from its ornamental value, however, but from its touchy disposition. At the moment it swam placidly— and healthily—through its liquid abode.

McCoy examined the fish carefully while Chapel peered into several connecting cages filled with small creatures, paying particular attention to the large specimen in the far corner. The cages themselves were worthy of note, not just for their inhabitants, but because they were constructed entirely of black materials. Had they been of a lighter color, observation of any kind would be difficult if not impossible.

The little mammals inside were nearly transparent, to a far greater extent than the albino, sometimes translucent cave dwellers of Earth. Here was a true transparency, like fine quartz.

McCoy mumbled something at Chapel, and she shook her head. He pressed the lab intercom.

"McCoy again, Jim. Nothing in the experimental animals indicates anything out of the ordinary has happened. The gossamer mice show no signs of shock, and our halo fish. . ."

"Halo fish, Bones?"

"We acquired them two visits ago at Star Base Science Center. The ones that lose all color at the least environmental shift? They're as radiant and healthy looking as ever."

"You sure, Bones? Isn't it possible that something subtle could affect them without their showing any signs?"

"Not in these two species, Jim. But wait a second

and I'll double-check." He beckoned to Chapel and indicated the aquarium. She walked over, rolling back one sleeve on her uniform.

Carefully, she slipped her hand into the water just above the slowly swimming fish. As soon as her fingers contacted the surface, the multicolored ring vanished and the zebraic array of colors on the body turned a pale white to blend in with the white sand bottom of the tank. When she pulled her arm from the water, both ring and colors returned.

"No, Jim. The animals are healthy. No sign of any disturbance."

"Good to hear. Thanks, Bones." He clicked off and turned to Spock, more relieved than he cared to show. "Your mystery wave seems harmless enough, Spock. You may as well continue your analysis while we conclude orbit. We'll hold here another few minutes.

"Mr. Arex, summarize sensor sweeps, please."

"Commencing condensation, sir. Condensation completed."

"Further detail on surface conditions?"

Arex studied his viewer, now linked to the *Enterprises*'s elaborate system of computer cells. "Sensor scans show a far more unstable surface than the old drone probe reported, Captain. Activity appears to be increasing almost exponentially. We may have arrived in time to witness a major blowup, though we do not have enough information to know for certain whether such a cataclysm is cyclic or extraordinary.

"Both eruptive and steady-flow disturbances are present. Given the current rate of tectonic activity, the emission of subterranean noxious gases will render the oxy-nitrogen atmosphere unbreathable in a few decades."

McCoy had hurried to the bridge, curious as to what had prompted Kirk's tense check of their life-systems status. Now he studied the main viewscreen and commented, "Not that it looks very inviting right now."

"What about composition, Mr. Arex?" Kirk went on. Pronounced seismic activity often brought other, more interesting things to a planetary surface than poisonous gases. Heavy metals, for example.

"Composition appears normal, Captain," the navigator replied, turning his gaze back to the viewer. "As far as evidence of ore-bearing formations is concerned, I believe. . .," his voice changed unexpectedly, "Captain . . . a light below. It appears to be shifting. I think. . ."

And then he was staggering back from his console, clutching at his narrow face. "My eyes. . . !"

The suddenness of the outburst had shocked everyone into immobility . . . doubly shocked them, coming as it had from the near-whispering Arex. Then Sulu rose to help his friend. Grabbing at the steadying support of the helmsman with one hand, Arex kept his other two over his eyes.

Meanwhile, Spock's eyes had been affected, too. The reason Sulu had been first to Arex's aid was because the science officer had been stunned by the abrupt explosion of lines on the upper screen—lines similar to the one that had so troubled him when it first passed through the ship moments ago.

Now the sensor in question was receiving that subtle, powerful impulse at a steady, unwinking rate.

"Captain," Spock said anxiously, "we are now under a non-communications beam of some potency. It's effects cannot. . ."

"Sound red alert!" Kirk ordered before the first officer could finish. He had no access to Arex's viewer, no sight of Spock's gauges. But the reaction of his navigator coupled with Spock's sudden announcement was sufficient to tell him something was definitely wrong.

"Uhura. . . !"

The lieutenant was moving too rapidly to obey. Her hand shot toward the alarm switch, stopped before she could reach it. Something froze her in her seat. Froze Kirk in the command chair. Froze Arex and Sulu standing together, Spock at his station—froze everyone on the *Enterprise.*

Simultaneously the crew, their instruments, even the walls of the ship flared with a pale white luminescence.

It was as if the ship were burning in the grasp of a cold white flame. They could hear a deep ringing sound, like the single toll of some great ancient bell.

Scott and Gabler were discussing the repair of a recalcitrant section of the ship's reclamation machinery when that awesome groan rolled through the ship. They stopped arguing—and moving.

In the main mess hall, hundreds of diners from the second shift were at mid-meal when all motion ceased and the light turned to creamy white.

It was the same from one end of the starship to the other—from Hydroponics to Astrophysics, from recreation rooms to sleeping quarters, from the salvage hold to the synaptic study center.

The *Enterprise* had been neatly pinned like a metal butterfly on a blackboard. It hung enveloped in an icy radiance produced by many beams erupting on the surface, forming an intricate webbing around the pinioned ship—a webbing woven by the multiple dish antennae that pockmarked the floor of a certain barren valley far below.

Trapped in that spectral radiance, the *Enterprise* drifted for long moments. Then the tired landscape below convulsed in a tremendous eruption. Several of the beams vanished as automatic antennae were thrown off their mounts. Others were buried by a steady avalanche of magmatic material.

With its interdependent, complex pattern broken, the rest of the beams shut down. On the *Enterprise*'s bridge the last reverberations of that thunderous peal died away. There was a brief moment of uncertainty as the ship lights flickered and finally steadied. They were somewhat dimmer than normal, but showed no sign of weakening further.

In the absence of sound there was motion, as those on the bridge began the comforting routine of checking first themselves and then their instruments for internal malfunctioning. Even Arex, still blinking away streaks from his sensitive eyes, was back at his station, hunting for the source of the surprise assault on their senses.

A good conductor keeps an eye and ear on tempo and rhythm but lets his players play. Kirk waited until his people had had a little time to sort themselves out before asking formally, "Anyone hurt here?"

A stream of murmured "No, sirs" came back to him from various seats. Uhura, Sulu, Arex, McCoy, Spock. He considered, made one concerned inquiry.

"Are you sure, Lieutenant Arex?"

The navigator looked back over his shoulder, the assurance of a dozen years in the fleet showing in every syllable. "I'm quite all right now, sir. I was only temporarily stunned, and most of that was surprise. There appear to be no lingering effects."

"All right, Lieutenant. Just the same," he continued firmly, "as soon as we revert from alert status, I want you to report to Sick Bay for an eye check-up."

"I was just about to order that myself, Jim," McCoy added. He looked over at the navigator. "You're positive there are no aftereffects, Lieutenant? No blurring of vision, strong retinal images?"

"No, sir," Arex told him. "I think—evidence supports it—that if there were any dangerous radiations in whatever hit me, the scope's sensors automatically screened them out."

"Let's hope so," the doctor muttered. Behind him, Kirk could hear Uhura talking rapidly over the intership com.

"All sections report in. Damage and casualties. All sections report in . . . damage and cas. . ."

Kirk had a sudden thought, caught Sulu's attention. "Mr. Sulu, any deviation in our orbit?"

"No, sir. Maintaining standard elliptical orbit. All instruments functioning normally." He looked back worriedly. "But we've been operating on impulse power since that whatever it was hit us."

Uhura broke in before Kirk could pursue the power situation further. "I have first damage reports coming in, Captain."

"Put them over the main speaker, Lieutenant."

"Aye, sir." In a second the bridge was filled with the

consecutive voices of various section chiefs, some confused, some slightly panicked, some admirably calm—all uniform.

"Mess section, no damage."

"Repair section intact."

"Cargo hold here, Captain, no damage observed."

And so on. Everyone had seen the white glow, recoiled under the ringing drone, been frozen in place. But there had not been any real damage. Not a broken eardrum or loosened plate seam. Odd.

Spock glanced up from his console, spoke quietly. "Captain, we are still receiving radiation from the surface, but it is greatly reduced—and altered. A most peculiar type. Our deflector shields are proving ineffective."

Kirk nodded quickly. "We just had ample demonstration of that. Let me know the second there's any increase in the intensity, Mr. Spock."

"Very well, sir." Spock returned to his instruments.

Kirk considered. After making sure to his own satisfaction that Arex was at least temporarily fit, McCoy had headed back for Sick Bay. He ought to be there any minute. Kirk pressed the intercom switch.

"Nurse Chapel here, sir," came the instant reply. "The doctor . . . he's coming in now, Captain." McCoy's deeper voice on the com, now.

"Sorry, Jim. Just finishing a quick check of my own. We've no casualties reported at all. Arex appears to have been the only one even slightly affected by the attack."

"Why 'attack,' Bones?" Kirk wondered. "We've suffered no damage and no casualties. It might have been a natural phenomenon."

"Call it my inherent pessimism, Jim. Anyhow, ineffectuality of method doesn't negate intent. Though I'll admit to the chance it was some random freak of tectonic activity. If that's what it was. I don't suppose. . ."

"As yet we've no idea what it was," Kirk told him.

"So then it wasn't completely harmless."

"Not hardly," Kirk observed. "Let me know if anyone walks in with any strange symptoms, Bones." A
light was flashing on the arm console. "Scotty wants in.
Kirk out."

"Sick Bay out."

McCoy flicked off the intercom and turned to
Chapel.

"No one seems to have been injured, Christine. Let's
hope it stays that way. Meanwhile, you can dig out the
tape file on Arex for me. Also the ophthalmological
standards and charts for adult Edoans."

"Yes, Doctor."

Engineer Scott turned and yelled instructions, liber-
ally laced with suitable comments on certain probable
ancestries, up at the four technicians who were running
on the catwalk above him. Then he turned his attention back to the intercom as a beep told him it was
clear.

"Engineerin' here, Cap'n."

"Let's have the details, Scotty. I know we're running
on impulse power. Anybody hurt?"

"No casualties, Cap'n," Scott reported, breathing
heavily. He had been doing considerable shouting and
running, often at the same time. "But trouble aplenty
with the engines. Every dilithium crystal's smashed in
the warp-drive circuitry. Damnedest thing I ever saw.
We're trying to rig a temporary bypass for them now."

"The main circuits, too?" Kirk asked incredulously.

"*What* main circuits?" Scott countered tiredly. "You
have to see it to believe it, sir." He shook his head.
"The big crystals in there have all come apart. Each of
them fractured and re-fractured and re-re-fractured
along its natural lines of cleavage until there's nothin'
left but powder. Try to imagine an elephant steppin' on
an opal, sir."

"What about spares, Mr. Scott?"

"I said *all,* sir. Even the spares. Whatever it was
took a whack at us didn't seem to much care whether
they were activated or not."

"And the other drive components?" Kirk asked, determined to know the worst.

"Nothin', sir. Only what shorted out when the activated crystals were pulverized. No problem replacin' them. Whatever hit us was damnably selective, Cap'n."

Somewhere in Scott's report, Kirk mused as he switched out, was the answer to the impulse beam they'd absorbed—and were still absorbing, according to Spock. He looked across the deck, found the first officer watching him.

"Though couched in emotional terms it would appear that Dr. McCoy's supposition may have some basis in fact," Spock ventured. "If this is truly a natural phenomenon, it has certainly chosen a sensitive portion of the ship to attack. Nor have I ever heard of dilithium crystals being affected in the way Mr. Scott described."

Kirk rose from his seat and started for the elevator. Spock followed. "We haven't *seen* it, either, Mr. Spock. But it seems that we're going to."

The chief engineer was waiting for them. They went to a small open hatch, stared into one of the dilithium holding cases for backup supplies.

"Not only is this situation different from anythin' I've ever seen, Cap'n," Scott was telling them, "but even if I had ever imagined dilithium breaking up, I wouldn't have visualized it happenin' like this."

"How so, Scotty?" Kirk asked.

"Well, sir, I would expect them all to go at once. Instead, whatever blasted us appears just to have initiated the process. The crystals are still in the act of disintegratin'. It's a steady process."

Moments later they stood before one of the operative grids. Scott made sure all activating circuits were inoperative, opened the double door and stepped back. Tiny crackling sounds, like glass popcorn, issued from within.

Staring inside, Spock and Kirk could see clearly what was left of one of the large dilithium crystals that not long ago had helped power the *Enterprise*. It had been reduced to a small pebble. And what was left was shedding tiny curlicues of itself, adding to the growing pile of dust in the grid. The curlicues were unique. Dilithium was the only mineral known subject to spiral fracture.

Kirk reached in, extracted a pinch of red-white powder. He studied the dust and tried to feel optimistic. The dust mocked his best efforts.

"This isn't going to power a toothbrush, much less the drive." He put the powder in Spock's outstretched palm and turned, heading for the engineering library. While Kirk and Scott looked on, Spock dropped the bit of dust into a depression set into one console. One switch sealed the depression; others activated the computer. Instructions were given.

"Any hope of recombining the powder into one or two usable crystals, Mr. Scott?" Kirk asked as they waited for the computer's verdict.

The chief engineer shook his head. "I know what you're thinkin', Captain, but the physicist who did that made a one in a million combination of heat and pressure work and he wasn't sure afterward exactly how he'd done it. It might take us a hundred years to grow one crystal from this powder.

"You can't play with dilithium like modeling clay. Too much of its peculiar potential is locked in subatomic structures. Even if we wanted to try it we haven't got the facilities here.

"No, Cap'n. Our only hope of gettin' out of here and back to a refuelin' station is a recirculatin' impulse from our stored emergency power cells—what's left of it. But before we can try that there are broken connections and linkages all over the place that have to be fixed."

Kirk looked thoughtful, considering their options. "Could we possibly. . . ," but he was interrupted by an anxious voice at the computer console.

"Captain, this is quite unprecedented."

For Spock to say something like that it would have

to be, Kirk mused, as he and Scott moved close to the instrumentation.

Spock had removed the sample of powdered dilithium from its holder and, following the directions of the computer, placed some of it under a electronic scope. He was peering into it now, but stepped aside so Kirk and Scott could have a look. Kirk put his eyes to the scope . . . and sacrificed a breath.

What had prompted Spock's typically understated comment was instantly apparent under the brilliantly illuminated circular field.

Dilithium was the only metallic substance whose molecules were arranged in helical instead of linear or linear-variant form. Now, even as he watched, the molecules were unwinding in various places, the chains spinning apart. In other molecules the chains were winding tighter and tighter until they broke apart, and then the fragments would begin to unwind or tighten.

In either case the resultant substance was no longer active dilithium.

This made his thin hopes of a minute ago obsolete. Even if they did manage to stumble across the near-magical process for recombining dilithium, soon there wouldn't be any honest dilithium shards left to recombine. Almost as remarkable was the fact that the breakdown was occurring without a hint of subsidiary radiation. It was a clean disintegration.

"Fracturing is spiroform," Spock went on, "as it has been theorized it would be. But it has never been observed to occur in an inorganic material like dilithium before—only in similarly built organic molecules."

Kirk leaned back from the scope, came down off his tiptoes. His mind was occupied by the impossibility just observed—otherwise he might have noticed what he had just done. He could be pardoned. It was the spiral structure that made dilithium the most rigid, stable. . . .

III

Kirk's thoughts were broken by the nearing voice of second engineer Gabler. He spoke while walking quickly toward them.

"Mr. Scott, more trouble with the circuitry clearance. It's just that. . . ."

"Blast," the chief engineer muttered. "What now?" He moved to the railing, looked down across the floor. "Now what, Mr. Gabler?"

"It's the tools, sir," Gabler yelled back up at them. "They're too big for us to handle."

Several other members of the engineering section came into view. All held up wrenches, pliers, liquid circuit welders and sliders and molly-pugs. All appeared awkwardly large in their hands.

Scott didn't know whether to be confused or furious. If this were some kind of elaborate joke on the part of his section, at a time like this. . .

"You sound like you're all of you blatherin' . . . no, wait a minute. Let's have a look." After what they'd just learned about dilithium molecules fracturing, he wasn't about to deny the possibility of anything. He moved to the nearest ladder and started down.

"That's an odd thing for Gabler to say," Kirk mused. Then he found himself frowning, staring. It seemed as if something were not quite right about Spock, all of a sudden. Nothing obtrusive—the first officer looked perfectly healthy.

Then why this sense of vague unease when he looked at him?

For his part, Spock's reaction was a dulled mirror of

Kirk's own. He was eyeing the captain, both eyebrows raised, an expression he reserved for more than idle occasions.

Kirk's frown deepened. He gestured at the computer console Spock was standing by, blinked. The light that had momentarily blinded Arex—was there some subtle variant of it at work in the ship now?

"Spock, are you slumping?"

"I've never slumped in my life, Captain," the science officer replied with considerable dignity. "But it is most peculiar. I was just about to ask you the exact same. . ."

"Security!" The violent call issued from the open intercom. "Any security, respond!"

Kirk rushed to the com., reached to turn it to broadcast and had to stand on tiptoes to do it. What was wrong with Spock, what was troubling Gabler—he was astonished at how calm he was in the face of the dawning catastrophe. Maybe it was the fact that, physically, he still *felt* fine. Or it might be shock.

"Kirk here. What's the trouble?"

His steady tone apparently reassured the voice at the other end of the line. It responded crisply, less hysterically.

"Mess Officer Briel, sir." The young officer was clearly trying to calm herself with the captain on the line.

"What's going on, Briel? Speak up—what's that noise behind you?"

"It's the second shift, sir. They're nervous and frightened and so am I. We need psycho assistance in the main dining area. At least, I think we need psycho. Maybe it's just me. Or maybe I just. . ." The voice was rising again and Kirk's tone turned hard, sharp, no-nonsense.

"Easy, Briel. I think I know what you're experiencing."

The voice was still tense, but the relief was audible.

"You do, sir? I wish you'd tell me. Tables, chairs, silverware—everything seems to have grown larger, too large to use. Women are losing their rings, hairpins . . . everything. The people here are near panic, Captain, and I don't know what to tell them. I'm the ranking officer present and I. . ."

"Do your best to quiet everyone, Sub-lieutenant. Get up on a table—if you can still reach it—and make an announcement. Tell everyone we're passing through a distorting field phenomenon. We don't know how far it'll reduce us, but we will eventually return to normal. Meantime everyone is to improvise. Tell them to use their imaginations."

"Thank you, sir," came the much-eased voice of the mess officer. "I'll do that. Frankly, sir, I was beginning to get more than a little. . ."

"Don't waste time, Briel, or you'll have your full panic. Relay the information to Lieutenant Uhura and instruct her for me to broadcast it throughout the ship. Quicker dissemination that way."

And also, he thought, the responsibility would take the sub-lieutenant's mind off her own fears.

"Aye, sir. Mess out."

Kirk clicked off, noticed Spock still staring at him.

"Well, what are you goggling at, Spock?"

"You lie with great facility, Captain."

"You have this constant aberration in which you persist in confusing diplomacy with prevarication, Spock," he shot back. "Let's get back to the bridge. Scotty will have to handle things by himself here."

Having absolutely no idea what to expect, their shock as they returned to the bridge was magnified severalfold.

At first glance it appeared that the *Enterprise* was being manned by a group of well-drilled children. All crew members were sitting on the fore edge of their seats. It was the only way they could still reach the controls. Heads swiveled as Kirk and Spock entered.

Uhura started in immediately. "Captain, reports are coming in from all over the ship. The most incredible thing is happening."

"We know," he broke in. "The whole ship and ev-erything on board has apparently expanded."

"An equally good possibility, Captain," hypothesized Spock, "is that the ship's personnel have contracted." He moved toward his library computer station and sur-veyed the abruptly oversized surroundings thoughtfully.

"And are probably continuing to shrink."

A moment of shocked silence on the bridge—some-how the idea that the *Enterprise* and its inorganic com-ponents were growing larger was merely ridiculously in-convenient, while the concept of the crew growing smaller held terrifying portents.

There was an element of grimness in Kirk's voice that hadn't been heard in some time as he turned to Sulu.

"Take us out of orbit, Mr. Sulu. Take us far out of here. Shut down all unnecessary systems . . . everything but defense and life-support. Draw on every ounce of remaining impulse power. We've got to get away from this planet."

Sulu and Arex worked furiously at the helm-naviga-tion console. Occasionally they were forced to shift awkwardly in their seats to reach a particularly distant control. There was a mild rising hum as fresh power was fed to the ship's engines, then a tense pause.

"Mr. Spock?"

"We're shifting position, Captain, but slowly."

A red light appeared on the console to the right of Sulu's hand. He eyed it, ignored it.

"Still moving, Captain," reported Spock patiently.

Gradually, painfully, the single red light by Sulu was joined by others. A brief hooting whistle sounded near Arex. He slapped a hand down on a switch and the hooting stopped. Sulu gave his companion a question-ing glance. Arex bent to his hooded viewer, studied its contents for a moment. Then he pulled away and gazed at each of the watching, expectant faces in turn.

"It's no good, Captain. The engines are completely dead."

"Confirmed, Captain," Spock added, studying

readouts. "We simply do not have enough dilithium left in the holding grids to activate the matter–anti-matter annihilation sequence. We retain enough emergency power to maintain basic life and internal ship functions, but nowhere near enough to drive the ship."

"Not even enough for a last try?" Kirk asked desperately.

"It would be foolhardy, Captain. The chances are on the order of thousands to one ... and we would surely lose life-support."

"Then that," Kirk murmured fatalistically, "is that." He glanced down toward his feet, shook his head and mumbled something Uhura strained to hear but couldn't. Then he thumbed a well-worn switch in the chair arm.

"Captain's Log, 5525.4. Our attempt to escape this world's gravity on limited power has failed after the ship's dilithium supplies have been wiped out. We are currently in a ... ," he glanced over at Arex. The navigator hid several controls.

Up to now the image on the main viewscreen had been a moving panorama of the planet's glittering surface. Now it shifted briefly to show a dull chart of the world with a blinking red dot floating nearby—the *Enterprise*. Kirk nodded and Arex banished the chart back to distant cells of memory. The roiling surface picture returned.

"... low but stable elliptical orbit. Main engines and circuitry are one hundred percent incapacitated." Again a look to the library station.

"Mr. Spock, what about that diffuse wave bombardment?"

Spock checked his viewer, barely able to reach it now. "We're still receiving a light amount, Captain, but it shows no sign of thinning further."

"Thank you, Mr. Spock." He spoke into the Log pickup again. "Unidentified radiation bombardment continues, resulting in either a contraction of our bodies or an expansion of the ship by a factor of. . . ," he glanced to Spock again and the science officer held up three fingers, ". . . by a factor of three." He switched off the recorder.

"Lieutenant Uhura, broadcast a general mayday."

"Aye, sir."

"Lieutenant Sulu, I know how precarious our reserve power situation is. But see if you can't compute something that would give us a little higher orbit without risking a fatal drain on the reserves."

"I'll try, sir."

"Arex," Kirk's voice remained brisk and businesslike, "give me a power reading on all backup cells."

As everyone on the bridge busied himself about his immediate tasks, Kirk sat back in the command chair . . . and discovered he couldn't even do that. He'd shrunk—or the ship had expanded—to the point that the chair no longer fit him easily.

He glanced over at Spock and studied the first officer in relationship to his surroundings. Assuming he was right and they were contracting, they now averaged about a meter and a third in height.

Then he stared tensely up at the main viewscreen and the glowing, angry landscape brought in close by the telephotos. Normally it would have been enough to examine the giant volcanoes, the lava lakes and strange movement in the burning, tortured crust. But now he found himself straining for sight of something more.

His first theory—that they'd been subjected to some unexpected burst of natural radiation—was being rapidly eroded. What natural effect would hit them for a microsecond with no discernible effect, come back full force, and then suddenly change to a steady low-power beaming?

But what if Bones was right and they were under attack? What kind of an enemy were they up against—and why? What could their tormentors want. There had been no attempt to contact the *Enterprise*. The only explanation that seemed logical was that the world below held a low-population race—living underground, perhaps—that was inherently inimical to all outsiders.

They are other than us, therefore they are to be destroyed was the usual rationale of such races.

Yet how could they know that the *Enterprise* contained creatures different from themselves? A problem, he reflected, that had plagued mankind throughout much of his own history. If they were under assault by an intelligent civilization, its founders must have a philosophical orientation radically different from the Federation's. Kirk watched the surface they hovered over, watched it trying to tear itself to pieces, watched and tried to visualize what kind of beings it could support.

What must they look like.

Sulu's voice roused him from contemplation. "New parameters established, sir." The helmsman sounded pleased with himself. Considering the miniscule amount of power he'd had to draw upon and the effect he'd achieved with it, he had reason to be.

"Our perigee has been raised by a significant amount."

Kirk made a positive gesture. At least they didn't have to worry about losing altitude until they crashed into the boiling crust below.

They could sit up *here* and rot.

Uhura's report was less encouraging. "No reply to our universal mayday, sir. I don't believe we have enough power left to push a signal to Star Base Twenty-three. And there's no reason to expect any other ships to be in this region."

Kirk nodded somberly. "All right. Keep trying, Lieutenant." He glanced to the library. "Spock, anything new on the wave bombardment we're taking?"

The first officer looked up and shrugged slightly. "Only that it is complex beyond anything in my scientific experience. As a weapon it would appear to be not only extraordinarily effective, but the product of a devious mass mind. And yet, there are psychological overtones that make me wonder. . . ."

"It's the physical ones I'm concerned with at the moment, Mr. Spock."

Scott's voice came over the ship com.

"Engineering to Captain Kirk."

"Kirk here," he acknowledged. "How are you doing back there, Mr. Scott?"

The chief engineer didn't try to hide the exhaustion in his voice. "We've replaced all the damaged circuitry and bypassed what we can't replace or repair."

"Will they hold up if we have to press them, Scotty?"

"Well enough, Captain. That's not the problem. We can only run so long on impulse power before the emergency cells go. Then it's restart the reaction chambers or. . . . The well will run dry soon enough, sir."

"I know, Scotty. You've done what you can. Kirk out." He considered. Somehow they had to conserve even more power. They might have to try a last breakout, Spock's warning notwithstanding. Then they would need every erg the reserve cells could muster.

"Uhura, reduce mayday signal repetition. One broadcast per ten-minute cycle."

"Reduce range, too, Captain?"

"No." Frequency would have to do. "Maximum signal strength for the isolated broadcasts . . . otherwise they'll be worse than useless."

"Yes, sir."

"Mr. Arex, cut down on all sensor sweeps of the planet."

"Visual sweeps are already impossible, Captain," the navigator told him. He gestured at his finder—*up* at his finder. "My eyes no longer properly fit the optical pickups."

"And I can't reach the dial I turned five minutes ago," added Uhura, a rising note of alarm in her voice. She was reaching for the control in question, stretching on tiptoe and still falling short.

Damnation! If they didn't shrink much more they could cope. But if they continued to lose height? He had had no compunctions about having the deflector shields turned off—they had proven useless anyway. If they couldn't break out of orbit and remained under the influence of the mysterious radiation, would they contract to the point where they could no longer operate the controls?

He was hunting for a miracle in a fog. What do you do in a fog first? Stay in one place, he reminded himself, and establish some reference points.

He hit the intercom again. "Kirk to Sick Bay."

"Sick Bay," came the familiar response, worried now. "Sick Bay ... McCoy here, Jim."

"Bones, I've *got* to have some answers. I know what's happening to us—what I must know is how, and why."

"Come down to the lab, Jim. Spock too. I was just going to call you. I may have something . . ."

Despite the fact that they ran, Kirk and Spock took much longer than usual to reach the lab. Not that they moved any more awkwardly, or that their strength was sapped, but they were now less than a meter tall. Sheer distance was making it more time consuming simply to get around the ship.

McCoy had to call out before they spotted him. The doctor was standing part way up a metal stepping stool, necessary now if he was to reach the instruments on the counter above. The cabinets above the counter proper were as much out of his reach now as the planetary surface.

He gestured at the laser scope on the counter, then stepped down to make room for Kirk. Fortunately, the device had a swivel eyepiece which could be tilted down as well as up. Kirk glanced in, feeling uncomfortable at the unnatural size of the scope lenspiece.

The slide was a hybrid, two sections joined side by side. The difference between the healthy stable tissue and the radiation-poisoned tissue was obvious.

Nonetheless, McCoy explained helpfully: "That's the test tissue I've been using on the right, Jim. From my arm, not that it matters. The stabilized normal tissue is on the left."

Kirk studied the accusing slide a moment longer before muttering, "Then Spock's theory is confirmed." He didn't look away from the scope. "We're contracting."

"No question about it, Jim. That's why our weight remains about the same, and why we haven't gone floating up to the ceiling with every step. The number of atoms remains the same. The wave bombardment is simply causing them to tighten, reducing the diameter of electron orbits. Just like the dilithium. Not to the shattering point, though—I guess organic structures have more resilience. Otherwise we would start breaking up like glass figurines. At least, I don't *think* the shrinkage will get that extreme." He looked uncertainly to Spock.

"Though I can't really make any assurances about an effect that's never been observed before."

"Agreed," the first officer said. "A most unique phenomenon. It is quite interesting. I should like to study it at more leisure. . ."

"Except that we haven't got any leisure time left," McCoy finished grimly.

"An accurate if not particularly scientific description, Doctor. I believe the process is accelerating."

Kirk finally turned away from the depressing evidence displayed by the scope. Obvious perversions of nature held a horrible inevitability about them that no amount of rationalizing could dispell.

"How long could it keep on?"

Spock stared around the lab as he reflected on the captain's question, the lab which had assumed the proportions of a coliseum.

"Perhaps infinitely. Considering that the distance between electron orbits and nuclei is relatively as great as the distances between suns, even if the rate of reduction continues to increase it should take some time before we . . . disappear entirely."

There was numbed silence in the lab.

"Dr. McCoy."

They turned as Nurse Chapel appeared from behind a row of cages. "It's the experimental animals, doctor. They're getting too small to be contained by some of the cages, the ones with wire mesh walls. All the gossamers are out already."

She held up one of the transparent quasi-rodents for them to stare at. It was perfectly proportioned and the proper size compared to the rest of them.

"Look how tiny they've gotten," she went on. "Just like the halo fish. It's tadpole size now." She looked back and pointed up toward the aquarium. They could still discern the sensitive swimmer, spectacularly colored as always, its satellite circlet fluorescing brightly—though now it was barely the size of a finger ring.

"And that," noted McCoy sarcastically, "is supposed to be a creature sensitive to the tiniest changes in environment." He snorted. "So much for the confident dictates of Starfleet Medical Center."

"Don't be too hard on them, Doctor," Spock advised. "No one could have forseen our present remarkable situation."

McCoy took several deep breaths and eyed Spock significantly. The science officer's attention had been diverted elsewhere, however. He was staring at a large band of metal which dangled from nurse Chapel's arm. He fingered the double twist of shiny alloy curiously.

"Christine, what is the composition of this decoration?"

Chapel blinked, looked down at her arm. "It was made for me by the Knight Smiths of Libra IV. It's a common piece of costume jewelry." She lowered her arm and the now greatly oversized circle of metal slid off easily. The arm bracelet was more like a necklace now.

"What about it, Spock?" queried McCoy. "I didn't know you were interested in jewelry of any kind."

"A moment please, Doctor. It is not its aesthetic qualities which intrigue me at the moment. Knight metal alloy," he repeated cryptically. "An artificial construct. Yet the uniform on which it rested fits as well as ever. Your uniform, all of our uniforms, is woven from algae-based xenylon, I believe."

"Naturally. All regular Starfleet-issue work uniforms are made of xenylon," McCoy observed, still not seeing what the first officer was driving at. But Kirk was only a couple of steps behind Spock and catching up rapidly.

"I think I see what you mean, Spock. They've all been shrinking proportionately with us, so. . . ."

"Exactly, Captain. I would be assured my theory is fact. . ." He was staring up at the aquarium, suddenly started towards the table it sat on. "One more example, I think."

Then he was climbing up the stool. Stretching, he reached into the water and brought out a small piece of floating coral which had become detached from the main mass. He examined it briefly before nodding to the others.

"The animals, the living corals, have contracted along with us—and so have their organically based limestone homes. Yet the rest of the material in the aquarium, the rocks on the bottom, remain unchanged and normal sized."

"I see. So that confirms it, then—only organic matter is affected," McCoy said. "But then how. . . ?"

"Remember, Doctor," Spock went on, climbing down from the stool, "the wave impulses cause only spiral molecules to wind tight. The only inorganic spiral molecular chains we know of are those which form crystalline dilithium. Which is actually analagous in structure to one we are quite close to."

"The doubled DNA helix in the nucleus of every cell in our bodies," Kirk recited, echoing a line from Academy biology. The remembrance was small comfort. He frowned. "I suppose we ought to consider ourselves lucky, Bones. Some of the dilithium crystals self-destructed when their internal structure unwound instead of contracting. If we were subjected to the same stresses we would all be puddles of jelly on the deck by now."

McCoy shrugged. "It's all the same in the end, Jim. I'm not sure that I wouldn't prefer that to being a candidate for a flea circus."

Kirk had a thought, hiked over to the computer console. "Bones, what happens when DNA is compacted to its ultimate limits?"

"I don't think the strands would break, Jim, as Spock says." He walked over to stand next to the Captain. "I guess they just stop winding."

"Well then, if that's the case, we can calculate the limits of our shrinkage. It shouldn't be infinite."

"It is possible," conceded Spock. "I'll feed the question to the library."

Kirk and McCoy wrestled with the stool set near the scope until it was set close to the computer console. Spock climbed up, carefully walked out onto the sensitive keyboard. The keys were now hand instead of thumb size. But he had no trouble depressing them.

"Something else that we had better calculate just occurred to me," Kirk yelled upward. "How long can we expect to maintain effective control of the ship?"

"I have considered that question also, Captain. The computer will project a point beyond which the systems switches and controls will be beyond our ability to operate efficiently.

"I might also add, Captain, that we had better take care where and how we walk. Remember, our weight remains approximately the same despite our smaller size. It is therefore concentrated on a smaller supportive surface. It would be dangerous to walk out on a glass surface, for example. We would tend to go right through it.

"It appears the calculations will take some time."

"Stick with it, Spock. I'm going back to the bridge."

"And I think I'd better make some preparations, Jim," McCoy told him. "At the rate we're contracting there're going to be some accidents soon. Maybe not quite the kind Spock is thinking of, but related."

"Check, Bones. Spock, report the moment you have some results."

"Yes, Captain."

The walk back to the bridge felt like a hike of kilometers, even though Kirk was expecting it. He was also expecting a new view of the bridge. Even so, his first glimpse of what had become a giant's playground was shocking. He walked slowly toward the towering command chair, thinking furiously. . .

While minutes and centimeters continued to tick away, the entire scientific complement of the *Enterprise* worked overtime trying to find a way to reverse, or at least halt the contraction that was literally taking their mastery of the ship away from them.

They knew the cause . . . the strange faint radiation from the surface they could not run away from. They could now calculate their rate of shrinkage. But no solution offered itself. They couldn't even identify the type of radiation.

The intercom buzzed insistently for attention. Kirk reached over to acknowledge the call, missed and had to readjust his reach. His arms had grown shorter in the last hour. That was the most frustrating aspect of the shrinkage effect. You had to constantly readjust your senses to a new size. A few crewmembers were reacting so badly to the constant change they had to be sent to McCoy for sedation.

"Spock here, Captain," came the voice at the other end. It was totally unreasonable to hope that the science officer had found any miracle solutions, but Spock had done it before. Unfortunately, this didn't look to be one of those times. The report was consistent only in its pessimism.

"Not only does our rate of contraction show no sign of halting, Captain, but it appears it may continue beyond our ability to adapt to it."

Still thinking about missing the intercom switch a moment ago, Kirk shot back, "How long can we anticipate retaining ship control, Mr. Spock?"

"I would say," the thoughtful reply went on, "that even with our most intensive miniaturizing measures and ability to design new compact backup systems, we will lose effective control of this vessel at the point when we become approximately one centimeter tall." There was a pause, then, "My present height is something like a third of a meter, Captain.

"I am coming forward to utilize the fuller resources of the library computer station . . . for as long as I can continue to operate it. Spock out."

"Kirk out."

IV

The next hour was a hectic race against rapidly increasing odds—reducing odds, actually—as the *Enterprise*'s construction engineers worked frantically to fashion an endless stream of ingenious, yet ultimately useless miniaturized apparatus.

Ladders mounted on wheels and built of metal strips; long clamp poles and flex tubes for manipulating simultaneous dials and switches now far out of reach—a host of intricate devices.

It was, expectedly, a losing battle. Eventually all operations and energies above bare life-support maintainance were directed toward retaining control in two sections . . . the bridge and Engineering.

Kirk leaned back and stared up at the cliff of the library computer station where Spock was running back and forth manipulating controls with tireless energy. But even with adroit manipulation of the new, miniature handling tools, Kirk could see that the first officer could not keep it up much longer.

Eventually he would grow so small he wouldn't be able to read the gargantuan printouts. He was minutes from losing the ability to use the hooded viewer.

"You said one centimeter was the critical point, Spock?"

Spock came to the edge, leaned over carefully and shouted down, "I beg your pardon, Captain?"

"When will we reach the critical one centimeter point?"

"At the present rate of compaction I should estimate in thirty-two minutes, Captain."

Kirk nodded, acknowledging the inevitable, then remembered an as yet unanswered question.

"How small will we ultimately shrink, Mr. Spock?"

"One moment, Captain." Spock turned his attention back to the instrument panel. Surveying the angular field of levers and switches, he mapped out a plan of attack. Starting with a red triangle close by he hopscotched his way across the controls. His only real worry was that his concentrated weight might shatter them, but fortunately the high-impact styrene remained intact.

Seconds passed. Then a billboard-sized series of figures appeared on the first screen in front of him. Spock studied them briefly, then marched back to the edge of the console. It wasn't the kind of answer he liked to give.

"There is not sufficient information to calculate our final reduction limit with any precision, Captain. I do have a projection on the time required for full analysis of the spiroid wave phenomenon, though, which could lead to a solution and method for reversing the process."

"That's great, Spock . . . follow it up!"

"I would, Captain, but there is one difficulty. The time required for such analysis is estimated at between seven and eight years. As we have perhaps several hours remaining to us . . ."

Across the vast valley of the bridge deck, Sulu heard Spock's fatal pronouncement and clenched his fists in helpless frustration. Sulu turned back to the helm console on which he now walked, the controls growing more and more difficult to manipulate. He stared up at the main viewscreen. It still showed the same quarter of fractured land below them.

This was not the way the men in his family had died! His ancestors would be ashamed to see one of their blood go down without fighting, without striking back. There *had* to be some way, *any* way. . .

"Bypass that analysis, Mr. Spock," Kirk instructed his first officer. He turned, looked over at the huge clock balanced carefully against the base of the command chair. The clock had recently rested on his wrist, but like all other inorganic material except the dilithium, his watch had remained normal size.

Hours—they didn't even have hours if the rate of shrinkage continued to accelerate. They had twenty-nine minutes. Twenty-nine minutes before they were too small to control the *Enterprise*.

Cupping his hands, he shouted to the busy cluster of crewmen moving around on the deck.

"Everyone continue to jury-rig control systems. There's nothing more we can do."

"But there is, Captain."

As the rest of the crew continued with their tasks, Kirk and Spock turned in the direction of the voice, staring up at the overhanging edge of the helm console. Sulu stood there, looking down at them. His tone was one of desperation.

"Sir, request permission to direct phaser fire at the surface immediately below," he implored, and then turned back to his own task at hand before the captain could reply.

Sulu shoved against a waist high needle set in a timing dial, pushing it back several notches. With his concentrated body weight he had no trouble manipulating the huge lever. But his mind was on something else.

When no reply from below was forthcoming, he turned and moved to the edge of the console again. "Ten seconds, sir, just let me set it for ten seconds and we'll destroy. . ."

"Destroy what, Mr. Sulu? Sensor studies have shown that the unknown waves originate from an area kilometers in diameter. We could assault that region for hours without disrupting whatever is generating the bombardment of the ship. We haven't got hours worth of power to divert to the phaser banks. We haven't even got minutes."

Sulu stood at the bottom of the circular timer, now clicking back along its present path, and continued to argue with the captain.

"What good does it do to wait like this, sir. Wait for a death *reductio ad absurdum* in the truest sense? Just one quick blast, Captain, to see what will happen."

In his concentration on winning Kirk over, Sulu had forgotten the timer completely. It clicked through the final notch . . . to club Sulu behind the knees. Both legs were taken out from under him.

Falling forward, he rolled once, took a wild, desperate grab at the edge of the console and fell floorward. There was a disproportionately loud thump as he hit. It sounded convincingly fatal, but wasn't.

"Sulu!" Kirk and Arex rushed to the injured helmsman's side. The same gestures that showed them he was still alive indicated he was far from uninjured. He was clutching his right leg and grimacing with the pain.

"Damn . . . mmphh!"

"Easy, Lieutenant." Kirk forced Sulu's hands away from the damaged area. He felt the leg gently, winced himself when he put miniscule pressure on a particular spot and saw the helmsman's face contort in pain.

"Leg's broken," he murmured to the watching Arex.

"Call Sick Bay for a bed?"

"No . . . the sooner we get him down there the better. Besides, Bones doubtlessly has his hands full already. Let's make a temporary splint." Arex made an expression of understanding, moved off to located the requisite material.

"Try not to move it, Sulu. We'll have you down to Sick Bay as soon as possible." The helmsman tried to smile back up at him, managed a slight grimace.

"Good thing I fell on my head, Captain. Beyond fracturing, I think."

"Something about you is." Kirk was studying the deck nearby. Sulu's heavy, compacted form had put a noticeable dent in the smooth metal.

"These should serve, Captain." Arex showed him a couple of small metal strips of the kind being used to make miniaturized holders and grips. He had also appropriated a couple of organically based belts from several crewmen.

Kirk straightened the leg slowly, while Sulu fought to stifle the pain. It couldn't be helped, they had to get the leg straight. He set one metal strip behind the leg, the other in front, and proceeded to tie them tight with the belts. The thick straps were awkward to work with.

"Couldn't you find anything better in the way of binding material, Lieutenant?" he grumbled.

"I'm sorry, Captain," Arex replied. "None of the cordage in the bridge storage lockers would work. It is all inorganically based and therefore has remained normal size."

"Of course." Kirk pulled harder on the bottom belt. Interesting how certain small items had suddenly become indispensable—and unavailable. While others, like these belts, were proving invaluable. He found himself fervently wishing that, of all things, starship's stores had included a couple of horses.

He finished the improvised splint. With the help of the captain and the navigator, Sulu managed to struggle to his feet. Arex slipped a pair of arms under him— one across his shoulders, the other across his front— and finally put the third around his waist. Kirk added an arm to the other side.

"Let's get him to Sick Bay." He glanced around. A small crowd had gathered. "Everyone, back to your stations."

Moving as quickly as they dared, they half dragged, half carried the injured helmsman toward the bridge doors. They seemed kilometers away.

"How are you doing, Sulu?" Kirk asked awkwardly as they struggled toward the elevator. He was at his best giving orders, not comfort. For all his sometime brusqueness, that was Dr. McCoy's specialty.

"Lousy, sir," Sulu replied, grinning. "I'll make it."

His expression twisted as he accidentally put pressure on the injured member.

"It would have been nicer, sir, if our ability to feel pain had diminished along with our size."

They reached the elevator doors—and came to a grinding halt. Nothing happened, even when they moved to stand right up against the metal. The now Brobdingnagian portal refused to open. Arex looked frankly puzzled. It took Kirk long seconds to recognize the reason.

"The body sensor. We've grown too small to activate it—beam's over our heads now." He left Sulu to Arex's support while he hunted around for something long enough. Everything seemed too big or too small, until he nearly tripped over a strangely shaped piece of metal.

It was barbed, thin, and bent in the shape of an elongated U... one of Uhura's fallen hairpins.

Hauling it back to the doorway, he hefted it carefully, then made a sweeping motion forward, overhead. Nothing. Another sweep, coupled with a little jump—and this time the colossal doors slid apart.

Slipping the hairpin over his right shoulder, ready for use at the next doorway, he resumed his support of Sulu. Together, he and Arex helped the injured helmsman through the door.

Even more depressing than the situation on the bridge was the situation in Sick Bay. Kirk was shocked by the number of injured there, many lying on the deck on makeshift pallets of bits of cloth and sponge. The fact that many of the blankets and sheets were woven from natural-based substances alleviated the problems somewhat. They'd remained in proportion to the growing number of patients, all of whom now averaged about eighteen centimeters in height.

McCoy and Nurse Chapel were doing their best to care for the injured. When the number of cases began to grow alarmingly, he had distributed the rest of the medical personnel to the various sections of the ship. That, he had decided, would be more practical in the

long run than trying to bring all the injured to Sick Bay
and would insure medical care throughout the ship no
matter how small they shrank.

And though some areas of the *Enterprise* were more
injury-prone than others, a large number still made
their way to Sick Bay for treatment.

Chapel spotted the new arrivals immediately, nudged
McCoy. The doctor bestowed a reassuring smile on a
communications tech with a shattered collarbone and
went with Chapel to meet the others.

He directed them to lay Sulu on an empty bed and
knelt to examine the helmsman. "What happened? No,
let me guess . . . another falling incident—people aren't
taking heights seriously, Jim."

"Broken leg," Kirk informed him. "He fell all
right—from the helm console." Turning slowly and
surveying the room, he counted the number of injured.
"I might ask you the same question."

McCoy was bent over Sulu, moving an improvised
miniature medical scanner over the leg.

"A lot more of the same, as I said. More and more
fall injuries being reported all the time." He clipped the
scanner on his belt, started to undo the makeshift
splint. "Compound fracture—how did you straighten
it?"

"Pulled," Kirk said curtly.

"Bedside-manner-wise you leave something to be desired, Jim. But it was the right thing to do."

"If we could only use a bone-knitting laser," Chapel
was muttering. At Kirk's questioning glance, she explained, "We miniaturized all the medical instrumentation we could, Captain, but we just didn't have time for
everything. We've been so busy." Her expression
brightened.

"Wait a minute, Dr. McCoy, what about the tiny
laser set in the auralite? The one designed to work on
the inner ear? Could it be used for bone work?"

McCoy looked away from his examination of the leg,
considering. "It ought to be easy enough to detach
from the 'lite—it's a self-contained, replaceable unit.

But bone work—I don't . . . no, it's better than splint-ing. At this stage anything's worth a try." He looked back down at Sulu.

"I haven't mixed a plaster cast since first year Med School. I'd sure hate to start relearning now—even if the supplies are still manageable." He was getting ex-cited. "Sure, let's try it. The 'lite's up on the shelf with the semi-surgical supplies."

"I'll get it," Chapel told them. She left while the oth-ers turned their attention back to Sulu. McCoy started to explain what would happen if the badly broken femur were allowed to heal by itself.

The lab room had taken on the appearance of a me-tallic replica of Zion Canyon on Earth, with sheer cliffs of white and gray closing in on narrowing channels. Chapel didn't need a map to find the shelf.

Up one of the movable stools to the table-top, from there up the angled base of the aquarium, and then an easy hike to the open shelf. Miscellaneous supplies were scattered about, hastily removed from containers as the people had begun to shrink. Spools of thread, small surgical devices now the size of shuttlecraft, all were strewn haphazardly about.

Several minutes of fruitless searching made the nurse think McCoy had been wrong about the location of the auralite. Then the long polished tube came into view near the far edge of the shelf. The laser module was in the front of the device. A couple of simple twists on a pair of screw clamps, a click, and it was free. She held it easily in one hand—an extraordinary piece of medi-cal engineering about the size of a small button.

It had its own self-contained meters. She stepped back to check the reserve power gauge in better light and stumbled. Her feet slipped onto a couple of large plastic skin-patches, now the size of folded tents, and the laser began to shift in her grasp. Clutching at it anxiously, she went over backward into the glass-sided lake of the aquarium.

The fall knocked the breath out of her and she had to fight for air as she swam back to the surface, still holding the laser. At first the incident seemed only embarrassing. The laser was well sealed and the water wouldn't bother it. She would climb out. . .

Only after regaining control of herself and her breathing did the first touches of panic set in. The towering glass sides of the aquarium proved unclimbable. And she was far from being the best swimmer on board the ship. She had to struggle to keep from thrashing about in the water and screaming in panic. Instead, she treaded water steadily and screamed at regular, controlled intervals.

Many of the patients in the main room were under sedation, so it was relatively quiet. Otherwise Kirk and the others might never have heard her.

Arex had returned to the bridge, but Kirk and McCoy heard the screams clearly enough. Kirk left the exhausted doctor attending to Sulu and ran toward the adjoining lab.

Chapel was already growing tired—she had no place to rest her legs and one arm had the double task of helping to keep her afloat while holding onto the laser—when Kirk finally located her. Following the same path upward he was soon standing on the shelf above the aquarium, looking over and down into the water.

He could hardly go in after her—that would leave two of them in need of rescue. Nor was there any miniature climbing gear in evidence. There had to be something on the shelf. . .

A now-enormous spool of metallic surgical thread caught his attention. Unwinding a sufficient number of loops—the thread looked and felt like electrical cable in his hands—he made a strong ring at one end and dropped it to Chapel.

She half swam, half flailed her way over to it. Maneuvering carefully, she put her head and arms through the loop. Using the spool cylinder as a brace he slowly hauled her up. A minute later she was standing next to him, gasping and coughing. Kirk found a shrunken lab smock that had somehow found its way onto the shelf, slipped it over her. Her shivering abated somewhat. The halo fish was a cold-water denizen.

"No more mountain climbing for you, Nurse. Understand?" Chapel ignored the warning. She was hunting through her pockets. Holding onto the laser and treading water had proven too difficult, so. . .

"Agreed, Captain," she panted as she produced the instrument, "but I've got it."

She insisted on carrying it herself as they made their way first to the floor and then back to the main room. McCoy studied it without speaking. Kirk watched him worriedly, waiting.

Finally, "What's the matter, Bones? Don't you think it'll work?"

"If you mean by work, will it still operate effectively, the answer is yes," McCoy responded. "That's not what concerns me. Normally this device locks into a much larger mechanism which in turn has standard size switches to operate it. I've never handled it directly— the contacts, of course, are far too small for our hands. I'm worried about getting the settings right." He looked at the deck, over at Sulu.

"No way to know without trying it, though. Nurse Chapel, shift the lieutenant's other leg to one side, please." Chapel did so. Then, while she and Kirk watched, McCoy improvised a stable stand for the laser. Hesitantly at first, then with growing assurance, he manipulated the tiny control contacts.

Eventually he sat back on his haunches and looked up at Kirk.

"That ought to be right, Jim, though I still can't be sure. I've replaced this component with tiny handlers often enough. It feels awfully strange working it directly." He directed his next words to the helmsman.

"Sulu, if there's any pain—anything that doesn't feel right to you—you tell me immediately, understand? Don't go overboard on stoicism—anything twangs out of tune, yell good and loud!"

Sulu responded with a quick, nervous shake of his head. No jokes, now. McCoy took a deep breath, exchanged an infinite glance with Kirk, then touched a tiny recess in the side of the circular instrument. A beam of bright blue abruptly took up the space between lens and leg. It touched the injured limb on black and blue skin, where McCoy had cut away the tunic.

"Nothing so far," Sulu reported without being asked.

McCoy bent over the laser, squinted at the screen set in the back of it and made a couple of adjustments. An infinitesmal shift in the beam was the only noticeable result. Thirty seconds, forty—McCoy touched another hidden switch and the beam vanished.

"All right, Lieutenant, move your leg." Sulu looked at him uncertainly. He gritted his teeth and started to pull his leg up. The grimace disappeared as it moved easily. Now he flexed it slowly, then with increasing confidence, moving it from side to side.

"It still aches a little, Doctor." McCoy moved over and started feeling the treated area.

"Here?"

"No . . . no . . . yes, there . . . that's the spot."

McCoy made sure of it, had Sulu straighten his leg again, then returned to the laser. Readjusting the device he activated the beam again, played it on the helmsman's leg for a couple of seconds.

"Try it again, Sulu."

The helmsman did, moving his leg at the hip, then at the knee, and finally raising it completely off the deck in a high arch.

"No pain now, Doctor. Only a kind of dull throb and a warm feeling."

"That's natural. No," he warned, as Sulu showed signs of getting up, "just stay there and rest for awhile Sulu."

"I'm going to need him, Doctor," Kirk said softly. "How soon before he can come forward."

"You mean you'll need him at the helm?" McCoy gave Kirk a look of admonition. "Isn't there a bit of wishful thinking there, Jim?"

"I try to think positive, Bones. If we have a second's

opportunity to blast free of here, I'll want my best people at the controls."

"Sorry, you can't have Sulu for a while yet. I'm not worried about the bone—it has fully knit. But sometimes rapid repairs have their own effect on the body. Severe injury isn't the only thing that can initiate shock. It will take time for the nerves and blood vessels in that area to readjust to the fact that they're suddenly not on a crisis footing. After that he'll be as good as new. But he needs to rest for a little while, at least." He lifted the laser carefully off its improvised platform.

"Christine, move the base, will you? Let's try Solinski's hip next." He looked at Kirk. "Excuse us, Jim, there are a lot of other casualties here I'd like to try this on."

"Of course, Bones." Kirk turned his attention back to Sulu. "I'm tempted to call Chapel's thinking of the ear laser a lucky break, Lieutenant, but. . ."

"Comments like that could result in a breakdown of command." Sulu smiled broadly up at him. "I understand, sir. Right now I'm too pleased with the results to care."

Kirk started to reply but was interrupted by a new voice. He turned to see Spock moving toward him.

"I have other results available now, Captain. Figures on the ultimate molecular contraction rate have come through."

"What are they?" Kirk asked, at once intensely curious and fatalistic.

The latter emotion turned out to be justified.

"Reduction factor of thirty-two-point-nine." Kirk did some rapid upstairs calculating, commented somberly.

"That means we're going down to one-sixteenth of a centimeter."

Spock nodded, spoke matter-of-factly, "Yes, Captain. While it is in a sense comforting to know we will not be tripping over dust motes, it is still well past the point at which we can exercise operative control of the ship. An interesting height from which to contemplate the world—and the remainder of one's life."

Kirk stood silently, watched by both Sulu and Spock. He thought back to Sulu's request of minutes ago. Everything was happening too fast. If they could spare the power from life-support, maybe by closing off all but a few remaining sections of the ship, maybe he should try phasers on the surface below.

No, they simply didn't have that kind of reserve energy left. Not enough for the phasers. But they did have power for something else. For one last choice.

If he was going to die, then the location didn't much matter.

"You have decided on a new course of action, Captain," Spock commented, evaluating the familiar thoughtful expression on his friend's face.

Kirk didn't even hear him. "Mr. Spock, can you calculate the approximate center of the wave-emitting region?"

"A simple enough task, Captain. But that will not necessarily be the point at which the waves are produced."

"I know that, Spock."

"May I ask the purpose then, Captain?"

Kirk shrugged, stared over to where McCoy and Chapel were busy repairing a yeoman's broken ribs with the laser.

"That is as good a place as any to beam down."

While Spock stood digesting this remarkable statement, Kirk moved to a nearby metal boulder. It had a flexible face bordered by projecting studs—a huge hand communicator. It would be quicker than climbing to a console and trying to operate the wall com. unit.

Putting his compacted weight behind the push, Kirk had no trouble opening the grid. Making his voice strong enough for the pickup to be activated was another story. He had to bend and shout into the mouthpiece at the top of his lungs.

"Kirk to Engineering! Scotty, can you hear me?" A pause, then the chief engineer's voice acknowledging, filtered, faint, and weak—but comprehensible.

"Just barely, sir."

"Get a crew down to the transporter room!" Kirk yelled. "We have twenty minutes left in which to operate ship's controls—including the transporters."

"How many beamin' down, Captain?"

"Just one, Mr. Scott. Me!"

"Aye, Captain," Scott replied solemnly. "Dinna worry . . . we'll rig somethin'. Scott out."

Kirk stop, kicked at the deactivation switch to shut off the communicator.

"I'll meet you in the transporter room, Mr. Spock. Meanwhile, see what you can manage in the way of a doll-sized communicator. Anything at all, even something that just broadcasts a pulse signal. I'll send in code, if I have to."

"Yes, Captain."

"I won't be long. I've got to make one more check of the bridge and issue final instructions."

"I understand, Captain."

Uhura, Arex, and the others took the announcements with typical calm. They had an advantage—nothing Kirk said came as any surprise.

As he headed for the distant transporter room, Kirk kept their faces, reactions in mind. There wasn't one among them who felt those last instructions would not be implemented in a dozen minutes or so. He still retained private hopes, though.

There was one last thing they could try to halt the lethal bombardment. If an intelligence was behind it, then one had to assume the waves could be shut off as competently as they had been turned on the *Enterprise*.

In the absence of any attempt at contact from the surface, Kirk had to assume paranoid reluctance on the part of any such intelligence. In which event a personal appearance might be the only thing that could convince "them" of the peaceful intent of their visitors. He would beam down and search them out.

Alternatively, they would reduce him on sight to something considerably less than a centimeter in height—a thin layer of smoking dust, for example.

With admirable foresight, the doorway to the transporter room had been locked open, and a metal plate had been secured over the sensor eye. As Kirk walked toward the transporter console he spotted Scott and Gabler working at its base. Chief Kyle was busy with a crew nearby. They were rigging a doubled-back piece of strong wire to the console, bracing it against an empty wire spool secured to the deck.

A rapid examination revealed that the other end of the doubled-back cable looped around the first manual lever of the transporter control. Fortunately, that crucial switch moved vertically. If a horizontal control had been involved they would have had all sorts of problems, requiring at least one and possibly more miniature pulleys.

The other end of the wire was being played out to a crowd of patient crewmen. Each was taking up a firm stance and a tight grip on the wire.

Kirk placed a hand on Scott's shoulders. Sweat dripping from his face, the chief engineer turned quickly, even managed a smile.

"We'll be ready in a minute, Captain. We can still manipulate the switches properly. It's workin' them at the proper speed that's goin' to be touchy, but I think we can manage it."

"Good, Mr. Scott." Kirk looked up, following the wire into the heavens to where it looped tightly around the handle of the transporter lever, now looking like a gray sequoia angling over the console cliff.

"I estimate our height is now down to about five centimeters," Scott ventured. "With maximum leeway I think we can manage controls for another fifteen minutes—no more."

"That will have to do, Scotty."

Kirk noticed Spock hunched down over a pile of material. He walked over as the science officer stood, trailing microscopic wire and hastily reduced hand tools.

The crudely made boxlike instrument he handed the captain looked ready to fall apart any second. Kirk hefted it, was gratified to see it was more solid than it looked.

"Unattractive but functional, Captain," Spock informed him. "This is the best I could do in rigging so small a communicator in such a short time."

"It's fine, Spock. Thanks."

"It is proportionately about ten times the size a hand communicator should be, Captain," Spock went on, still apologizing for the incredible feat of improvisational engineering he had just accomplished, "and its range cannot be guaranteed. How shall we locate you for return if it fails?"

"We haven't much time anyway, Mr. Spock, so that problem solves itself." He called back over his shoulder. "Scotty, set an automatic return for me. If there's anything to be found down there, ten minutes should do it."

"Aye, sir," Scott agreed. "We'll set it now." He turned, yelled to several crewmen hanging on another wire. "You there—Johnson, Massachi, Nikkatsu—let go of that wire and give me a hand with this servopole." The men hastened to obey as Scott started to take up a grip on the long hollow tube.

"A disconcerting thought, Captain," Spock ventured, "that I have been pondering while working here. The transporter relies on a banked record of the body's molecular structure. Will that record adapt as well to your present height?"

"There is the chance, I suppose, that it can't adjust to the transporter pattern," Kirk admitted, "in which case, either I simply won't go anywhere—or else I'll go everywhere, in pieces.

"We'll know shortly. And in fifteen minutes it won't matter whether the transporter can bring me back or not. Prepare to energize." Kirk started for the transporter platform. Spock took a step to head him off.

"Captain, may I wish you all. . ." Spock hesitated, unusually. "I hope logical eventualities prove that . . . good luck, sir," he finally finished awkwardly.

He and Kirk exchanged shoulder claps. Then Kirk

hurried off down the endless metal plateau toward the alcove.

Spock watched him for a minute, then moved to take up a place along the doubled cable. There was a short wait while Kirk scrambled up the low cliff of the single step leading to the platform proper. The super-strong wire made an excellent "rope" ladder.

Once on top, Kirk ran to the center of the nearest disk, turned, and waved both arms.

Scott, lost in other thoughts, eventually became aware Spock was speaking to him.

"What?"

"The captain instructed us to energize, I believe, Mr. Scott."

Energize. He had a job to do. First wire one, then the two servopoles were adjusted, turned. Spock took up a place in front of Scott, both hands on the wire. Speed was critical now. Five seconds, ten . . .

"Heave, lads, heave! Heave for your lives!"

The line of tiny figures on the floor started backward. As the slack in the cable was taken up the line grew taut, held. Straining, straining, for millimeters at a time, they pulled on the wire. Pulled until triceps howled with the demand and shoulders threatened to pull from their sockets.

The lever began to descend. Slowly, condescendingly, but it moved. Servopoles made minor adjustments again. A dial was turned as men broke their backs on twin wires.

On the transporter platform a waterfall, a cascade of color, splinters of a rainbow, began to form. It was normal in shade, normal in flickering speed, normal in shape—normal in all respects except for its incredible, abnormal *thinness*.

It completely enveloped the near-invisible figure standing at its base. The figure wavered, blurred, became a standard transporting silhouette . . .

. . . and was gone.

V

Even though he had seen it only from kilometers above, the landscape was far from alien to Kirk. He was studying it even as he materialized on the plutonic scoria.

What was surprising was the amount of vegetation holding its own against the threatening tremors underfoot, green-brown roots and branches offering defiance to lack of moisture, promises of sulfuric rain.

Kirk was aware of this, of the constant intrusive growl of smoking peaks all around—and something else, something indefinite and undefinable. Not the ash-filled purplish sky overhead, nor the thin layer of pumice that crunched under his boots. Something much more immediate. Something like . . .

A lessening of weight, weight on his right arm, weight that should have been nestled in the crook of arm and ribs and no longer was. Instead it rested neatly in his palm, a miniscule shard of badly worked metal and plastic.

The communicator Spock had presented to him only moments ago. He smiled.

Spock's suspicions about the touchiness of the transporter memory bank had been justified—only not in the way he had imagined. Instead of the transporter pattern adapting to his smaller size, it had operated on the old pattern stored in its cells, had forced Kirk's body to adapt to *it*. He was back to his normal size.

From a distant peak, an intense beam of light shot like a yellow bar across the valley and disappeared in a far-off crevice. To his right was another, beginning lower down but also meeting somewhere over a nearby ridge.

Turning a slow circle he saw that a network of light converged at one point just beyond his vision. He started walking toward it.

As he started up the slight grade he raised the communicator, handling it carefully. If it slipped out of his grasp he doubted he would find it again in the loose gravel and detritus. Peering at the tiny device he used his fingernail to put the lightest pressure possible on the activation lever.

A violent rumbling began in the distance, grew rapidly loud. There was a throaty ripping sound, like an underground freight-liner rushing past. A flank eruption burst the side of one of the volcanoes behind him.

He spared it only a brief glance. At the moment he was more concerned about the tiny beep from his palm. He spoke at the communicator, hoped Spock's improvised pickup would modulate his voice properly at the other end.

"Kirk to *Enterprise. Enterprise* ... do you read?" No reply from the tiny speaker. Maybe they were trying to talk to him, and his ears couldn't pick up their minute voices. He continued on the chance they were picking him up.

"I think we have the answer to the height problem. It seems the transporter beam returns our molecules to normal spacing. Nothing to indicate that once realigned and transported back aboard the whole compaction process wouldn't start all over again, but at least we've got a stop-gap now."

Still no reply. He tucked the communicator away in a pocket. The slope grew steeper here and he wanted to concentrate on keeping his footing. Also, the eruptions on the valley fringe were growing in violence and he wanted both hands in case of a fall. One particularly sharp tremor almost did knock him off his feet.

Once the dust and volcanic ash in the air grew so thick he had trouble breathing. And then, without sound or warning of any kind, the beam of light he was paralleling abruptly winked out. He looked around, across the valley, up the slopes of distant mountains. The network of lights he had observed on beam-down had been completely extinguished. He brought out the communicator, tried again.

"Kirk to *Enterprise,* do you read me?" This time there was an answer. Faint and unnaturally high-pitched, but for all that immediately recognizable.

"We read you, Captain," Spock told him. "It was necessary to readjust power flow to the main communications board to boost your transmission to audible levels. Your makeshift communicator carries less power than I believed.

"A most interesting thing has just happened. If sensors are to be believed, wave bombardment of the ship has just ceased."

"I think I know why," Kirk told his astonished listeners. But before he could elaborate he felt an agonized heaving underfoot and the ground bulged. A crack like a sonic boom followed, and this time Kirk was knocked completely off balance.

Bracing himself he landed without being more than dazed, but something he had feared had come to pass. Despite his best efforts the tiny communicator had gone flying. Flaming bits of ash and lava started to fall around him as he searched for it on hands and knees. The fiery fallout was dense behind him, though less so in the direction he had been headed.

Several minutes of fruitless searching failed to locate the lost communicator. The rain of lava was growing worse and the sharp-slivered pumice had nearly butchered his knees. It seemed a good idea to move on. He was nearly to the top of the ridge and he ought to find some protection from the sizzling hail on the other side.

Scrambling to his feet he started upward again. Occasionally a hot ash would land on him and he would beat frantically at the ember as it smoldered on his clothes. But he still found no sign of whatever existed at the center of the vanished lights.

Once, a lava bomb—a tear-drop shaped dollop of

molten lava cooled to hardness during its fall through the cooler atmosphere—shattered near him. It must have weighed a hundred kilos at least. It would take a far smaller bomb to make a real mess of him. No use wishing for a solid duralloy umbrella, nor could he dodge the unexpected missiles.

But it was hard not to think about them.

Another sharp tremor. Ready for this one, he kept his feet. A meter-wide crack opened in the ground to his left, forcing him to change the direction of his climb slightly. Even without the time limit imposed on him he didn't think an unarmored man could spend much time roaming this surface. Sooner or later the steady assault would either batter him unconscious or cause him to break an ankle in the plethora of tiny crevices and cracks.

He topped the rise, ready for a sight of the unexpected—but not ready for the mental shock he received.

Down in a steeply walled hollow, not five meters from the base of the slope he stood on, rose the walls of a city. Graceful towers and arching branch structures were brilliantly lit from within, the whole metropolitan network intersected by a complex webwork of covered highways.

To one side were stadiums and a huge amphitheater, while another boasted a large factory complex. Parks and lakes studded the landscape throughout, while the entire city was surrounded by concentric rings of cultivated land, farms and dairy country. In all respects it was one of the most thoroughly planned yet exquisitely wrought cities Kirk had ever seen. It differed from the great cities of Earth and Vulcan and the major colony worlds in only one respect.

The whole metropolitan area was just large enough to fill the floor of an average-sized room aboard the *Enterprise.*

He stepped over the ridge, sat down in the grinding pumice, and stared at the scene from a book of children's stories. The tallest spire of the city came just about up to his waist.

As he sat frozen with fascination, another cycle of tremors shook the ground. He was certain that the delicate towers and bridgeways of the tiny city would be shattered, yet they barely moved. Obviously those spires were built on some kind of flexible foundation, constructed to give with the constant quakes.

But this series of shakes opened a branching canyon near the outskirts of the farthest agricultural section. Kirk could have stepped over the largest crevice in the crack, but it would swallow the biggest building in the city with room to spare. Even as he watched, one arm of the canyon moved like a bolt of brown lightning in slow motion toward the city.

It was easy to conclude that despite its miniscule size, he had come upon an intelligent civilization which possessed enough science to immobilize and threaten the *Enterprise*. Despite the threat to himself and his crew, he still could experience a sudden fear that he might have crushed some outlying farmhouses on his approach. He resisted the urge to retrace his steps.

Right now he had to make contact with the inhabitants of the city. Clearly, their intellect was in no way proportional to their size. He studied the plan of the metropolis, decided the best thing to do was get as close to the city center as possible.

Rising, Kirk started carefully down the slope, edging around toward what appeared to be a section of farmland lying fallow. He could do the least damage by approaching the city center from there.

Even as he did so, a familiar tingling started on his skin.

"No, no. . . ! He repressed the shout. There wasn't a thing he could do. The ten-minute time period was up and the automatics were bringing him inexorably back to the *Enterprise*. And then he had a moment to consider a horrifying thought.

Was this pattern the one the transporter computer would retain? Or would he be rematerialized back aboard ship in his smaller size?

Too late to stop the action, too late to change, too

late to worry. His vision blurred; he felt a second of total disorientation and nausea, and then the tingling left him and his vision returned. He was back on board.

Kirk looked down at himself, around the room. He was still his proper size. He stepped off the disk, glanced around urgently.

"Scotty, Spock . . ." No answer, no gratified replies. Maybe they could not shout this far.

Moving rapidly to the transporter console, he examined the place where the crew of straining wire-pullers and pole-handlers had worked alongside the first officer and chief engineer only ten minutes before. No sign of them.

He took a moment to examine the whisker-thin wire still looped around the transporter lever, marveling from a new perspective at the ingenuity of Scott and his assistants. Dropping to all fours he commenced a detailed survey of the area, but found no sign of the crew.

Surely they could not have shrunken to microscopic size! That would be far beyond Spock's projected lower limit of a sixteenth of a centimeter.

Knowing the automatics would return him, they had probably gone to another part of the ship in need of their attention. The bridge, for example. He got to his feet.

After covering kilometers of scaled-down corridor, it was a pleasure to make it to the bridge at what seemed like superhuman speed. The door was still locked open, the metal plate still taped over the sensor.

A quick look showed all panels and instrument consoles still operating. Impulse power was still keeping the basic functions of the ship operational, then. But still no sign of any of the crew.

There was plenty of evidence of their activities, though. Discard remote handler poles, wires running to dials and levers, doubled-over cables attached to other controls in the same fashion used to manipulate the transporter lever, tiny ladders and stilts made of metal bands.

But an uncanny silence. Clicks and snaps of relays

going over. The hum of still-powered machinery. And—he strained to hear it—something more?

High-pitched, barely audible, like the mewing of a small kitten tucked away in a drawer somewhere. Bending, he tried to follow the sound, finally saw the line of ant-sized figures emerging from behind one edge of the helm console.

Dropping to hands and knees, he looked closer. The figures took on familiar shapes and forms and even individual features. But they were so *tiny,* so incredibly tiny.

"Scotty, is that you?"

Scott was staring upward, past the towering peninsulas of Kirk's fingers, up into the monolith of his overhanging face. It hung in the sky like a great pink thundercloud.

He cupped his hands and shouted, "Aye, Captain, for the love of heaven, be careful where you step!"

Kirk nodded slowly, then dropped his face to the floor in an attempt to get as close as possible to eye level with his miniaturized crew. Scott and the others backed up nervously. It was like a mountain falling.

"IS EVERYONE SAFE?"

Scott staggered backward, hands clapped to his ears. "Easy Captain, you'll deafen us for sure."

Kirk dropped his voice to what he thought was a bare whisper. To the shrunken crew his voice still sounded like distant thunder. "Everyone accounted for?"

"All but the regular bridge complement, Captain!" Scott yelled back. "They were all at their posts, when according to the ensign who witnessed it, they were suddenly beamed away. Every living one of them. That's why I moved my people up here, to keep things runnin'.

"No warnin', no indication of what was comin'—and not a blessed hint of what did it! Only that something was using standard transporter technology."

That was the end, the final assassin of somnolent diplomacy. Now they would not deal so amiably with the inhabitants of the miniature city. Considering their attitude toward the *Enterprise* thus far, Kirk didn't think their treatment of the captured bridge staff would be very benign. Sulu would get his wish, if he were still alive.

Kirk put the tail end of that thought out of his mind.

Turning his head, he had another look at the main viewscreen. He could still see the same quadrant of tortured surface seething below. Transporter records would show precisely where he had been set down. He could pinpoint the city easily. He whispered downward again.

"All personnel away from the helm area. Move to the far bulkhead. I don't know if those people down there—I think I flatter them—have any kind of defense other than their compaction beam, but they might have a more physical way of jolting us. I'd hate to fall on anybody."

As the crew moved at top speed, with infinite slowness, to scatter across the floor, Kirk got to his feet and walked to the helm. His gaze went to certain boldly marked controls—controls which the now-vanished Sulu had pleaded to use before.

Kirk set the phaser control thoughtfully, pressed a couple of attendant switches, read the results of his request on the appropriate gauge.

Yes, the phasers were lined on his desired region. Yes, they still retained enough impulse power for a couple of mild bursts. But that was all it would take to melt the jewel-like little metropolis with its belligerent inhabitants into a shining puddle of metal slag.

Anyone else in Kirk's position might have done that immediately, on the chance of being whisked from the bridge by some irresistible transporter effect himself. Anyone else might, but *they* would not have been a starship captain.

Kirk's anger was moderated by one overriding factor—the chance that Sulu and the others might still be alive somewhere in that honeycomb of towers and roadways.

With the phaser controls set, he moved to Uhura's communications console, checking to make sure Scott and his companions were far from his path between there and the helm. After a second's thought, he selected the general interspecies frequency, composed his thoughts, and addressed himself to the pickup.

"Message to the inhabitants of the city on the planet below. I hope you can receive this frequency and understand my words. Your continued survival depends on it." He paused, gave any listener a chance to fine tune.

"All this ship's armament is locked in on the coordinates of your city. In case you doubt our ability to operate effectively, I've timed a demonstration." He checked his wrist chronometer, counted seconds, looked up at the screen.

The brilliant beam of the secondary phaser bank vanished into atmosphere. On the surface, another steep-walled valley appeared in the ground alongside the one which held the city. Reduced in strength as it was to a trickle of its usual self, the beam was still powerful enough to annihilate the entire city at one touch. The illumined towers and gilded rectangles trembled slightly from a new, artificial quake.

Kirk turned back to the pickup. "You have one minute to restore my bridge crew unharmed or you will receive a full barrage from my ship's armament."

Opening the speakers and setting part of the instrumentation to *Receive*, he moved back to the phaser controls, set one switch, and put his finger on the fire button. He had reversed the field effect in the fluid switch. Now, if he took his finger off the button—if he were suddenly beamed away—the phaser would fire.

He considered the possibility of destroying an entire city. He found it impossible to be objective, yet the situation had come to the point where someone below had to make the ultimate decision. It was no longer his responsibility. He told himself that, repeatedly. Sulu, Uhura, Arex, Spock—all might be dead already.

A glance at his wrist. Half a minute gone, forty seconds—and then a rapid series of high beeps and sputters filled the bridge, pouring over the main speakers. On the main viewscreen the image of the surface fluttered, was consumed by static, and then suddenly sharpened.

Kirk saw the interior of a huge room—huge on the screen—with a vaulting roof soaring far overhead. Highly intricate machinery was set nearby, and tunic-clad creatures were clustered around it.

One of the beings stepped suddenly into the visual pickup from the left side, blocking out most of the view behind. Kirk thought he had seen enough aliens to be prepared for the sight of almost any creature imaginable—any creature unimaginable.

This was unimaginable and shocking. Overpowering.

The alien was male, tall by the standards of its people, vigorous-looking and topped with gray hair. If it resembled anything Kirk had seen before, it was his own father.

Gulliver had been right all along—only his geography was inaccurate.

Kirk underwent some localized tremors of his own as he tried to readjust his thinking.

The man spoke in a high-pitched but nonetheless impressive voice, a voice filled with a dignity and earnestness that bespoke long experience as a leader of men living in desperate circumstances.

"In the name of the Terratin people," he said formally, "I forbid you to take offensive action against this city, Captain Kirk."

Kirk spoke into the helm pickup mike, trying to put as much sarcasm into his voice as possible. "You forbid me, after what you've done to my ship and to my friends?"

"I am Mandant of all this city," the figure told him with assurance, "superior in command to yourself."

"Sorry," Kirk informed the speaker grimly, his finger quivering on the fatal button, "Mandant is not a recognized Starfleet rank."

At this point the leader's tone softened noticeably.

"We are a people of considerable pride, Captain. Equal in pride to your own. We neither suffer insult, nor give apology for actions we deem necessary, but...," and here he hesitated, obviously struggling with himself to find the words for something he was quite unused to saying, "I give apologies now for the inconvenience done your ship and crew."

Inconvenience!

"To make amends I may tell you that this world contains . . ."

"I'm not interested in what your world contains just now," Kirk replied angrily. "Where are Mr. Spock, Lieutenant Sulu, and the rest of my officers?"

"I order...," the Mandant began and then he stopped, glanced away. "No . . . no. Not order. Please try to understand, Captain Kirk. Our adopted world is dying, has been dying for many years. No ship of an intelligent race had passed this way until yours came exploring.

"We tried to tell you of our plight as you entered orbit, but our great communications antenna was buried too deep by sequential flows of lava and ash. We were, we are, desperate, Captain. We *had* to make some kind of contact with you. The only device we had remaining to us which conceivably could have made you take notice was our invasion defense system, and . . ."

"You still haven't answered my question," Kirk interrupted him. "Either you tell me what's happened to my people . . ."

The Mandant abruptly moved aside . . . to reveal a healthy Sulu and Arex. Both were carrying tools of unfamiliar design, yet vaguely familiar in outline. Neither showed any sign of mistreatment.

"Here we are, Captain." Arex speaking, normal, relaxed.

"We're in the capitol building of the Terratin city, sir," Sulu explained. "As you've probably guessed, they beamed us down with their transporters."

Now why didn't they just do that in the first place? Kirk found the answer immediately after the thought occurred. If the Terratins had tried to make contact by transporting down members of the *Enterprise,* even one person would have obliterated not only the transport station but probably half the city as well.

That's why they had to use their invasion defense system first, to reduce the crew sufficiently in size to where they could be brought into the city.

Kirk wondered if the Terratin engineers knew that the crew members would return to their normal size once transported back to the *Enterprise.* That was a question best side-stepped for the moment. The important thing was that Sulu and the others were all right.

But he didn't let himself relax until he had reset the phaser controls to normal and lifted his finger from the red button.

"What's going on down there, Lieutenant Sulu?"

"See for yourself, sir." He stepped out of view, favoring his injured leg. Arex and the Mandant did likewise.

As the pickup panned the great hall, Kirk saw McCoy and Chapel tending to a mass of people scattered on beds about the chamber. The room was packed to overflowing with people. Normal, human-type people, except for their size. Many of them appeared to be burn victims. Kirk rubbed idly at a hole on the shoulder of his own shirt where one of the flying embers had burned through. He did not need to be told what the sufferers in that hall were experiencing.

Even as he watched, the picture shook visibly and the people in the building reacted to the new quake. There was no panic, however, only a few gasps and the shushing of crying children. These people were used to such shocks by now, if not resigned to them.

Panning further, the pickup finally settled on Spock. The science officer was working with several Terratins. They appeared to be struggling to repair what resembled a video-broadcast unit of extremely ancient design. His anxiety over the condition of his companions now satisfied, Kirk permitted his curiosity full flow.

"Mr. Spock!" The first officer looked up. "Who are the Terratins? Where did they come from?"

The first officer of the *Enterprise* spoke toward the screen. Kirk could hear him clearly.

"An intriguing historical sidelight, Captain," he began, with typically scholarly reserve. "From the records I have had time to examine, they appear to be the descendants of an early lost colony ship. They are, despite differences in size, of the same Terran stock as yourself.

"Believing their colony to be the tenth to be founded, they named this world Terra Ten—which over the years has become the present corrupted form, Terratin."

"All very plausible, Mr. Spock, except for that slight difference in size. I doubt we would find any records of Earth ships carrying colonists a sixteenth of a centimeter tall."

"The original colonists were normal-sized humans," Spock continued. "The remarkable radiation which they have incorporated into their unique defensive system is present naturally in a transuranic element quite common on the surface here. This defensive system intensifies the compaction effect of that radiation tremendously.

"The naturally present wave effect took several hundred years to reduce the colonists and their descendants to their present size. Once aware of what was happening, they were able, as were we, to predict the ultimate dimensions of the compaction. And to plan far in advance for it, designing all the miniature machines and devices they would need for survival."

Suddenly the Mandant reappeared on the screen, now standing beside Spock. "The colony ship was well equipped, Captain. But even with many years to prepare for this, our current state, our ancestors were forced to direct all their energies to insure their descendants' survival.

"In concentrating on survival technology, many other abilities were lost or degenerated—our ability to build deep-space communications equipment, for example. Nor could we escape, since the material inherent in a colony ship's construction is designed to be incorporated into the colony itself. Colony vessels were designed for one-way trips only. Once our ancestors began to cannibalize it for material for the first city, there was no hope of using it for travel again.

"We had to build a new way of life on this world, Captain Kirk. We had to adjust to our changing size, create a new form of defense against any potential attackers, master this planet's unstable ways. We encountered no outsiders, had no help of anyone." The screen shook again, more violently this time. When the shaking had stopped and the cries of the children in the hall had faded once more the Mandant continued, his voice growing thick with emotion.

"But as you now see, Captain, we are forced to seek outside help, for we are about to lose everything. The geologists of the original colony selected what they believed to be one of the most seismically stable regions on the surface. Yet even here we were never wholly immune to quakes and tremors. Their intensity has grown alarmingly in recent months.

"We began to hunt frantically for outside aid. And we began to despair of contacting another vessel. When your *Enterprise* went into orbit here we were hysterical with hope, despite the earlier destruction of our communications system. We are only able to contact you now," he made a gesture off screen to his left, "due to the knowledge of your Mr. Spock.

"We had to contact you and request if we could, compel if we must, your help. Many thousands look to me to preserve their lives, Captain Kirk. Even so, I hesitated before ordering the defense system brought into play. I apologize again if in gaining your attention we caused any anguish to you or your crew."

"Your actions all but lost us our ship," Kirk responded, his tone turning milder even as he spoke the words. "If I hadn't accidentally discovered that our transporters could return us to normal size, we would have lost total control of the *Enterprise*. That would have been the end of us and any help we could have given you."

"Again, I am sorry, Captain Kirk," the Mandant replied, torn between natural pride and the utter desperateness of his situation, "if in gaining your attention we utilized the first rule of politics—do that which is expedient rather than that which may be right. Really, we had no other choice." He paused, and all traces of arrogance vanished in a naked plea.

"I do not know how to beg, Captain Kirk. I can therefore only request, ask you to save as many of my people as you can. My counselors and I decided to use our defensive system to contact you. If you bear any grudge against us, we will submit whatever judgment you deem fit.

"In any case, we of course insist on being the last to be taken off."

"Don't be idiotic," Kirk found himself mumbling. He was vaguely aware that the Mandant was manipulating his emotions with a skill born of long practice, but somehow it didn't seem to matter. Not with the lives of a city at stake.

Uhura had entered the field of visual pickup and was looking out at Kirk. "They had no other way left to them, sir. They meant us no harm."

Kirk had already arrived at that opinion independently. But there were other things that had to be done first, no matter how it made him look to the anxious Terratins.

"I can help no one under present conditions," he told the Mandant, staring firmly into the pickup. "I can't run the *Enterprise* myself. All bridge crew, prepare to beam aboard. See to it, Lieutenant." She nodded, disappeared from the screen.

"Oh . . . and Uhura?" Her face reappeared. "The Terratins are a Earth colony. That means they have Federation or at least pre-Federation technology. Is their city by any chance powered by. . . ?"

"Dilithium, Captain?" The communications officer

smiled. "Lieutenant Arex has already checked on that. It sure is, Captain." Kirk allowed himself to mirror her grin.

"Mandant, are you still there?" The leader of the Terratin colony reappeared a moment later.

"Yes, Captain Kirk. This difficulty, at least, has been anticipated. Your officers informed us of your difficulty in this regard. This world contains substantial deposits of dilithium. The natural wave radiation here is not strong enough to affect its internal structure in the way our defensive beams do. We have a certain amount of refined crystals on hand not essential to the operation of the city. It was this I tried to tell you before.

"My people have been transferring a stock of the largest crystals to a storage area near our main transporter. The move is nearly completed. They will be made available to you for whatever use you require."

"You realize, don't you," Kirk ventured, "that once I have the rest of my bridge crew aboard and the engines repowered, we might easily destroy your defense system and leave you stranded here."

The Mandant looked solemn.

"This is all obvious, Captain Kirk." That was all he said. The directness and openness of his reply made Kirk feel uncomfortable he had even considered such a thought.

"Okay then. Lieutenant Uhura?"

She reappeared on the screen.

"Captain?"

"As long as we retain power I'd just as soon use our own transporters. The Terratin computer has patterns of you only for your present size. As long as you're coming back aboard you may as well do so at the proper size.

"It's going to take me a minute or two to get down to the transporter room. The dilithium crystals are ready to come aboard?"

"Nearly, sir."

"Tell the others to stand by."

"Yes, *sir!*"

He had one bad moment in the transporter room. It looked as if he had misjudged the amount of reserve power remaining and would not have enough to beam them back aboard. But by shutting down all life-support in several unoccupied storage compartments, plus the shuttlecraft hanger, he was able to divert a fair amount to the transporter. It wouldn't run forever, but by the time reserve power ran out they should have the Terratin dilithium aboard and the engines powered up.

Kirk studied the image in the transporter console viewscreen as he prepared to beam the bridge crew up. They were in another chamber of the capitol building. This one was also filled with refugees from the rain of hot ash outside.

The picture jerked a couple of times. Not from a planetary, but from a human-induced tremor, as Terratin technicians moved the pickup around. It finally settled on Spock and the rest. They were arranging themselves for beam-up while the Terratins divided huge masses of crystalline dilithium among them.

At least, they appeared huge beside the compacted crew. Actually, they were normal-sized crystals and Kirk knew he could hold the entire amount in one palm.

Terratins driving powered carts continued to arrive with more and more of the vital mineral. Kirk allowed them to heap the crystals around the feet of Uhura, Sulu, and the others until it was overflowing outside the range of transporter pickup.

"That will have to do, Mr. Spock. We can get more the next time. Prepare to beam up."

"Very well, Captain." The first officer turned away for a moment and said something to one of the Terratin technicians. He nodded and backed out of range, but Kirk could hear him speaking to the crowd.

Immediately both colonists and the cart unloaders moved away from the waiting crewmembers. Spock turned to take up his place in the group, stared straight ahead as the Terratins moved their visual pickup further back.

"We're ready, Captain. You may energize at any time."

Kirk worked the transporter controls in proper sequence, his gaze moving constantly from the console to the viewscreen. Familiar sparkling cylinders formed around the crew as the transporter effect took hold. His gaze moved to the empty alcove in front of him as the whine of shifting energies filled the chamber.

The multiple shapes were materializing in the alcove, fullsize, along with irregular clumps at their feet. Dilithium, visible as gravel now instead of boulders. He shifted down, turned a dial, and the effect faded around darkening silhouettes.

"Nice to be back aboard, sir," Uhura murmured with undisguised relief, "and back at one's natural size."

Kirk nodded, spoke quickly. "Everyone watch where you step. We had enough trouble finding this dilithium. Before you move off those disks, gather up those crystals." As they all bent, he turned his attention back to the console, flipped on the ship-wide com.

"All crew personnel report to the main transporter room immediately. Prepare to beam down to the surface. Beam-down and return will bring you back to normal size. Repeat, all crew report to the main transporter room immediately. Move along the walls. Normal-sized personnel will take proper precautions."

Spock came over, both hands cupping the precious load of accumulated dilithium. It looked appallingly small compared to what he had seen on the viewscreen.

"The Terratins are making available every crystal they can spare, Captain. The specimens are small, but I believe they will provide enough power to operate the ship efficiently until we can get a mining crew down to the surface."

Kirk made a sign of agreement, looked past Spock. "Mr. Sulu, take over the transporter, please. Mr. Arex, you will move to B deck to handle transportation problems there. See that Mr. Scott and his engineers are in the first round trip, Sulu." The lieutenant nodded.

"They can handle the rest of the transporting, then," Kirk continued. "As soon as everyone has made the circuit and is restored to proper size, see that Mr. Scott gets a geotech crew down to dig out a sufficient supply of dilithium." He grinned.

"At least we won't have to go prospecting for it. That's another way the Terratins can be of help."

"Excuse me a moment, sir." Sulu was beginning to adjust the transporter controls for the next beam-down ... but slowly. "What *about* the Terratins? The people in the city are in a state of barely surpressed panic and . . ."

"You have your orders, Mr. Sulu."

"Yes, sir." All hint of expression disappeared from the lieutenant's face as he turned full attention to the instrumentation.

Kirk took half of the double handful of vital crystals, eyed Spock. "Ever on-loaded an active dilithium reaction chamber by hand, Mr. Spock?"

"No, Captain. But the process is reputed to be fail-safe. As I evaluate the steps involved, I forsee only a very small chance of our destroying the ship."

"Thank you, Spock. I can always depend on you for a feeling of security and reassurance. Let's go." Together the two officers started for the elevator doors.

"Slowly, Captain," Spock advised his friend, as Kirk started off at a run from the elevator. "It would be awkward to drop the crystals—or not to see some of our still compacted companions until too late . . ."

"Don't worry, Spock. I'll choose my steps with as much care as you choose your words." The first officer jogged silently alongside as they neared the door to engineering section marked in bold red characters . . .

DILITHIUM REACTION CHAMBER—AUTHORIZED PERSONNEL ONLY!

VI

His disclaimer of experience notwithstanding, Spock managed the loading of the new supply of raw dilithium into the minutely balanced chamber with all the skill of a reaction specialist—just as Kirk had known he would.

Impulse power was fed to the chamber to spark a greater reaction. A number of gauges on the nearest monitor immediately jumped upward with gratifying speed.

Spock was ready with the results by the time Kirk had re-established life-support and power in the sections he had shut off earlier.

"We will not be able to travel to the nearest starbase, Captain, but essential functions no longer have to be checked as closely and we could break out of orbit at any time.

"And the next load of dilithium should make us fully secure until Scotty and his mining crew can get to work." He let out a sigh of relief, moved to the intercom.

"Mr. Sulu?"

"Main transporter room here, Captain; but it's Third Transporter Engineer Lefebre in charge. Mr. Sulu has returned to the bridge, sir. I was directed to take charge here as soon as I was returned to normal size."

"Carry on, Mr. Lefebre. Is Mr. Scott there?"

"Mr. Scott left some minutes ago for Engineering Central, sir. Said something about working on the engines. He did request that I inform you when you called in that Second Engineer Gabler and a party of five

have beamed down to the surface with appropriate
equipment and are already engaged in extracting an ad-
equate supply of raw dilithium for future needs—under
the direction of geologists from the Terratin city."

"Thank you, Lefebre. Kirk out."

"Transporter Central out." Kirk started for the elevator, Spock at his side.

"It appears that we shall soon be fully powered up
once more, Captain."

"Yes, Mr. Spock. As soon as we've taken on all the
dilithium we'll need, we can leave this place."

Spock raised a questioning brow, but Kirk had
moved slightly ahead of him and didn't notice it.

Or if he did, he chose to ignore the suggestion behind it.

The ship's transporter facilities worked overtime for
the next several hours, beaming ant-sized humans down
to the Terratin city and rematerializing them on board
in their normal guise moments later.

The Mandant stood in the crowded chamber,
watching humans come and go via transporter. Now
and then he leaned to confer with one of his aides or to
eye the visual linkup which had been hastily set up in
the room.

It showed several views of the city outskirts, now
menaced from three directions by abysses and crevices
which grew with even the slightest of tremors. Another
screen revealed the interior of the Terratin science center where worried geologists hurried back and forth.
They paused only long enough to deliver increasingly
desperate reports.

The Mandant acknowdged every report, spoke steadily and reassuringly to his aides . . . all the while trying
to keep a calming hand on the metropolis itself. The
macropsychosis of the city was fast approaching chaos
proportions.

Already a mob was forming outside, threatening to
storm the hall and hold the next group of aliens who
beamed down as hostages until guaranteed rescue was
effected. What kind of rescue was not specified, but

that made the demonstrators no less virulent in their demands.

The Mandant smiled sadly to himself. Such people would always exist, never to be calmed, never to be satisfied.

We exist for such a minute time, he mused. We perform a great many inconsequential nothings and call them Acts of Significance, realizing the futility of our lies all the while. Yet we constantly strive for the postponement of the inevitable end which would bring peace to all. Such is the nature of man, and it does not change with his physical stature.

For himself it mattered not what the captain of the starship chose to do. For the young adults and children it mattered a great deal. Some of his aides still had confidence in the remnants of their defensive system. The Mandant knew better. Now that the location of their city was known, they were completely helpless.

Their eventual fate depended on the whim of a man whose ship and command they had nearly destroyed for their own need. Even so, if he were forced to go back he felt he would be compelled to do everything exactly as it had been done before.

But while he could control his fear of death he still had a responsibility to the people.

So when the next group of crewmen appeared in the room, he moved rapidly to stand next to them before the transporter took hold and asked, "Please inform your captain that the reports from our remote seismic research stations are very discouraging. It is apparent now that the former stability of this area is fast diminishing. We doubt we can survive continued quakes much longer without some form of aid.

"Our entire city is constructed on an interlocking series of precision bearings and gimbals mounted in a viscous fluid. These serve to keep us upright and steady despite the severity of successive jolts. Though we are rocked a little from time to time, as your fellow crew members can attest.

"But while we can withstand the most violent shakings we cannot withstand the peril that faces us now. A number of enormous—by our measurements—cracks in the ground are forming outside the city . . . and are expanding with each new quake. According to predictions from our science center, they will undercut the city in a very short time and drop us to our doom.

"Your captain must tell us—shall we prepare to be rescued, all or part of us? Or to die—all or part of us."

The young yeoman who stood nearest looked back at the Mandant with wide eyes. "I don't know, sir, but. . . ." The air began to glow around him. "I think I have a pretty good idea what Captain Kirk's decision will . . ."

His words were cut off as the transporter energies surged around him and stole him from sight.

Kirk glanced at his wrist chronometer again before turning his attention back to the gauges, dials and readouts he was inspecting in his walk around the bridge. The *Enterprise* was back to battle efficiency again—fully manned and fully powered.

More than fully powered. If the dilithium Gabler's hastily improvised crew had brought back was anything less than a mother lode, the Terratin world might one day become a major source of that fabulously valuable material. Though he doubted it would ever be much of a colony world.

"How's the helm now, Mr. Sulu," he asked.

The lieutenant looked back at Kirk. "Fully responsive, sir. All instrumentation appears normal once again. All readings are up to red-alert capabilities."

"Subspace radio now operational too, sir," Uhura put in from over at communications. "I have had contact with Star Base Twenty-three and have informed them of the situation prevailing here. They are recording currently."

"Very good, Lieutenant. You might also relay to them tapes of everything that has taken place in the past twenty-four hours."

"Yes, Captain." Uhura turned back to her mike, began talking into it low and steady.

Kirk heard the elevator door hum, turned to see Scott step onto the bridge. All questions about the state of the ship's engines were answered by the broad smile on the chief engineer's face.

"The last of the crew has been through the double transporter trip, sir. Everythin' runnin' smooth as a mother's lullaby. To look at the power levels you'd think we'd never had any trouble here."

"Almost, Mr. Scott." There was one last problem to be dealt with. He turned to face the helm. "Mr. Arex, prepare ship for immediate departure from this region."

Arex looked ready to say something but another listener beat him to it.

"I beg your pardon, Captain."

Kirk turned to the science station. Spock was staring at him evenly. His voice was a monotone. "What about the people on the planet?"

"I haven't forgotten them, Mr. Spock. I know exactly what to do. I thought about it while the rest of the crew were beaming up. It's the only thing that can be done." He looked to the helm.

"Mr. Sulu, direct forward phasers to the region of the Terratin city."

"Captain, I. . ."

Kirk moved to stand next to him, smiled reassuringly. "It's all right, Mr. Sulu. We'll require pinpoint fire control. There are some precision adjustments necessary—but believe me, this is the best way."

Using the computer linkup to phaser control, he proceeded to trace with the electronic stylus a certain pattern of fire on the targeting screen. Behind them, Uhura, Scott and Spock had all turned from their responsibilities of the moment to watch. All but Arex, who continued with his part of the preparations for leaving the area. Of all of them, only he had some idea of what Kirk was going to try.

"Can you handle that, Mr. Sulu?" he asked when he'd finished with the computations. The helmsman studied the carefully wrought fire pattern and nodded slowly.

"I'm sure I can, sir. I would like to incorporate a fail-safe into it, if I might."

"No time, Mr. Sulu," Kirk objected firmly. "We'll have to do it right on the first try. Those people down there must not be made to suffer any longer."

"Very well, Captain," Sulu acquiesced. He turned and commenced programming the phaser control computer. Once he stopped, to request some information from Spock. When that was granted, Scott and Uhura grew more curious than ever—since Spock now appeared to know what was going on, too.

Neither dared interrupt what was clearly a harried operation. But when Spock was finished relaying Sulu's needed statistics, Scott moved to stand next to the first officer.

"For the love of Loch Lomond, what's happenin', Mr. Spock? What's the captain up to?"

Spock turned unblinking eyes on him. "Nothing more than what the captain has already stated, Mr. Scott, though I confess to having been somewhat mystified as to his intentions at first, myself." He turned back to his console. "I suppose one might describe it by saying we are about to embark on a program of long-range geologic dentistry."

Scott mulled this over a moment and then his face twisted into a quizzical expression. "There are some people down there I think I could grow fond of, Mr. Spock, from what I've seen of them. Don't play word games with me."

"We are attempting an extraction, Mr. Scott," Spock elucidated.

"An extraction?"

"Only instead of removing the infected region from the healthy, the captain is simply reversing the process."

Scott's expression of uncertainty lasted only long enough for a few seconds concentrated thought . . . and then his face settled into a pleased highland grin as the truth was revealed.

On the west side of the city two yawning crevices—soil-sided, rock-toothed—pierced the outlying farmland. The atmosphere behind the tiny gilt spires and soaring steel buttresses had turned orange with the burning hills in the distance. Thunder rattled the valley and sharp slivers of blue flame broke through the orange at distant intervals.

The continued existence of intelligent life on this world was becoming impossible.

"Now, Kyle!" Kirk yelled into the intercom. Long pause while everyone held his breath and waited—until Transporter Chief Kyle's voice sounded over the com. with an air of exhausted accomplishment.

"Got 'em, Captain."

"Are you sure, Kyle?"

"Aye, sir. It took a helluva lot of power for so broad a subject, but we're holding."

"Outstanding, Mr. Kyle. I'm on my way down. Hold it in stasis until we get there, just in case."

"Will do, sir."

Kirk and Spock hurried from the bridge. They moved impatiently through elevators, down corridors, heading for the bulk transporter room near the Shuttle Bay.

Minutes later they were standing beside Chief Kyle, staring at the considerable object which had appeared in the cavernous chamber. It was the Terratin city, neatly sliced from the planet's surface.

The city proper rested on about a half meter of crystalline bedrock, it's gimbal-bearing support system buried within and keeping it steady as always.

An astonishingly efficient system, Kirk mused, which when increased in size and adapted to other Federation colonies on active worlds would save thousands, perhaps millions of lives.

At the moment, the city was still enveloped in the shifting spectral phosphorescence of the transporter effect.

"Set it down, Chief."

"Aye, sir," Kyle replied. He activated the necessary instrumentation, pushed slowly up on a certain lever.

The three men watched as the fairyland of towers and domes materialized on the deck. The city, complete to farmlands and forest belt, fitted neatly into the chamber.

If the city had appeared unusual on the surface, Kirk reflected, here on board it was thoroughly unreal. Unreally beautiful, too. No, he wasn't worried about the Terratins finding a useful niche in Federation society. Any people who could construct a habitation of pure loveliness under the incredible stresses imposed by the world below would contribute more than their share to any society they joined.

If anything, their participation in Federation affairs would be outsized.

He took a couple of steps closer, peering into the depths of the transported metropolis and wishing he could see and hear the inhabitants clearly. Spock again proved himself open to suspicion of mind-reading—or perhaps clarvoyance!

"I took the liberty of having this made up in bioengineering as soon as I divined your intentions toward the Terratins, Captain." Kirk turned and saw that Spock was bringing a large device out from behind the transporter console. It looked very much like a telescope pointing the wrong way. It was all of that—and a good deal more.

There seemed to be a great deal of activity around the open platform which girdled the tallest tower in the city. Kirk helped Spock aim the narrower end of the device toward it.

"Speak normally, Captain. The instrument will project and mollify your tones simultaneously." Kirk cleared his throat, adjusted the focus on the visual. One of the people on the platform looked familiar, though more composed than Kirk remembered him—which was understandable.

"Mandant?" The figure smiled, nodded. "We welcome your people on board the *Enterprise*."

The leader of the Terratin colony stared up at the monstrous machine. Behind him, his counselors and aides grew gradually less timid, moved out to stare up in their turn, look 'round in wonderment. To look at the Mandant, you would have thought he traveled with his city by starship at least once a year. A very cool individual, Kirk thought. He had no more worries about the Terratins' ability to handle themselves in Federation politics.

"Captain Kirk, we welcome your eye upon our city and hope you find it fair."

"I would tend to say stunning rather than fair, Mandant," Kirk responded honestly. "Right now it's about the most gorgeous thing on the *Enterprise*. Much as I hate to lose you, I'll have to admit my ship's not a sufficient setting for it."

"What do you have planned for us then, Captain?"

"There is a small world named Verdanis in a system ten days' cruising from here, Mandant. Verdanis is a lush world, much like Earth itself, but devoid of an animal life. It is also about the size of the solarian asteroid Ceres. Too small and too far away to support a normal colony, but I think more than sufficient for your people. Under Federation protection I think you will thrive and grow there—in a relative sense, of course."

The Mandant smiled back at him. "It sounds idyllic, Captain. I do not know how to begin to thank you."

"Thanks are not in order, Mandant. However, it may please you to know that while your adopted world will never support a large population, it looks to become a mining world of considerable importance for its dilithium deposits alone."

"The rescue of a portion of our population was all we could ever hope for, Captain Kirk. To be saved such, with our homes and city too, and then to be given a new, friendlier world, is beyond prayer."

Someone whispered in his ear—one of the aides—and the Mandant paused to listen to him. He turned and appeared to engage in conversation with several of the counselors.

When he turned back to Kirk, the counselors could be seen smiling in the background.

"I believe it is appropriate for me to make a very short speech, Captain." Kirk waited quietly. "People of the *Enterprise*," the Mandant intoned importantly, "we have no way we can possibly pay the debt we owe you. But this one little thing we can give, and upon this one thing we are all agreed." He gestured around, his arms taking in the city surrounding him. "We name you all honorary Terratins, now and for all time to come."

"A singular honor," observed Spock drily, "insofar as we came rather close to making it more than merely an honorary title." Kirk looked away from the eye piece.

"Somewhere along the lines of one sixteenth of a centimeter close?"

"I would say about that, Captain." Kirk grinned back at him.

Maximum attention was paid to the Terratins as the ship moved towards Verdanis. Once Starfleet deciphered the first reports on the lost miniature colony, a flood of requests for information kept Uhura and M'ress bound to the communications console.

A missing link in Federation prehistory was filled in as the ship's historian took tape after tape from the city's miniscule library stacks. Ship geologists spent days in conference with their bug-sized brothers discussing living under constant quake conditions. And all the engineers marveled over the construction of the city itself, with particular marveling reserved for the remarkable Terratin city gimbal support system. Nothing like it existed anywhere in the Federation.

There was a brief ceremony of departure when the *Enterprise* went into orbit around Verdanis. The world was officially renamed Verdantin, good wishes were exchanged, formalities of possession signed, and then the city was transported down onto a broad plain filled with miniature streams and—to the Terratins—Sequoia-sized fungi.

"What do you think will become of them, Jim?" McCoy wondered. He was staring at the main viewscreen, which showed the city nestled in among the towering vegetation. A nearby pond formed a broad lake at the far end of the transplanted metropolis.

"Their location will be on public file with Starfleet Central, of course. Eventually it will become common knowledge throughout the Federation. But from what I've seen I don't think the Terratins will be satisfied with protectorate status for very long. They'll want full membership. That means trade, the exchange of ideas and material. With first settlement rights to their original home planet—and its mineral wealth—they'll wield considerable financial clout."

"That's fine for the immediate future, of course ... but what of the day after tomorrow?"

Kirk looked over from the command chair, considered. "One's tempted to say they'd be in trouble, Bones, but I think not. You should hear what the engineering people are saying about some of their quake-resistant machinery. It looks as if they're going to become a much sought-after group. Some of their techniques and references are badly dated, but skill and ability do not go out of fashion." He returned his attention to the screen.

"Why, I'd be willing to predict for openers that when population controls are released, Verdantin is going to become one of the biggest exporters of precision machinery in the Federation." He looked at his wrist and smiled.

"Do you know, Bones, that the Mandant and some of his counselors wear wrist chronometers every bit as accurate as the one I'm wearing? It takes a forty-five-hundred credit instrument under the control of a master timemaker nearly an hour to properly adjust the timing pin where it sets into the vibrating crystal. One of the Terratin engineers fixed it for me before the city was transported down ... in a couple of minutes.

"Do you know what precision, super-miniaturized

tool he used, Bones?" He eyed the doctor challengingly. "A crowbar."

"I see what you're driving at," Bones confessed, suddenly excited. "In fact, I begin to see some possibilities myself. Damn! If I'd only spent some time with their best surgeons, instead of setting bones and treating burns. . . !" He was thinking furiously.

"I wonder, Jim . . . do you suppose some of the Terratin doctors might consider a little experimental surgery . . . wearing diving suits?"

Kirk didn't comment, but McCoy rambled on, his voice taking on a reverent tone.

"Wouldn't it be wonderful, Jim, if we could perform heart operations as an inside job. . .?"

PART II

TIME TRAP

(Adapted from a script from Joyce Perry)

VII

Kirk tossed uneasily in his sleep. Strange, unknown energies were buffeting the *Enterprise*. No matter what maneuver, no matter what speed, no matter what attitude change he ordered, she seemed unable to break the grasp of the malignant invisibility.

Around them, space was solidifying, tangible tendrils and fingers and ropy tentacles materializing out of the black depths. All reaching out, out, for the ship.

An inky pseudopod looped itself tightly around an unsuspecting engineer. A long finger folded crookedly over the bridge itself, while somewhere in the distant well of infinity a mad voice giggled.

He ordered full phaser fire, but the beams simply assaulted space itself, the ravening fire passing harmlessly through semisolid members. The *Enterprise* rolled, pitched, shook, unable to loosen the slowly contracting grip of those gigantic digits.

Two of them entered the bridge, one from either wall. They started to move toward each other. Kirk, frozen in his command chair, was in the exact middle. Someone screamed. He tried to rise from the chair and discovered he couldn't.

The black thumbs moved nearer and nearer, closing off his view of the rest of the bridge, blotting out Spock and Uhura and Arex and Sulu and the main viewscreen and the phaser controls and the black cat slinking along the deck. Spock and the others had shown no sign, no awareness, of approaching oblivion.

Didn't they see? Couldn't they feel the massive claws flowing in upon them like black glaciers to crush and squeeze and pinch? He tried to call to Spock but seemed to have lost his voice along with his mobility.

All ignored him as he tried to shout; all went about their usual tasks as the life was taken from them. Only Bones turned, once. Incredibly, his gaze went right through Kirk as if he weren't there.

The black fingers tensed tighter. The harder he struggled, the more firmly rooted he was in the chair.

And all the while the ship continued to shake as dozens of other cyclopean tendrils and fingers pulled and wrenched at it. No one paid the least attention. Pressing hard now the fingers dug in. Now they were at his very shoulders, squeezing, pressing tighter and tighter. Compression started a ringing in his ears and he felt pressure on both sides of his head.

Ringing . . . a mocking, insistent ringing that grew and grew as he tried to shut it out. Struggled to shut it out. Fought to shut it out.

And failed.

He shot to a sitting position in bed, hands behind him, eyes wide and unwinking—instantly wide awake. Then he slumped ever so slightly and ran a hand across his forehead. He rubbed at both eyes, but the buzzing and ringing didn't go away. Instead, they were transformed into a steady, almost familiar hum. It pulled at his attention insistently.

Thought . . . he turned, saw the winking red light set over his bunk. Pressed the *acknowledge* button. At the same time a strong tremor jolted the covers around him.

"Kirk here."

"I think you had better come forward, Captain. We have just impacted the perimeter of the Delta Triangle. As you can tell from the recent shake, things are beginning to happen already."

"All right, Mr. Spock." He paused while another, more violent vibration rattled his living quarters. "I'll be forward in five minutes."

He dressed rapidly. His mind raced as he hurried toward the bridge.

Following the establishment of the lost Terratin colony on the tiny world of Verdantin, the *Enterprise* had received orders to proceed to the Delta Triangle. The order had been transmitted and accepted with a quiet assurance at both ends of the transmission that neither broadcaster nor receiver felt.

There were too many unanswered questions about the Delta Triangle, none of them inspiring to a starship captain.

Kirk leaned against a corridor wall as yet another jolt shook the *Enterprise*. Noticing the uneasy, almost frightened look of two young yeomen who were walking the opposite way, he smiled confidently at them as he passed. Their incipient fears vanished, but not his own.

The Delta Triangle had a reputation that was well known. It was a vast, uninhabited, unexplored sector of the galaxy in the outer reaches of the Federation's influence. Its reputation stemmed from the number of disappearances occuring there of both manned and unmanned starships. Some dated from ancient times. Nor were they all Federation ships. Whatever was responsible for the multitude of disappearances made no distinctions as to race or region.

For awhile it had been enough simply to prohibit ships from entering the area. Nonetheless some persisted. Miners, traders, religious fanatics—the Delta Triangle was an irresistible magnet for them all.

Sometimes they came out, unharmed and having seen or found nothing. Often they disappeared, without a message, without a trace.

Now the expanding Federation found its frontiers pressing hard against the Delta Triangle. Should they avoid it and grow only in other directions? Or were there worlds within worth exploring . . . and exploiting?

Starfleet Command studied, thought, considered the problem. They decided the time had come to risk a full-scale exploration of the sector with a major research vessel. That meant a ship of the *Enterprise*'s class.

That meant, specifically, the *Enterprise*.

The alarm lights were flashing to suitable aural accompaniment as he stalked onto the bridge. His first glance was for the helm navigation console, where Sulu and Arex were working frantically. Moving near, he peered over the Edoan's shoulder.

An area roughly triangular in shape was projected on the navigation grid. A tiny, regularly-flashing blip sat just inside the bottom edge of the triangle. Neither blip nor triangle were to scale, but it was enough to show how little of the mysterious region they had managed to penetrate.

And trouble already.

Kirk nodded to nobody in particular, turned and took up his position in the command chair. Sulu cut off the alarm lights and sound. Another jolt rocked the ship as the captain took his seat. The jolts were getting stronger. For a second he thought he was back prowling the unsteady surface of the Terratin world.

It was time for facts.

"Situation, Mr. Spock?"

Spock spared him a brief glance before returning his attention to the library computer console. He looked more than usually preoccupied with his instruments.

"Indeterminate, Captain. Many of our sensors have become completely unreliable. Some continue to function, while others give readings which are patently impossible. And this wholesale disruption of detection sensors shows no internal pattern.

"The phenomenon commenced the moment we entered the Triangle sector. I do have one positive external reading, however. A solid object lies directly ahead, though it barely registers on the long-range sensors."

Kirk considered this information thoughtfully. "And

this object is the source of the instrumentation disruptions, Spock?"

Now the first officer did take the time to look away from his readouts. "That is the odd thing about it, Captain. This newly detected mass appears to have nothing whatsoever to do with the addled sensors. Interesting."

"Very," Kirk agreed. "Has visual identification been tried?"

"Not yet, sir," Sulu volunteered. "The object Mr. Spock refers to has just come within range of our maximum visual scan."

"Let's see if we can't pick it up, then, Lieutenant. Magnification ten on forward scanners."

"Magnification ten, sir," Sulu echoed, working the controls just to the right of the phasers.

Kirk's gaze shifted to the main viewscreen. It showed the speckled blackness of deep space just ahead. Another of the unexplained jolts rocked the ship. The static that momentarily appropriated the screen was of unique and unfamiliar nature.

It sputtered out, leaving a grainy, pebbled picture behind. Despite the lack of clarity, there was no difficulty in identifying the object picked up by Spock's operational detectors.

A Klingon battle cruiser.

It appeared to hang motionless against the distant star-field, hovering against the emptiness like the great bird of prey it was vaguely patterned after, though Kirk knew it was anything but motionless. The scanners compensated for its actual speed.

It was a surprise to see an Imperial Klingon vessel here. The Klingons were not considered to be among the more adventurous races where abnormalities of time and space were concerned. The Delta Triangle was one of the last places Kirk would have expected to encounter them.

Somehow he had a feeling that their presence here was unrelated to neutral exploration.

"Klingon battle cruiser," he announced, his tone becoming brisk. "Deflector shields up, Mr. Sulu."

"All deflectors up, sir."

"Recognize her, Mr. Spock?"

Spock studied the screen. "No, Captain. *Klolode*-class ship, though." Kirk nodded.

"Equivalent to our own." He directed his next order backward. "Lieutenant Uhura, open a hailing frequency and . . ."

Further conversation was cut off as several pulses of lambent color suddenly erupted from the front of the Klingon ship. The scanners were momentarily blinded. A soft rumbling was heard, and the deck trembled slightly underfoot as the barrage of disruptor bolts impinged on the *Enterprise*'s deflector screens and were repulsed. A moment later the screen cleared, showed the image of the battle cruiser shrinking rapidly with distance.

"Mr. Sulu," Kirk began angrily, "will you. . . ?"

"Following, sir," Sulu said tightly. The helmsman was obviously controlling his voice and emotions with difficulty. Kirk didn't have to ask why.

No doubt the Klingon commander had hoped to catch the *Enterprise* unprepared, her screens down, with that first attack. Seeing that it had failed, he was running now.

The Klingon's logic was not hard to follow. Were the *Enterprise* to disappear in the Delta Triangle, her demise would be recorded as just another in the age-old series of mysterious disappearances. Clever . . . and thoroughly slimy.

"He's running in a high warp arc, Captain," Sulu reported, handling the pursuit course, "but we've got her. She won't get away."

"Plotting confirmed," added Arex in his usual calm, soft tones. No sign in his voice that anything out of the ordinary had occurred.

"Ready phasers," Kirk ordered.

If the Klingon commander expected his surprise attack would go unanswered, he was badly mistaken. Letting such a provocation go would be tantamount to an admission of cowardice. That was something the

Klingons would immediately rationalize as *carte blanche* to try similar adventures in other sectors—perhaps against less well defended Federation vessels. If nothing else, a strong response was required as a deterrent to such thoughts.

"Phasers ready—approaching attack range, Captain," Sulu told him. Minutes later, "Phasers locked on target, sir."

Intolerably intense beams of deep blue lit the blackness between the *Enterprise* and the Klingon cruiser that sat squarely in the center of the main viewscreen.

The Klingon had looked normal to Kirk until just before the phasers were fired. Then he had noticed—or thought he had noticed—a peculiar wavering of space around the alien warship. A suggestion of motion where there should have been no motion. A hint of light where light was absent.

Probably a trick of the eyes. In any case, he had no time to consider it. The two bursts from the ship's forward phasers impacted on the Klingon's deflector screens.

One of two things should have happened.

The shields should have flared brilliantly with the strain of absorbing the phaser energy or, if the bursts were strong enough and contacted the shields at a weak enough point, the ship should have shown damage from the powerful attack. Neither took place.

Instead, the Klingon cruiser vanished.

Not in a burst of incandescent flame, not in a sudden supernal explosion—it just vanished. One second the ship was there, awaiting the counterattack of the *Enterprise*—and then there was only the silence of space in its place, nothing to indicate the cruiser had ever existed.

At least, that's how it appeared to a flabbergasted Kirk.

The first step was outside confirmation of his own observations. His attempt to secure same was not subtle, but had instead the virtue of directness.

"Mr. Spock, did you just see what I think I just saw?"

"Not only did I just see what you think you just saw, Captain, but I am now observing what you think you don't."

"So we concur on analysis if not on grammar. Explanation?"

Spock's attention was divided between the main viewscreen, numerous gauges set above the computer keyboard, and his double-hooded viewer. Several moments of intense study of all three areas produced a reply tinged with the faintest hint of uncertainty.

"I can offer nothing plausible at this time, Captain. However . . ." Studying yet another new bit of information, he hesitated. "Playback of sensor readings taken just prior to the disappearance of the Klingon ship, when examined at ultraslow speed, indicate that the ship was not destroyed, repeat, *not* destroyed, by our phaser fire.

"Replay further *implies* that the enemy vessel's shielding was operating at full strength and successfully deflected both phaser bursts though no direct evidence of such shielding was detectable."

Kirk paused a moment, asked, "What about the possibility they're using a variety of the invisibility shield we've encountered before?"

"I do not think so, Captain. That produces definite, detectable reactions, measurable stresses in the fabric of space. Nothing of the sort has been observed."

"*Ummm.*" Kirk thought back to the strange phenomenon he *thought* he had noticed just before the battle cruiser vanished. "Seconds before we counterattacked, Mr. Spock, I think I saw a certain—well, a kind of fluttering around the Klingon's hull."

"I observed a smiliar field-effect, Captain," Sulu said excitedly. "I thought it was a distortion in our scanners, an after-effect of the disruptor bolts."

"It is not a distortion, of either our eyes or the scanner's," Spock added. "I saw it, too."

"I'll assume visual confirmation, then," Kirk went

on. "We should have a record of the effect, Mr. Spock. Sensor analysis?"

Spock returned to his computer, made demands on recently employed tapes. "The instruments are still not registering with regularity, Captain—a disruption still unaccounted for. But I believe I can say with assurance, after scanning the pertinent information, that the Klingon ship was not in any way responsible for the effect we observed and exercised no control over it.

"As there have been numerous ship disappearances in this region, I would venture the opinion that . . ."

"Whatever caused the disappearance of the Klingon ship was a natural phenomenon," Kirk concluded. "Clearly the Klingons were expecting it no more than we were. But what kind of natural phenomenon absorbs starships without a trace?" He turned his gaze back to the viewscreen.

"At least we have some idea what to expect . . . instant, quiet annihilation. How comforting. All duty personnel, yellow-alert status."

Sulu touched the necessary switches.

"Give me a three-hundred-sixty-degree visual scan, Mr. Sulu. Horizontal plane first, then forty-five degrees, then vertical."

"Aye, Captain," the helmsman replied, making adjustments. "Scanning three-hundred-sixty-degrees horizontal." The starfield on the screen began to move from right to left as they watched.

The scan was barely a fourth completed when the scanners picked up a new phenomenon. Unlike the odd fluttering that had appeared around the vanished battle cruiser, this one was immediately identifiable. The moving blot could be only one thing.

"Captain, we have another vessel on the screen," Sulu reported. "No, make that a double pickup, sir. Both vessels moving toward us at cruising speed, angle of approach. . . ," and he spat a rapid stream of threatening figures at Kirk.

"Visual pickup holding . . . stepping up magnification, sir," the helmsman continued. The image on screen shifted, changed, held.

Two Klingon battle cruisers appeared on the screen now, and they were between the *Enterprise* and her entry point into the Triangle.

Spock had moved over to stand next to the command chair, eyed the screen. Kirk's voice was grim as he studied the pursuing vessels.

"Mousetrapped." He glanced up at his first officer. "If the surprise attack by the first ship doesn't succeed in blasting us out of existence, they have a pair of reserves ready to make sure we don't get away to tell the story."

"Speaking strictly from the standpoint of objective tactics, Spock commented drily, "an excellent idea. They are apparently most concerned that word of this altercation should never reach Starfleet Central."

"With good reason," Kirk noted. Both men turned to face the communications console as Uhura spoke up.

"Sir, we're receiving a Class Two signal from the nearest Klingon ship. Shall I acknowledge?"

"One moment, Lieutenant." Kirk looked to his helmsman. "Mr. Sulu? On my command, I want you to turn us from our present course and head for the exact coordinates where the Klingon cruiser disappeared. Warp-eight."

"Yes sir." Sulu puzzled over the order even as he made the necessary preparations. Sometimes he wished the captain would be a bit more communicative about his intentions. It occasionally seemed to him that the *Enterprise* was governed as much by surprise as by forethought.

"All right, Lieutenant," Kirk told Uhura. "Put the visual on the main screen. And I'll want this entire exchange recorded and beamed back to Starfleet Command." Uhura looked doubtful at this last.

"It will take three weeks to reach the nearest Starbase, sir. And additional time before it can be boosted and relayed to command headquarters."

"Nonetheless, let's have it on the records . . . provided the Klingons don't try to jam it."

"Aye, sir." She turned back to her board, fiddled a moment. "Signal coming in." The main viewscreen flickered briefly. Then the view of the two Klingon cruisers was replaced by a portrait of a high-ranking Klingon officer.

This particular Klingon was heavy-set and stiff-faced. He also affected a beard and mustache, the latter a thin, drooping kind once favored by Oriental mandarins on ancient Earth. It gave him an especially displeasing appearance. His eyes were impressive, his manner standard for a Klingon commander who believed himself to be in a position of incontrovertible tactical superiority . . . blunt, overbearing, irritatingly condescending.

"You have been identified as the Federation Starship *Enterprise*, Captain James T. Kirk commanding at last record." The words came out clipped, accusative.

Kirk shifted slightly in his chair, making sure the small visual pickup trained on him was giving the Klingon as good a picture of himself as they were receiving. His voice he held carefully neutral.

"Your information is correct. This is Captain Kirk speaking."

A grunt of satisfaction, then the Klingon went on. "I am Commander Kuri of the Imperial Klingon fleet. We have just witnessed the destruction of our sister ship, the *Klothos*, and we hold you responsible. Surrender immediately or we will destroy you."

Nothing like getting to the point. Diplomacy figured in Klingon requests about as much as semantic inventiveness . . . meaning not at all.

Kirk took a pained breath, hoped Kuri was enough of a reader of human expression to know what it meant; and he continued, his voice tinged with just the proper amount of exasperation.

"We did not destroy the *Klothos*—and you are well aware of it, Commander."

"Surely you don't expect me to believe it just vanished," Kuri replied furiously.

Spock leaned over, still staying out of range of the visual pickup, and whispered, "The Klingons are not good poker players, Captain. From this one's attitude and expression, I would say he is as confused as we are—and not a little bit frightened."

Kirk had no time to consider Spock's observations in detail. He went on sharply. "You may believe what you like, Commander. We were fired upon first, without warning of any kind. Naturally we returned fire. Our instruments record that the *Klothos* successfully turned back our phaser attack . . . and then disappeared. I have no more idea than you what caused it.

"But, as you are no doubt aware, we are now in the Delta Triangle. You are familiar with this region's reputation?"

Kuri suddenly seemed unsure of himself. Clearly he had believed the *Enterprise* was responsible for the disappearance of the *Klothos*. Kirk's explanation sounded plausible.

"Yes, certainly, that was why . . ." He hastily took another tack, aware of what he had almost confessed openly. "I am familar with the numerous ship disappearances recorded in this sector, yes. But that it should happen now, at such a time, is a coincidence of proportions I am not prepared to accept." He confessed the last in such a way that Kirk couldn't be sure if it was meant for his ears or for those of unseen persons hovering invisibly around them.

Kirk was the only one who responded, however. "Frankly, Commander, what you accept is of little concern to me. *Enterprise* out." He flicked a switch in the armchair console which shifted the viewscreen back to external scan. Once more the two battle cruisers dominated the picture.

At the same time he said, "Now, Mr. Sulu."

The Klingon ships vanished as Sulu drew power from the engines. Kirk called for further magnification, but the Klingons had been lost in the starfield. That wouldn't last for long.

The view on the bridge of the lead Klingon cruiser was reversed, where it was the *Enterprise* that seemed to disappear.

"Fools, idiots!" Kuri shouted. "Thinking they can escape." He had already forgotten Kirk's protestation of innocence. It was confession enough that the Federation ship was running. He turned to his own helmsman.

"Accelerate to maximum . . . use emergency power if necessary—but *do not let them escape*! Prepare to open fire."

Moving in tandem, both cruisers leaped forward in pursuit of the *Enterprise*. Using emergency power, they sprinted, closing on the Federation craft.

Range had been reduced from excessive to marginal and several minutes had passed when the gunner on board the lead Klingon cruiser looked back at his commander wonderingly.

Kuri was aware of the scrutiny. Undoubtedly the officer was wondering why the order fire was being withheld. Kuri fully intended to give the order, but he had just the least bit of hesitation, the tiniest touch of uncertainty, at the back of his mind.

He did not know Kirk personally, but he knew both his reputation and the reputation of his ship. It was not like the *Enterprise* to turn and run, no matter what the odds. A quick frontal assault, at least, a passing attempt to damage one of his two remaining ships—but instead, she had turned and run.

Nevertheless, they *were* within range.

"Both ships, fire at will," he ordered, waiting expectantly for the *Enterprise* to do . . . what? What if Kirk had been right about the disappearance of the *Klothos* being due to natural phenomena? Might not the same be waiting out there, poised to capture yet another vessel?

Disruptor bolts fled across the intervening space. A

feathery nimbus flared repeatedly around the fleeing *Enterprise* as her screens handled the assault.

The steady barrage of disruptors blanked out the rear scanners. Kirk switched to the forward pickups. By now he was more concerned about where they were going than what was behind them.

Scott was working the engineering console on the bridge. He had held off speaking as long as he could. Now he felt it was time to speak up.

"Sir, aren't we going to defend ourselves?"

"Your deflector shields are doing that quite nicely, Mr. Scott." Scott struggled to maintain a respectful attitude. This wasn't like Kirk.

"But sir, just to . . . run away, sir. We *were* attacked . . . and there are only two of them left."

The chief engineer might have felt better if he could have seen how Kirk was fighting his own instincts. "We'll turn and fight if we have to, Mr. Scott." He looked to the helm. "Mr. Sulu, are we on course for the exact spot where the *Klothos* disappeared?"

"Dead on, sir," Sulu responded, checking his readouts. "We'll arrive in . . . ten seconds. Mark, nine, eight . . ." He counted down the seconds. At six, Scott whirled from his console to announce in a stunned tone, "Captain, our deflector shields have just gone out."

Sulu commanded his attention before Kirk could reply. "Sir, the helm instrumentation has gone haywire. I can't orient myself."

"Everything is quite abnormal, Captain," Arex added. "None of the navigation readouts are behaving sanely."

"Subspace radio channels are all dead, sir," put in Uhura.

By way of mechanical afterthought, alarm lights began flashing, blinking on the bridge. None of them could see, of course, the gentle shimmering light which had suddenly appeared around the ship.

For several seconds the *Enterprise* lay enveloped in a faint, ghostly halo. Then the halo winked out, and with it, the *Enterprise*—both presumably gone to the same unimaginable, unknown destination.

Not too far away in the relative sense, a senior Klingon officer suddenly jumped halfway out of his seat, staring in disbelief at his main viewscreen. A Federation vessel had been depicted there only seconds before.

"Where did they go? Where did they run to? Navigator!" The officer in question examined his gauges and telltales, looked back helplessly at his commander.

"I do not know, Exalted One. Their ship has vanished from range of every one of our detectors—as did the *Klothos*."

Kuri sat down slowly.

It was not permitted a cruiser commander to appear frightened before his men. However, nothing in the manual of battlefield posture prohibited him from sounding concerned.

"Slow to minimum speed. Spread out, search this area. And remain in contact at all times. The second any abnormal phenomena are detected, both ships are to retreat at battle speed to the perimeter of the Delta Triangle." He turned to his communications officer.

"Keep all hailing channels open." The officer nodded. "Federation and Imperial frequencies." Now there was nothing more he could do.

First the *Klothos*—and now the *Enterprise*. Kirk had been right, then, in his explanation of the *Klothos*' disappearance. Little good it had done him!

Unless . . . unless this was another Federation trick. If there was one thing Kuri had learned through the years it was never to underestimate the deviousness of the Federation mind. But he was grasping at *f'korr*. Some gross abnormality of space-time was at work here.

It was time to proceed with the utmost caution.

On the *Enterprise* something had happened to the vision of the bridge crew. Or else something had affected the atmosphere in the room. Whether the thing was in their eyes or air, it caused everyone to see his neighbor through a faint haze. One couldn't judge distances, discern outlines; and whatever it was made the eyes hurt—and the brain, which had the responsibility of trying to sort out the distorted images and reconcile them with known memories.

No one was having much success. Those who had not fallen from their seats were hanging on for dear life. The sudden displacement was not due to any violent shaking or tumbling, although a weird vibration was running through the metal underfoot and in the hull walls. Rather, everyone was experiencing an abrupt and disquieting loss of balance. Something was causing a gross distortion within familiar surroundings.

Sulu had both arms around the back of his chair and was leaning crazily around one end, staring back in Kirk's general direction.

"Captain, coordination's gone ... dizzy."

Even Spock spoke without his usual assurance. "Captain, we appear to be suffering from a sensation akin to mass vertigo. Remarkable."

"Sulu," Kirk managed to mumble, "are we still locked into the same course?" The effort to concentrate on the weaving outline of the helmsman was making him feel sick. Somehow he controlled it.

"I can't tell, sir," was Sulu's reply. "I can't read the instruments clearly. They're all running together. Running, blending, and ..."

As abruptly as it had begun, the strange haziness abated. Vision and balance returned with unnatural speed. Only the lingering queasiness gave any indication something unusual had happened.

Spock, characteristically, was the first to recover. His gaze was directed not to Kirk or any of the others but to the main viewscreen.

"Captain ... ahead of us."

Still feeling slightly ill, Kirk looked over at his first officer and followed his gaze to the main viewscreen. His first reaction was that somehow the two Klingon battle cruisers might have gotten ahead of them. But that was not the explanation. *Oh, no.*

There were other starships ahead of them, though. Several starships. Dozens of starships. Starships of every age and origin. Starships representing every known civilization—and some unknown.

Some looked so ancient it was difficult to believe they contained even the most rudimentary form of star-drive. Others were sufficiently advanced looking to boggle Scott's mind.

All drifted motionless against an alien starfield, tightly packed, a chaotic confluence of uncounted relics in overwhelming numbers.

There was unconscious awe in Kirk's voice as he studied the slowly shifting panorama. "It's a graveyard. A graveyard of ships from every part of the galaxy—maybe from Outside, too. Ships I've never seen before. Look at that one."

He was indicating a monstrous jumble of spikes and pylons bound together by a webbing of translucent arches. Not in his considerable experience nor in the recognition tapes Starfleet issued regularly had he seen anything remotely like it.

Nor, he ventured to guess, had he ever encountered anything like its unknown builders—wherever they were.

"Where are we, sir?" a voice asked hesitantly. Uhura's.

"I have no idea, Lieutenant," he said huskily. "I don't *think* we've traveled very far in space." He nodded towards the screen. "Some of those farther constellations looked unchanged. It's the nearer ones that look distorted. That means we may have traveled a respectable distance . . . in time."

He broke off to stare at another vessel passing close by to starboard. It showed a more familiar outline—an interstellar cargo transport of a type and design discarded as obsolete some three hundred years ago.

"If we check" he went on, "I'll bet we'll find that many of these ships are ones designated by history as having been lost in the Delta Triangle."

"Where . . . ," Uhura started to say, but Kirk had other concerns in mind.

"Mr. Arex, can you give us any idea of our present spatial position?" Arex worked at his console for several minutes. Eventually the bony skull swiveled round on its thin neck and he stared back at Kirk out of deep, soulful eyes.

"I'm afraid not, Captain. Our sensors are operating properly once more, but the star-field is not cooperating. I cannot place our position with any certainty, given the apparent position of the nearer stars. Nor can I pick up anything like a navigation beacon."

Kirk was nodding. "I suspected as much."

"An alternate universe, Captain?" Uhura wondered.

"Perhaps something of the sort, Lieutenant. If we were in the same universe but behind some form of energy screen then we ought to be able to plot our position. But as Mr. Arex says, everything is changed around here. Same universe, different continuum—it's all a matter of semantics."

Alternate universe, different continuum . . . amazing how easily the words came when you were presented with an astrophysical *fait accompli*.

"Observations and comments, Mr. Spock."

"I can find no fault with your evaluation of the situation, Captain. I would add a thought, however.

"It must be remembered that many vessels which enter the Delta Triangle traverse it with no incident whatsoever. It would seem therefore that the contact between the two continua is erratic, the point of tangency shifting. In this case the *gate* remained open long enough for us to follow the *Klothos* in." He momentarily turned his attention back to a readout.

"Possibly it closed before our pursuers could follow us on through."

"I'm not sure they tried," Kirk ventured.

Scotty added a heartfelt "Aye."

"Speaking of the *Klothos,* Captain, I've been scanning for her ever since we threw off the lingering effects of the entry." Sulu continued to probe the space around them with full scanners. "But there are so many ships here, it's near impossible to locate a specific one."

"Stay with it, Mr. Sulu."

"Yes, sir."

Kirk studied the viewscreen. Somewhere in that sargasso the *Klothos* drifted, perhaps disabled, perhaps as intact as the *Enterprise* seemed to be. The *Klothos*, which had sprung a totally unprovoked, premeditated surprise attack on them, he found himself looking forward to meeting again ...

VIII

At slow speed the *Enterprise* moved deeper into the swarm of dead ships—and dead they surely were. Not a sign of life or hint of motion from any of them.

Every member of the bridge complement experienced related reactions to the sight of so many abandoned vessels, the thought of so many vanished crews. But for Chief Engineer Scott the experience bordered on the religious.

Naturally the man to whom starships themselves were reason for existence was most profoundly moved of them all.

"Sir," he told Kirk, his voice hushed, "there are ships here I've only seen crude drawings of. Pictures in museums. Ships I've only seen bare outlines of on the Federation's unconfirmed-sightings charts. Ships hinted at by rumors."

Spock added additional information, his library working overtime. "Sensor scans have provided a rough approximation of the age of the metal in some of the hulls, sir—those hulls which are metallic in composition. I have already catalogued several whose base is plastic. There is also one of a unique ceramic-metal alloy and even one of wood." ·

"Wood! Come on now, Mr. Spock!" Scott admonished. But Spock remained confident in the findings of his sensors.

"That is what the detectors reported, that is what the spectrograph confirmed, Mr. Scott. A wooden starship. The hull was composed of a celluloid material of a density not believed possible in an organic substance.

"As to the age, Captain," he continued, turning his attention back to Kirk, "while none of the vessels here have deteriorated, of course, there was sufficient degeneration of some material to indicate that many have been here for centuries. That may be a conservative estimate."

Scott's voice rose in a yelp of sudden recognition. He pointed at the screen. "My Great Aunt McTavish's haggis, Captain, isn't that the old *Bonaventure*?"

Kirk looked at that hulk. He had no question which of the myriad ships on the screen Scott was gesturing at.

Among the alien helical, parallelopiped, and conic ships floated a metal shape much like that of the *Enterprise*, only smaller. Its hull was not as smooth, festooned with awkward-looking projections and tubes, its design not as sleek—but nevertheless, a powerful vessel in its time.

Scott's voice was reverent. They were looking upon a piece of the interstellar cross. "The *Bonaventure*, the first ship to have warp-drive installed. The first of us all."

"She vanished without a trace on her third voyage." Spock spoke from over by his hooded viewer. "The crew's descendants could still be living, Captain."

"Their descendants?" Kirk threw his science officer a look of puzzlement. "But I thought . . ."

"The vessels in our immediate vicinity are indeed dead, Captain. But there is a chance some of their crews could have transferred to other ships. Specifically, to the cluster directly ahead of us, from which I am picking up faint energy and, I believe, life readings. They are increasing in intensity as we move nearer."

While Spock and Scott and Kirk studied the *Bonaventure* and this new possibility, the *Enterprise* was being observed on another screen.

With its life-systems screened out, and nestled carefully into the melange of empty hulks, the *Klothos* waited like a trap-door spider at the edge of its hole—all systems poised, only its eyes showing.

Senior Officer Kaas looked back from his station at the main sensor console. "It is the *Enterprise*, positively, Exalted One. Scanners indicate her shields are fully down."

"Excellent!" Commander Kor viewed the hated silhouette on his bridge viewscreen with satisfaction. He still did not understand what had happened to him and his ship, and for awhile it had seemed as though nothing good could come of it.

But now . . . "All hands to battle stations, quietly. Prepare to open fire on the *Enterprise* the moment she comes within range. Full disruptors—let's get her the first time, this time.

"First Engineer, I want minimum motive power to the engines. Navigator, intercept course. And rotate the ship slightly. It is imperative that we resemble one of these derelicts as much as possible."

Spock turned away from his loaded viewer for a quick glance up at the screen. His gaze started to turn back . . . and lingered. One eyebrow rose a millimeter. Then he returned his attention to the viewer.

"Strange," he muttered.

"What, Mr. Spock?" asked Kirk idly.

"I had thought that the only sign of life here was in the cluster of ships lying directly ahead of us, but there appears to be . . ."

Before he could finish, Sulu was leaning forward in his seat, staring at the screen. His eyes suddenly bugged as he recognized one shape in the crowded scene, and his brows went even higher than Spock's.

"Captain . . . the *Klothos* . . . twenty degrees port!"

"Sound red alert," Kirk ordered sharply. "All deflectors on full—phasers lock on target."

"Aye, sir," Sulu responded, his hands moving faster than his reply. "Screens up . . . phasers locked on."

On board the *Klothos*, sirens and horns suddenly howled in warning. Commander Kor shouted an obscene word, made a violent gesture.

Every disruptor that could be brought to bear immediately cut loose with a tremendous discharge of destructive energy. The *Klothos* shook with the release.

The wave-particle tide got halfway to the *Enterprise*—and the enormous charge shimmered and dissolved into nothingness. First Officer Kaas stared at his gauges with an expression he might have used if they had suddenly confronted a Kalusian sand serpent a hundred *kuvits* long.

"Sir, I don't . . . our entire weapons system . . . it's frozen."

Kor started to rise from the command seat, an appropriate comment on his lips—then there was a sudden crackling in the air. A brief whiff of ozone, the commander was outlined in a sharp flare and then he was gone. Utterly dumbfounded, the rest of the crew stared at the chair where their commander had sat seconds before.

On board the *Enterprise*, Kirk had a brief comment of his own, directed in this case to the helm. "Fire, Mr. Sulu."

"Firing phasers." It was the *Enterprise*'s turn to tremble with the release of annihilating energies.

Seconds passed before Kirk prodded Sulu. "This is no time for daydreaming—report, Mister."

"There's nothing to report, sir," the dazed Sulu finally managed to blurt. For a moment he thought the sensors might have gone berserk again, but no, they were operational. But the readings made no sense.

"No indication of damage, or even that the deflector

shields of the *Klothos* registered contact. All instrumentation appears functional and . . ."

A sharp report, like the discharge of an ancient projectile weapon, sounded on the bridge. Sulu whirled in time to see Kirk outlined by a radiant nimbus. It closed over him, and was gone.

So was Captain Kirk.

For once, Spock had nothing to say.

The chamber conveyed a vastness of spirit rather than mere space. To a Terran it would have seemed more like a gothic cathedral rendered in pastel tones than anything else. A curved wall backed one end of the chamber, fronted by a raised dais.

Twelve beings sat behind a sloping table running the length of the dais. Male and female, human, humanoid, and other—no two members were of the same race.

A Klingon sat next to a Tallerine, who seemed tiny compared to the huge Berikazin on his right. Next to the representative of that warlike race sat a beautiful woman from the Orion system. An Edoan was near her, from the same world that had given Lieutenant Arex birth. A Vulcan rested at ease beside him. One could also see a Gorin and a human in the assembly.

There were also three aliens representing races no one in the Federation would have recognized, for they were as foreign to Federation knowledge as was the Tetroid ship the staff of the *Enterprise* had observed here. Yet they waited in harmony with their nine spiritual brothers and sisters.

There was an air of purposefulness about this place which transcended mere species. No seat was more prominent than another, no being of the twelve higher than his neighbor. At the moment an air of expectancy hovered over them, though none could say what they awaited.

A peculiar electrical discharge appeared in the room immediately before the dais. The flickering vanished and a large simian shape stood there.

Kor's reaction was typical of a Klingon warrior suddenly thrust into an inexplicable situation. He reached for his sidearm.

The clutching hand never touched the handle of the pistol. A secondary discharge formed in the region of the gun and he stumbled backwards. The electrical shock he had taken was not strong enough to hurt him badly. The import, however, was sufficient to discourage him from trying it again.

Near the center of this alien collage, a tall Romulan stood. His eyes were oddly sunken for a Romulan and his voice soft yet firm.

"My name is Xerius." He nodded in a way that was unmistakably directed at the weapon, and his voice turned cold. "That will not be needed here, Commander Kor."

Before Kor could offer the objections that occurred without thought, a golden cloud of charged particles formed at his side. He stepped hastily out of range of the tingling field. A moment, and Captain Kirk had materialized beside him.

Kirk spared Kor a barely contemptuous glance. Other things claimed his attention.

"My name is Xerius," the aged Romulan repeated. "Welcome to Elysia, Captain Kirk." Turning, he gestured at the exquisite Orionite woman who sat next to him.

"This is Devna, our interpreter of the laws. She will speak to you both, now."

As the woman stood, she cleared her throat—the first sign Kirk had that while remarkable, this place was not Olympus and its inhabitants not gods.

She bowed formally, her gaze shifting from one starship commandant to the other. "Gentlemen," she informed them in clear, bell-like tones, "you stand now before the ruling council of Elysia. Our nation, confederation ... call it what you will. Our world without a world.

"Representatives of one hundred and twenty-three races participate in our government. Our existence dates back over a thousand Terran years. During this time these diverse peoples, many of whom were bitter enemies on the Outside, have learned to live together in peace. Learned to do so because they must.

"Any act of violence is strictly forbidden here and will be dealt with swiftly and with utmost severity." This directed primarily at the scowling Kor, though she didn't neglect Kirk.

The ritual speech ended abruptly. She smiled. "You are now each permitted a question. Captain Kirk?"

Kirk considered a moment before asking, "Are we in an alternate universe, truly?"

"It is not certain, but we believe otherwise," Devna told him. "This tiny universe has no stars or planets, though we can see many such. Exploration here has been most extensive. There is a barrier that cannot be pierced to the outer galaxy." Her smile grew wider, her attitude sympathetic.

"Those who were first here have had much time to explore. The finite limits of our environment is one reason why all must cooperate. This place is best described as a pocket in the fabric of normal space-time."

"A restrictive Elysium," Kirk murmured, but to himself.

"Never mind all that," Kor broke in roughly. "How did you freeze my weaponry?"

Overlooking his tone, Devna endeavored to explain. "We have among us many individuals gifted with psionic powers unknown to most races. On the Outside such people were often required to use their powers to exploit, terrorize, and kill. Here those powers are employed only to preserve the peace.

"All our energies are directed to the maintainance of that peace. You, a moment ago, were attempting to break that peace, Commander Kor. We will not allow that."

There was a significant pause while she stared at both men in turn, then a look at Xerius.

"Pronounce the law," the Romulan intoned solemnly.

Once more the Orionite bowed, this time to the Romulan, then turned back to the two commanders. "Under our law, as ship captains you are each responsible for the behavior of your crews at all times. Should a crew member engage in any form of violence against another intelligent being here, you will suffer the maximum penalty. Total immobilization of your ship and selves for a century. There is no lesser penalty for such an abomination."

Something had finally taken a little of the cockiness out of Kor, Kirk noticed. His startled reply carried little of its natural bile.

"A century!" he exclaimed. "We will all be dead by the end of the penalty period."

"No, Commander Kor, you would not." Kirk looked closely at the Romulan. "This small universe of ours is a most curious trap, you see. Time passes here other than it does Outside. It moves with a most extraordinary patience. A century means nothing to us." He gestured at his colleagues.

"Our council appears fairly young, yet all of us are centuries old."

And *that* took some of the self-assurance out of Kirk. "No war, and near immortality," he murmured softly. "Your life here must be almost perfect."

Xerius smiled wistfully. "The same laws that enable us to exist here over the decades in peace compel me to tell you the truth, Captain Kirk. At one time or another, not one among us has not experienced a desire to leave this place, to return to the normal universe. Such desires can be tamed.

"We have made the best possible existence here, Captain, our lasting peace, because we have found there is no choice. There is no escape from Elysia—as you will find."

Each word of the Romulan's last sentence fell like a steel weight on Kirk. It had a similar effect on Kor. Incredible as it seemed, the confidence in Xerius' pronouncement belied any attempt to deceive them.

And with a thousand years in which to explore and attempt, it was possible that he was right—though every molecule of Kirk's mind rejected such a possibility.

"No escape . . . no escape . . . no escape . . ." The words rattled around in his head maddeningly. There had to be a way. He'd seen little enough of this paradise, but one thing he did not doubt was Xerius' contention that everyone had tried to leave it at least once.

It was like the children's fable of the man who became a billionaire, had himself transformed into the handsomest man in the galaxy—and then found himself trapped on an empty world. Money is valueless with naught to spend it on.

The same was true of life. Yet . . . it might be merely years of practice, of concealing truth, but as he read those expressions he could on the faces of the twelve, there were none that looked mad or unbalanced. These people had come to believe in their isolated immortality. It wasn't surprising, really.

Sanity dictated it.

Well, they could swim in it if they liked. He wanted no part of it. Right now all he desired was to be back on the bridge of the *Enterprise* where . . .

. . . Spock, Scott, and Sulu suddenly entered from the elevator, Kirk between them, still talking.

Otherwise the bridge was empty. The viewscreen remained on, still showing a panorama of the metal constellation swirling about them.

". . . and that's the whole of it, gentlemen," he finished, sitting down in the command chair. Spock and Scott arranged themselves nearby while Sulu took up his position at the helm. Kirk gestured at the screen.

"They may not be able to get out of here; they may be resigned and even happy with their *perfect* society—but *we* are getting out."

"Then we'd better do it pretty quickly, Captain," Scott said warningly. Kirk eyed him uncertainly.

"I'm afraid speed may not be possible," Spock ventured. "As the captain has told us, these people have been here for centuries, and their escape plans have failed. We'll need time to find an answer." Typical

Spock, Kirk thought admiringly, understatement and complete confidence in the same breath.

His confidence did not rub off on the chief engineer. "Time is just what we haven't got."

"What's wrong, Scotty," Kirk said calmingly. "I thought time was the one thing we had an unlimited supply of here."

"Only in the abstract sense, Captain," Scott replied crisply. "Not in the practical. No wonder no one's been able to work out an escape plan from this continuum.

"It's the dilithium crystals. They're deteriorating again, breaking up—and rapidly."

"But how . . .?" Kirk began, and then looked exasperated. "I sometimes wish, Mr. Spock, that Professor Jenkins and his associates had found a more stable substance on which to base their successful warp-drive."

"It is this very instability that gives dilithium crystals the triggering power necessary to drive starship engines, Captain," reminded Spock.

"I don't know how it's happenin', sir," Scott continued. "It's not like the last time . . . the breakdown is fast, but not as bad. And it's a basic atomic breakdown, it's not in the molecular links this time.

"I've no doubt it's somehow connected with the same energies that slow time here. At any rate, I calculate that we've another four days our time before the power goes completely."

"It's a gradual breakdown, then?"

"Aye, Captain. That's the odd part of it. The crystals lose power uniformly."

Kirk nodded. "Otherwise we would lose every function on the ship. Be unable to maintain life-support. I wonder what the other ships here use as substitute for dilithium. Their drives don't appear radically different from ours.

"There are other races here whose engineering abilities we know nothing of, Captain. Think of the unique transporter, for example, which took both you and Commander Kor at a moment's notice. Clearly they possess an alternate energy system sufficient to keep them alive, but not sufficient to drive a ship at a decent rate of speed."

"Four days to get out of here, then." He threw his science officer a questioning glance. "Got any miracles in your physical-science tapes, Mr. Spock?"

"The basis for producing miracles does not exist in the system, Captain."

"I'll settle for a natural solution, then. You'll start work on the theory immediately, Spock. When you have something worked out, talk it through with Scotty. If his objections get too strenuous, go back and start again.

"Requisition whatever you need. Work around the clock until you arrive at a formula for getting us out of here." He looked away, back up at the screen. "If you can't find one in ninety-six hours, you'll have plenty of time to catch up on lost sleep . . ."

On board the *Klothos,* in the pseudo-barbaric chamber that was the commander's quarters, Kor looked up suddenly from the sheaf of forms he was studying. His attention was focused on the erect figure of First Officer Kaas, who stood stiffly at attention.

"You call yourself a science officer!" Kor sneared, suddenly throwing the forms and printouts in Kaas' face. The first officer flinched only slightly.

"These computations are useless. You couldn't compute your way out of the defecatory." Standing, he jabbed a finger at the other officer's nose. "Get out of my sight and don't come back until you have a plan that will work. Not one that delineates at length the reasons for your ineptitude."

Kaas saluted smartly, his upper lip trembling only a little. "Yes, Exalted One." Then he knelt, quietly gathered up the scattered forms, and left the cabin.

Kor watched him go. He paced nervously for long minutes before throwing himself on the circular sleeping platform. Rolling over, he stared up at the multi-depth picture set into the ceiling. He felt caged—by this room, this ship, this accursed pocket in time and space.

His sole consolation was that Kirk must be as frustrated as he was.

Only three of the twelve who had welcomed the newcomers now waited in the council chamber. Devna and Xerius were seated at the far end of the dais.

Between them sat a female from a world in the little known Omega Cyna system—a world of light gravity, as shown by her long slender limbs and slimness across the body. There was a quality of ethereal suppleness about that form. Otherwise it was fully humanoid.

Her head was bent, her eyes shut tight in concentration. The lights in the chamber were dimmed.

"What do you see beyond your eyes, Megan?" Devna whispered softly, putting her lips close to one nearly transparent ear of the Cygnian.

Long, long pause. The female's head rose slowly. The lids slid back to reveal a pair of silver mirrors, blank, pupilless.

"The two newcomers . . ." The voice was delicate, fairylike—wind blowing through high grass. "In each ship, beings strive to solve a riddle."

"Name the riddle," demanded Xerius.

"The riddle of the time trap. Escape, escape." The wind blew harder. "They are desperate for a way out. A way back to their own space-time, to their own universe." Boneless hands fluttering in agitation, in helpless empathy. "Escape, escape . . . !"

Devna reached out hurriedly and took the woman's nearest hand, rubbed her own palm gently along its back. "Gently . . . gently, good Megan. Easily . . . return to us now. See us now."

The Cygnian named Megan let out a sibilant sigh, an almost imperceptible whisper of air as thin lungs contracted. The mirrors of her eyes appeared to dissolve, to break up like blots of silver ink. The eyes turned to a light gold color, and from a tiny pinprick in the center, black pupils appeared, expanded to full size. Vertical, they were, slitted like a cat's.

The Cygnian smiled sadly at her companions. "The new ones wish only to get away, to run. It's always the same for the new ones. I'm sad for them."

"You're sad for everyone, Megan. That's part of you and your people. The sympathy you feel for others, intensified by your mind, enables you to see with sympathy all that others do."

"They may wish to escape all they like, fight as hard as they want," commented Xerius. "It is quite impossible. There is no danger from that."

"Still," Devna countered, "it is natural that they do so. They cannot help themselves, Xerius. They *must* try. They would not be normal if they did not. All must try before they come to accept. Best to leave them so and not try to compel."

"That is truth," Xerius admitted. "All will be well in four days' time when they have no hope. I wish it were now. Even to keep the watch, to see that in their fear they do no harm to themselves or others, feels unnatural to me. It implies the threat of direct physical restraint.

"When I was forced to prevent Commander Kor from drawing his weapon in the council chamber, the action made me almost physically ill. Eventually they will feel the same—even the one named Kor."

"You controlled yourself well, Xerius," agreed Devna. "I think the effort it cost you was worth it. The lesson was taken to heart by Captain Kirk, at least. I felt as sick as you. All of us on the council did.

"It is something we must go through. A close watch is especially vital in this case because it seems that these two are natural antagonists."

"So it would appear," Xerius admitted. "It is difficult, not knowing what is happening in the socio-political universe about us."

"But we do have our compensations, Xerius," Devna reminded him quietly . . .

Spock was working at the library computer station, Kirk staring over his shoulder. Both men were examining a series of figures the astrogation computer had just coughed up.

More than a little time had passed since Scott's ultimatum. Kirk was growing by turns tired and depressed. Initial results had not been encouraging. It seemed impossible that Spock would not be feeling the same emotions; but, of course, even if he were it would never show.

The most one could say for him was that his usual precision of manner was showing some wear. Spock held his fatigue inside. Kirk glanced back up, at the viewscreen.

Nestled squarely in its center and surrounded by ancient derelicts lay the *Klothos*. Behind it was the tight cluster of ships that still held power and life. Elysia's inhabitants tended to group tightly together for company and companionship, shifting from one ship to another as internal arrangements permitted.

In this way they achieved a certain amount of variety in companionship over the years. Over the centuries, Kirk thought. The image held before them was far from cheering. He turned from the thought and the view of the *Klothos*.

"This is the very best you and your theoreticians could come up with, Mr. Spock?"

"Yes, Captain. I was personally astonished we could produce a plan so efficacious in so short a time."

"I was hoping you could pull a whole rabbit out of that computer instead of part of one. You've done it before."

"I do not ever recall nor do I see any reason," Spock replied in confusion, "why you should suddenly expect me to produce a Terran mammal of the leporid family from the computer banks at this, or any other time."

Kirk waved it off. "Slip of the tongue, Spock. What I meant was that when there seemed to be no possible answer, no conceivable solution to a problem, you and that machine operating in tandem have produced one time after time."

"Not this time, it appears, Captain," Spock confessed, never one to offer an encouraging word in place of the truth.

"Have you covered every possibility?" Kirk pressed desperately. "Every factor—I don't care how extreme the mathematics."

"*Every* possibility, Captain, several times. The facts are, simply, that with our maximum drive we do not have the capability to pierce the continuum barrier. I do not wish to surrender all hope, but the facts do not offer reason for much encouragement. This was the best we could do."

Kirk looked around, suddenly stood up and stared uncertainly at the screen.

"Well, he isn't giving up, at least."

Spock turned away from his console too, as did everyone else on the bridge, to watch the screen.

The *Klothos* had begun to move. It was leaving its parking position and moving off at high speed. Automatic trackers, preset on the *Klothos* to free Sulu and Arex for research, adjusted themselves to follow the Klingon cruiser. Kirk spoke without turning.

"If they can do it, why can't we?"

"I do not believe they can, Captain," Spock said with assurance. Kirk stared at him. "I consider it the unlikeliest of possibilities. Clearly Commander Kor believes otherwise.

"Their S-Two Graph unit, which is roughly the equivalent to our warp-drive, began giving off depleted energy readings at the same time as engineer Scott reported the start of dissolution among our own dilithium supplies. Their situation is no different from ours, their abilities to react to it no better.

"Kor has apparently decided to try it anyway, regardless of the attempts of his navigator and engineers to dissuade him. I am certain they have tried. The attempt may cost them all their dilithium, even to the loss of power to their life-support systems."

"So he's going to try, contrary to the advice from his own experts, without a chance of getting through?" Kirk looked skeptical. "I don't see even a megalomaniac like Kor trying that."

"You are momentarily forgetting the Klingon mentality, Captain," Spock reminded patiently. "It concludes that the guiding law of life is that all laws are made to be violated. To them their treaties with the natural universe are as tenuous as those they make with other peoples. That is why their advancement in the physical sciences was held back for so long.

"I need not add mention of their pride, which is everything to a Klingon—especially to a commanding officer like Kor. He would do personal battle with a sun if his pride was at stake."

"You're right, as usual, Spock," Kirk turned back to stare at the screen. The *Klothos* was now passing beyond the last row of desiccated starships and out into the blackness beyond.

Kirk should have thought of that himself. Kor could not live with his trampled ego without at least making the escape attempt . . .

IX

A subtle trembling had begun to run through the bridge of the accelerating *Klothos*. Kor and his officers ignored it, as they ignored the alarm lights which had begun to flash around them.

The forward scanners showed a strange mix of light and faint color. Sensors indicated a concatenation of immensely powerful forces centered ahead.

The first officer of the *Klothos* struggled to keep his

voice normal as he reported to his commander. "All power beyond minimal life-support has been diverted to the engines, sir. We're continuing to pick up speed."

Kor looked over at him, showing equal control—control he didn't feel.

"Continue on course for the coordinates indicated."

"Yes, Exalted One." Kaas' attitude was that of a Klingon warrior about to plunge into battle against overwhelming odds. He was prepared to die, he only wished for a less indifferent opponent.

"Approaching maximum drive, sir," he reported, after a glance at the controls.

The center of the glowing vortex appeared to take on a slight spinning effect, its flanks bursting with erratic flares of violet light. The *Klothos* impinged on the outer edge of the luminescent matrix.

A high-pitched whine began to build on the bridge, accompanied by a steady increase in the trembling beneath Kaas' feet. It built to the point where Kor had to hold tightly to the arms of his command chair to avoid being thrown to the floor.

Several other members of the bridge staff were not so lucky; they were thrown off balance and had to fight to regain their seats. The whine grew to deafening proportions.

The ship's lights went out and were replaced by a faint purplish light something like the color of the Terran sky seen from the bottom of a spaceport lift shaft. The whine became a scream, a howl. One officer clapped both hands to his ears, forgetting his controls. Another severe jolt rocked the bridge. Then they were all tumbling, falling, as the *Klothos* spun suddenly on its axis and the artificial gravity failed to compensate in time.

Instantly, their speed started to diminish. Though no one was able to report this immediately—least of all Kaas, who had been thrown against a far bulkhead and knocked unconscious.

Spinning, tumbling, rolling crazily, the *Klothos* had been thrown back along the path it had come. Its speed reversed, it was slowing perceptibly by the time it neared its original parking position.

Attitude control was far from being reestablished, however. A slight deviation in its return path was enough to send it crashing into and through half a dozen of the unoccupied, drifting starships. Mangled and dented, it finally came to a complete stop as some desperate engineer shut down its engines completely.

Broken compartments released a small cloud of frost ... frozen atmosphere bleeding from a broad crack near the rear of the tilted hull.

On the bridge the shrill whine had been replaced by a wail of another sort—a mixture of the overworked alarm system and the cries of injured personnel. Kirk and Spock were not privy to such cries as they studied the damage to the once powerful battle cruiser, now centered in the main viewscreen.

For a moment, Kirk's pent-up anger at Kor's earlier actions was replaced by a grudging admiration. "You were right, Spock, but I almost wish they had made it."

"I am glad they did not," the first officer replied easily. Kirk gasped in surprise.

"Spock, *you* hold a grudge?"

"Not at all, Captain. I would never experience such an unreasonable, long-term emotion. It is rather that their unsuccessful attempt has given me an idea as to how we may be able to break through the barrier."

Kirk waited a moment, then, "Well ... what is it, Spock?"

"I would suggest that everyone concerned with the eventual attempt hear this together. There will be emotional as well as physical requirements."

"I don't understand."

"Neither may certain members of the crew, Captain. Especially any who have been involved in serious conflicts with the Klingons before. I suggest, therefore, that we and the principal officers concerned adjourn to the central briefing room."

"I'm not sure what you're leading up to, Spock, but if you think this is the way to handle it ..."

"It is for the best, Captain."

Unlike previous gatherings in the spacious conference room, no one ventured any jokes in an attempt to lighten the atmosphere. McCoy in particular wondered at the absence of Uhura. The reasons for excluding her from the conference would become clear as Spock explained his intentions.

Uhura had more reason than any of them to dislike the Klingons.

Beside Kirk and Spock, the conference included Scott, Dr. McCoy, and Sulu. Lieutenant Arex was on duty on the bridge along with Uhura, primarily to keep an eye on the *Klothos*, though it appeared certain that Commander Kor would be unable to mount any surprises for quite a while.

Aware the others were watching him expectantly, Kirk began immediately. "Mr. Spock has come up with a formula which has a chance to extricate us from this paradise. Here is one instance where figures speak louder than words."

So saying, he hit a switch just under the edge of the table top. A standard three-sided viewer popped up in its center. Another adjustment, and a complex set of computations began to appear on the three screens.

Kirk and Spock already knew what the computations meant. McCoy could hardly follow them at all. So it was a toss-up between Scott and Sulu as to which man would see their significance first. The first expression to become quizzical, then lopsided, then finally appalled was Lieutenant Commander Montgomery Scott's.

"But this involves combining, in close-order maneuvering, with the *Klothos,* Captain. Closer-order maneuvering . . . hell, it means combining ships!"

"That's right, Mr. Scott," agreed Kirk quietly. The chief engineer did not try to conceal his disgust at such a prospect.

"You mean you want us to work hand in hand with those vipers? Engine dregs, murderers . . ."

"It's our only choice for getting out of here, Scotty." The chief said nothing more, but continued to mumble under his breath. Were Uhura present, further discussion would have been impossible. Someone would have to break the news to her later.

Meanwhile, Sulu had been working furiously with his pocket computer, occasionally glancing up at the nearest of the three-sided screens to cross-check his own work with the original equations.

"As a problem in navigation it has more loose ends than a millipede, Captain. Trying to guide two such disparate vessels through such an intricate maneuver ..." His voice trailed off and he shook his head wonderingly.

"How difficult, Mr. Sulu?" Kirk pressed. The helmsman tried to hedge his reply.

"I can't say for sure, Captain." He squirmed mentally. "Just ... difficult."

"Impossible?"

"No ... no, not impossible."

"Do you really believe that?" That forced a half-grin from the helmsman.

"I'm not sure whether I do or not, Captain. But I am sure that if Mr. Spock is confident enough to propose it, then he thinks it isn't impossible—though I'm not going to press him too hard for the exact odds. I think I'd rather not know.

"If he considers such a plan workable, then it's up to Arex and myself to find a way to make it work."

"That's that, then." Kirk turned his attention back to his chief engineer. "Mr. Scott, your comments?" Scott appeared to wrestle with himself a few moments longer. He too had little reason to love the Klingons. But eventually, he capitulated.

"Considerin' that we've only two days left before our supply of dilithium has deteriorated to the point where we can no longer drive the ship, I'd say we've no choice but to go with Mr. Spock's plan, Captain. Though I don't like it. Not one bit."

"I know how you feel, Scotty," Kirk sympathized. "I'd prefer just about any alternative. We haven't any. If it makes you feel any better, consider that Kor and his people will like it even less." He smiled sardonically.

"Our dislike of them is founded on reality, which enables us to consider such a plan rationally. Their pathological hatred of non-Klingons would prevent them from thinking of one—but it won't stop them from going along with it."

"That's just my point, Captain," Scott wondered. "Can we trust them?"

Kirk spread his hands. "That we don't know." Sulu finished his own figuring, stated his position.

"I agree with one thing, though, Captain, we have to try it."

"As for the Klingons being trusted . . ." Kirk turned to McCoy. Having nothing to contribute to an argument on astrophysics, the doctor had sat quietly through the entire discussion. "What do you think, Bones?"

"Emotionally," McCoy began, "I tend to concur with Mr. Scott. The idea of combining ship functions with that crew of backstabbers automatically sends my hand for a phaser." He looked resigned.

"But to get out of here, I think they'll restrain their inherent animosity toward us. Anything to escape this elephants' graveyard."

"Exactly," agreed Spock.

McCoy shot him a look of surprise.

"Now there's a reference I would not have thought you'd know, Mr. Spock."

"Reading the great fantasies of Terran fiction was one of my mother's favorite pastimes, Doctor," Spock informed him. "As a child I read through all of them avidly."

"Then we're all agreed on this," put in a smiling Kirk. "I'll get in touch with Kor immediately . . ."

"Escape, escape, *escape* . . ." Megan fairly vibrated with the violence of the emotions and thoughts she was reading. Devna had to reach out quickly again to soothe the Cygnian.

"Softly now, Megan," she whispered reassuringly, "softly."

But Megan had no control over modulating such emotions.

"It burns them . . . it consumed them . . . it is a . . . *fire*." Her voice shook dangerously.

"Return to me now, Megan," Devna husked quickly. "Gently, gentle, return . . . see me . . . *now*." The bright mirrors shattered like a pool of quicksilver. Their normal light gold color returned, the cat-pupils emerging.

"It is a violence in them. They have no control over it."

"Not yet, perhaps," countered Devna, "but they will come to accept. All do, eventually. There is no other choice."

"What has been learned?" queried a new voice. Both women turned to see Xerius materialize in the chamber.

"These new ones," Devna went on, "they learn nothing from their first attempt at escape. Now there is a new plan . . . to combine their two ships and try again. Can you not stop them, Xerius?" The speaker of the council looked troubled.

"It is not against our laws to try to escape."

"But they may kill themselves in these mad attempts. Already one of their ships has been damaged and people injured."

"That is how it must be, then, till they are convinced," Xerius replied stolidly. He looked thoughtful, reminiscing.

"Remember, Devna, how I tried and tried to flee? Tried till my ship and my people and even I were beaten. Only then did I begin to accept. So long as they do not break our laws we must not impede them. Were we to do so *we* would be breaking the laws. Not only that, but doing so would lead them to think they were our prisoners, and then they might never come to join us in peace.

"No, they must learn the futility of escape for themselves."

"Even if they kill each other in the process?" Devna wondered bitterly. "Our laws forbid violence. Why then do we allow them to do violence to themselves?"

"It is only violence against others that is . . ." Xerius looked up at Megan. "You have been looking into them, Megan." The Cygnian nodded. "Tell me, then. If a majority are being *forced* to try these escape attempts . . ."

But the Cygnian shook her head. "One word branded indelibly in all, their minds, that word is *escape*."

Xerius looked slightly downcast. "It is as I remember it, from long ago." He smiled sadly at Devna. "You see, Devna? They must try. They must burn this desire out of themselves. This thing we cannot do for them."

The main briefing room on the *Klothos* was far more elaborately decorated than its counterpart on the *Enterprise*. The central table was inlaid with rough-cut gemstones. Spotted and striped, diamond patterned and tight-curled furs padded the seats. Archaic heraldic banners were on the walls, sealed in transparent plastic. Only four officers were present. Kor and Kaas representing the *Klothos*, Captain Kirk and Mr. Spock from the *Enterprise*. The discussion had been going on for over an hour now—Kor's screeches alternating with Kirk's taut replies, Kaas' aloofness bouncing off Spock's invulnerable calmness.

At last all suggestions had been made, all inferior arguments rebutted.

"Then it's settled," Kirk sighed finally. "Our science and engineering teams will get to work immediately at integrating both warp-drives and navigation systems so that we can maneuver as a single ship. Exchange of personnel and beginning of computer interlock will commence as soon as we return to our ship."

Fourteen natural objections leaped to the fore in Kor's mind. He forced every one of them down. These were extraordinary circumstances. So all he muttered was a curt, "Agreed."

They rose. Or at least, three of them did. Spock remained seated, his face blank, almost dreamy.

"Mr. Spock," Kirk said. The first officer suddenly became alert. Rising, he started for the door.

Spock pushed his way between Kor and Kaas and threw an arm around the shoulders of both men. "I cannot tell you," he confessed, his voice bordering on true emotion, "how impressed I am by your splendid spirit of cooperation." There was total amazement in the room. It was impossible to say whether the two Klingon officers or Kirk stared at Spock with more astonishment.

"I realize we have had our differences in the past," Spock continued unctuously, "but now we can be brothers in the face of adversity."

Kor's natural reaction to such intimate and uninvited personal contact would have been a fast stab to the throat with his nails. Had Kirk tried a similar move, that might have been what would have happened. But coming from Spock, the action so stunned the Klingon commander that all he could do was squirm uncomfortably in the Vulcan's grasp.

"Mr. Spock," Kor muttered, "if you will please . . ." Kirk, in a state bordering on paralysis, continued to stare. Spock released both mortal enemies then placed his hands on Kor's shoulders.

"Forgive me, Commander," he said gently. "I was overcome by the import of this moment. May I shake your hand?"

"I suppose so," the dazed commander replied. He extended his hand as if it were no longer a part of his arm. Spock took it, shook firm and long. Releasing the still befuddled Klingon, he turned to his own counterpart on the *Klothos*. That worthy was staring silently at him with an expression usually reserved for the more interesting specimens of previously unknown alien life.

And yours, Science Officer Kaas." The first officer of the cruiser extended his own hand . . . somewhat reluctantly—and Spock shook it, hard.

"Goodbye, for now," Spock said. Then, apparently

overcome still further, he turned and started for the door, shoulders heaving, concealing his face.

Kirk followed, glanced back at Kor and Kaas, rather embarrassed. "Goodbye, Mr. Spock," mumbled Kor. "Captain Kirk."

The door slid shut behind them. Kaas stared at it for several seconds after the two Federation officers had left before breaking the silence.

"The stories of his being half human must be true."

"More than true," agreed Kor. "Or perhaps passage through the continuum gate affected his hybrid mind more than most." That shook the first officer from his lethargy. He turned to eye his commander with something less than mindless subordination.

"I wonder," he began pointedly, "if perhaps we all haven't been affected."

"Explain yourself," Kor ordered, but not as sharply as he should have.

"This willingness of yours all of a sudden to work closely with an old enemy like Kirk. With one who has thwarted so many thrusts of the Empire. It is not like you, Commander. What do you really have in mind?"

Kor relaxed, let out a Klingon chuckle—a sound as devoid of humor as a cobra's hiss. "You've been my first officer too long for me to conceal much from you, Kaas. Very well.

"What would you think if the *Enterprise* were suddenly to disintegrate after our dual ship had pierced the space-time window?"

"I would think my Commander had maneuvered brilliantly."

"I think the implications are clear?"

"Perfectly," Kaas responded, understanding what was required, now.

"And it can be arranged?" The first officer hesitated before replying, ran clawed fingers over the polished wood of the briefing table.

"It involves a high risk factor, given the lack of time to prepare and Kirk's naturally suspicious nature. Yet I think it can be arranged."

"Very good, Kaas. I'll leave it to you to attend to the details of the *Enterprise's* destruction." The two Klingon officers exchanged vows.

Of all the hundreds of ships drifting in the blackness of the pocket universe, none were stranger than the two that hummed with activity near its center. Blue and purple from tiny phaser welders surrounded the doubled vessels with shifting motes of light, and it wore a corona of suited figures busily weaving about its multiple hull.

The *Enterprise* had been maneuvered to a point just above the *Klothos*. Now the two ships were being joined together with cables and plates, bars and impulse connectors.

Kirk leaned back in the command chair, studying the changing view on the main screen. Multiple external scanners provided a constantly changing picture of the work in progress. They were racing a clock with too few hours left.

They had to finish by tomorrow noon, ship time. That was the point at which the power supplies of both ships would be depleted to such an extreme that they could not reach the minimum speed necessary to satisfy Spock's figures. Time and navigational requirements were inflexible.

If they failed, they would be trapped here forever.

McCoy was nearby, chatting with Sulu. The doctor was trying for the eighth, or possibly the ninth time, to get an explanation in layman's language of the complicated physics through which it was hoped they could break back into the normal universe.

"Beg your pardon, sir," came a voice from behind him. Kirk swiveled in his chair, was confronted by Second Engineer Gabler and another crewman he didn't recognize immediately. A drive tech . . . Bell was the name.

Slouching between them—rather reluctantly, Kirk thought—was a Klingon engineer. With a thousand other things on his mind, Kirk forced himself to devote full attention to the men before him.

"What is it, Mr. Gabler?"

"Sir, Bell and I are the relief watch for the dilithium storage tanks." Gabler's way of telling Kirk that the suspicious Scott had placed guards at certain vital points in his section. "We arrived a few minutes late and found this one and a couple of his buddies poking around."

"Where are the buddies?" Kirk inquired, glancing behind the Klingon and seeing no one else.

"Being watched, sir. This one appeared to be in charge."

"This is absurd, Captain Kirk," the Klingon engineer broke in. "We were lost, that is all. What is more natural when one is performing hurried work on a strange ship?"

"Lost, my foot," protested Gabler angrily. "It's clearly posted as a restricted area. You didn't have any trouble reading any of the more complicated symbols. *Keep Out* is one I'll bet you recognized easy enough. You knew all along you weren't supposed to be in there."

"Gentlemen, I'm sure there's been a mistake." Everyone turned to stare at Spock as he moved toward them from his position at the library computer station. He put a comradely arm around the shoulders of the Klingon. The engineer couldn't have been more shocked if he'd been bitten by a malachite tree viper.

Once again Kirk found himself at a loss for words. "Now then, my good fellow," Spock inquired pleasantly, "where were you supposed to be working?"

"Ah ... your pardon, sir, but ..." The Klingon found an answer quickly. "Engineering subdeck five."

"Close enough to the dilithium storage area. A natural enough error, I'm sure you'll agree, Captain."

"If you say so, Spock," Kirk responded uncertainly.

"There, you see?" Spock said to Gabler. "A perfectly natural mistake. Allow me to escort this young man back to his work area, Captain."

"Very well, Mr. Spock."

Spock, his arm around the Klingon engineer, turned and steered him toward the elevator, talking easily with the alien. The latter continued to eye the Vulcan uneasily. As soon as the doors closed behind them, Kirk looked firmly at Bell and Gabler.

"Return to your posts—and don't leave until you've been formally relieved."

"Aye, sir." Gabler saluted stiffly, making no attempt to hide his displeasure at the way things had proceeded. He and Bell turned and left the bridge.

When Kirk turned the chair back he found McCoy had been standing behind him. There was a note of real concern in the doctor's tone.

"Are you as worried about Spock as I am, Jim? Taking into account what you told me about his actions on board the *Klothos*, and now seeing it for myself, I'd say it would be the understatement of the millennium to say he's not acting quite normal."

Kirk rubbed a hand across his forehead. "He's been performing under a lot of pressure, Bones. All of us have. Spock's been working around the clock for the past two days—almost three, now, and we're not finished yet. Arex and Sulu have checked his calculations, but this is still being done at his say-so. And the most crucial moments are still ahead of us, when he has to be at his sharpest."

"I know that, Jim. So listen to the say-so of someone who has not been under so much pressure recently, when I say that there's something wrong with him. I've never known Spock to act like a pal under any circumstances. Least of all toward the Klingons."

Kirk frowned, clearly worried. "That's true, of course, Bones, but . . ."

"If he's coming apart, Jim," McCoy continued relentlessly, "then we're in real trouble. He handled all the original computations for this escape try himself. If he's not, as you say, a hundred percent when we start to move, he could go under the pressure—and take the rest of us with him."

Kirk reflected on the situation. Bones was right, of course. Maybe he had become so exhaust himself these past couple of days he had not paid enough attention to the condition of those around him—especially Spock's. Particularly since the science officer's work had not suffered.

Still, you never knew for sure what Spock might be concealing.

"All right, I'll talk to him, Bones. That's about all I can do. I can hardly recommend he see you for medication without something more positive."

"No, you can't, Jim. I don't even know if unnatural friendliness on the part of a Vulcan is a sign of illness. I only know it's not part of Spock's normal behavior."

Kirk rose from the command chair. "He's in the main briefing room. I'll take care of it now."

"Good. And Jim?"

Kirk paused. "Yes, Bones?"

"Whatever you find out, let me know. So I can be prepared. In case."

Kirk nodded once.

The briefing room, where Spock could work in absolute privacy, was crowded, but not with people. The table was littered with piles of computer tape, cards, tiny cassettes, diagrams and computations. Material spilled off the desk onto chairs, dripped onto the floor like white moss.

At the moment, Spock was totally absorbed in the study of a series of projected energy abstracts on the three-sided central screen. Kirk didn't remember when the first officer had last slept, but he rose promptly when Kirk entered the room.

Kirk smiled reassuringly. Spock took this as a sign that nothing of an emergency nature had developed, sat back down and concentrated once more on the tiny lists of figures. Kirk examined another side of the triple viewer for a few moments, then looked evenly at his first officer.

"Everything seems to be moving on schedule. But

then, you're the only person who can really be sure. Everything devolves on you, doesn't it, Spock?"

"I would suppose so, Captain."

"Any final determination of our chances?"

Spock replied without looking up, though there was a note of puzzlement in his voice. "That is an odd question to ask at this stage, Captain."

"Nothing serious, Spock. It's just that Dr. McCoy and I were thinking—well, there has been something about your recent behavior of late—particularly toward the Klingons . . ." He trailed off uncomfortably.

Now Spock looked up, spoke thoughtfully. "Yes, I grant you it is not my usual pattern."

Back went his gaze to the viewer. He touched a control and a new set of abstracts appeared on the screen.

"Well," Kirk finally pressed, when it was evident Spock wasn't going to add anything, "is something wrong?"

"I believe there is, Captain. But not with me," he added quickly, noticing the sudden look of alarm on Kirk's face. "With the Klingons.

"I sensed something odd about their attitude when we were aboard the *Klothos*. Kor was far too agreeable to our proposals."

"You think so?" Kirk wondered. "He objected to every suggestion we made."

"And ended by agreeing with all of them. I believe his objections were mere verbal camouflage. And his first officer, Kaas, seemed to me more at ease than our mere presence would explain."

"It might be due to their desire to get out of here as desperately as we," Kirk countered. "There could be a host of reasons for both Kor and Kaas acting the way they did."

"I would agree that their behavior might have other explanations, Captain, had I not touched them. But even though the physical contact was necessarily limited, and their minds were uncertain, I did detect a number of subtle indications in Kor—physical as well

as mental—connected normally with victory and c-
quest in Klingon physiology.

"It is not a simple thing to convey with words, Captain. You have to experience it. I can only infer that
Kor had an attack on the *Enterprise* in mind even as he
agreed to cooperate with us."

"Attack? How can they attack us when our ships are
maneuvering as one?"

"I don't know, Captain. But I would hypothesize
some form of delayed action. Something that will affect
us when we have successfully broken the barrier and
the *Klothos* has separated from us."

"Could you gain any hint from Kor's mind, Spock?"
Kirk leaned over the table intently.

"No, Captain. At the time Commander Kor may not
have decided on the method, only the course. I am not
that telepathically gifted, you know.

"I also studied the mood and mind of the Klingon
engineer who was discovered in the dilithium vault.
There was nothing specific in his thoughts—only a
vague feeling of animosity, which is to be expected,
and expectancy, which is not. I cannot escape the feeling that some kind of sabotage is being planned against
the ship."

There was silence while Kirk weighed possible action. "Whatever they have in mind, they can't do anything until after we've finished our run at the barrier.
They need us to get through. That gives us time to
uncover anything they try to plant on board." He activated the desk com.

"Security, this is the captain speaking. I want all security teams on round-the-clock duty now. Watch every Klingon who is working on board the ship double-
close. Interior or exterior. I don't want one of them to
go to the bathroom without our knowing about it."

"We've been watching them all along, Captain,"
came the reply.

"I know that. I want the most intense surveillance
you can mount, Mister. Is that understood?"

"Yes, sir," came the abashed response. Kirk switched

off, looked satisfied. "If they try anything, we'll be ready for it."

"I hope so, Captain," Spock mused. He turned his full attention back to the screen. "I sincerely hope so."

The other members of the bridge complement on the *Klothos* ignored the conversation of the three officers grouped around Commander Kor's chair. As any good Klingon crew ought, they attended strictly to their assigned tasks, closing ears and eyes and minds to all that occurred around them that did not require their personal concern.

Kor and the female, Lieutenant Kali, cast expectant eyes on the first officer.

"All is in readiness, then," Kor announced. "You have the device Kaas?"

In reply, the first officer reached into a belt pouch, pulled out a small, deceptively innocent-looking device. It was about the size and shape of a throat lozenge and looked to be about as dangerous. It gave even Kor pause when he considered what was bound up inside that tiny package.

"My compliments to Engineer Kanff," he said in open admiration. Kor always appreciated fine workmanship. "A wonder that they got it so small. Kanff and his staff are due a decoration for this."

"Yes, an extraordinary job, considering the requirements and the lack of time in which to fulfill them," Kaas agreed.

"How is to be triggered?"

Kaas turned the compact device over in his hand, displaying casual disregard for its capabilities.

"According to Engineering's calculations, we must achieve at least warp-eight to have a chance of penetrating the barrier. At the time our dual vessel reaches that speed, a sensing crystal within the device will shatter, setting the timer.

"Reaction time will commence approximately three minutes after we have pierced the barrier, assuming the Vulcan Spock's predictions to be correct. Our engineers concur. The reaction will backflow until it reaches the dilithium chambers themselves. At which point the *Enterprise* will disintegrate."

"An admirable plan with an admirable end," grinned Kor, retaking his seat. "Engineer Kanff has carried out the first half of the mission in producing the machine." His gaze wandered up to Lieutenant Kali. For a brief moment he considered virtues other than those of a top officer. It passed.

"The other half, Lieutenant, will be up to you."

"Yes, Commander. I have been briefed and understand what is needed. How will I recognize the diversion?"

Kor looked temporarily pained.

"Unfortunately, that is the one factor we cannot plan for in advance, Lieutenant. For it to succeed, it must be at least partly spontaneous in nature. The choice of the crucial moment will be up to you. However, there should be ample opportunity at the joint gathering this evening-time."

Kali's expression became one of disgust. "To mingle on a social basis with humans and Edoans and their kind," she almost spat. "It will be difficult to maintain an aura of civility, Commander."

"It is necessary to be more than civil, Lieutenant. We must endeavor to appear openly friendly." He eyed her sternly. "We can do nothing until we escape this trap. Remember that if your resolve weakens ... and smile."

"Yes, Exalted One," she answered compliantly.

Kaas handed her the tablet-sized machine. She took it carefully and tucked it away in a waistband pocket.

"Tonight they entertain us," Kor observed, barely controlled excitement in his voice, "and so it is only just that we provide them with some entertainment ourselves. It will only last for a few milliseconds, but it should be most gratifying."

"If that device does what Engineer Kanff assures me it can," added Kaas, nodding in the direction of the now hidden tablet, "I almost regret that

none on board the *Enterprise* will have the opportunity
to observe its entertaining capabilities at greater
length."

X

It was all the better for Kor's machinations that the
party had been suggested by the psychology staffs of
both the *Klothos* and the *Enterprise* and then mutually
agreed upon by himself and Kirk. That should lull any
suspicions of ulterior motives on the part of the
Klingons.

The rationale behind the gathering was that since the
Elysians felt so strongly about the personnel of both
ships co-existing in harmony, it might be an excellent
idea for them to observe members of both crews min-
gling in a spirit of good fellowship and cooperation—
even if a little faking was required.

As a further indication of their desire to cooperate
with their new friends, invitations had been extended
from both ships for members of the council to attend.
When locale had been called into question, Kor had
magnanimously agreed to have the event staged on the
Enterprise.

One of the large briefing rooms had been made over
for the occasion. Klingon and Federation trappings
were placed side by side. They did not blend well, since
conflict carried over even into decorations.

Long tables were set up around the room and loaded
with food and exotic drink from both ships. Natural
antagonisms momentarily laid aside, the celebration
commenced surprisingly well. Klingons, crewmembers

of the *Enterprise*, and representatives of the Elysian council mingled easily in the large chamber.

Taped music played over the concealed speakers. At first it had been mostly martial Scottish music, angry fifes and drums, until Kirk ordered the selection changed over engineer Scott's objections.

Then the speakers poured forth a tape requested by Devna, the Orionite member of the council, and promptly turned out by the *Enterprise*'s vast library.

She was dancing in the center of the floor, to the admiring stares of numerous onlookers. Sounding clearly over the hum of constant chatter, the music was lush, full, impressionistic. Devna danced sensuously, completely relaxed. Only occasionally did a movement seem forced. It was as if she were desperately striving to demonstrate that there was a different side to her than the formal interpreter of laws who sat on the council.

Now she was interpreting with her body instead of her voice. There was nothing abstract in her movements. They were basic ... primal, even. The performance ended with a flurry of difficult moves lithely managed—ended with her lying prone on the floor.

There was applause, varying according to diverse styles of artistic appreciation. The music changed to something simple, gentle, purely melodic. Almost embarrassed, Devna made a slight bow and disappeared into the crowd, leaving the dance floor free for others to try their Terpsichorean skill.

Kirk was engaged in a somewhat forced conversation with one of the Klingon library technicians. He turned to speak to Devna as she hurried by. He was glad for the chance to break off the discussion without becoming insulting, finding it increasingly difficult to control his emotions around the Klingons. Their ever-present, unsubtle sense of supercilious superiority generated in him most undiplomatic urges.

"That was beautifully rendered," he told her.

"I thank you, Captain." She was barely breathing hard.

"Especially that grande finale."

Her eyes suddenly seemed to light, and a glow came into her face. "You've seen the dances of Orion before, then?"

Kirk nodded. "Many times. Always with pleasure, never without admiration."

"I wish ..."

Interpreter of laws, council member or not, the look on her face was unmistakable.

"Wish what?" he prompted. She stared hard at him.

"I wish I could return through this space-time barrier and see Orion again. We tell, we lie, we say to ourselves," she continued tightly, "that homesickness is a mental abstraction and easily avoided. We have put our former lives behind us ... and so we have.

"But ... the walls we've built in front of those memories are not always as strong as we would wish them to be."

"You could go back," Kirk told her. "We're perfectly willing to take passengers."

"No," she said, gazing at him tiredly. "You see, we've all seen the absurdity of trying to escape. Many times each of us here dreamed of breaking out, till we came to understand it simply cannot be done. We have accepted our new lives here. To dwell on the possibility of returning is only to open emotional wounds best left closed. Such speculation is unhealthy."

"We're pretty sure it can be done," Kirk countered.

"Do you not think," she half shouted, "that each of us has not believed that same thing as intensely, as strongly as you? Did you not see the *Klothos* fail? Did you ..." She stopped, staring at him.

"You still do not believe. You still fail to admit to reality. When fact has replaced dream, I will dance again for you, Captain Kirk. You will find, when you have been here a hundred years or so, that the appreciation and companionship of one's fellows is among the finest ends anyone can live for.

"Until then, I will intrude on your dream no longer."

"Funny," Kirk murmured. "I've always felt exactly

the same way about appreciation and companionship on the other side of the space-time barrier."

She gave him a friendly, pitying smile of the sort usually bestowed on a stubborn child, turned and walked into the crowd, heading for the place where Xerius stood in earnest conversation with another council member—a Tallarine male, Kirk noted absently. He knew better than to go after her, better than to repeat his offer of escape.

Usually the outright refusal to consider another way of looking at something was a sign of advancing age. It appeared that physical deterioration of the body was not a prerequisite for turning so obstinate. Repeated discouragement would only contribute to such an attitude.

The music issuing from the speakers had turned faintly romantic. A number of couples were dancing on the floor now. There were also one or two triples.

Kirk might have intervened if he had seen what was happening across the room, but his view was blocked and no one else saw fit to step in. McCoy, overcome by the enforced spirit of the occasion, had imbibed rather too much. But so what if his emotional gauge was running a bit high? His judgment was unimpaired, he thought—and member of an inimical race or no, that Klingon lady was one of the most beautiful gals in the room.

The doctor made a gallant, if unsteady bow before her, smiled broadly.

"Miss . . . would you care to dance?"

Not surprisingly, the offer took her utterly unawares. She made a pretense of looking away, in reality searching for Kor. He saw what was happening, nodded slightly. She forced a smile of her own and stood.

They started to shuffle around the floor—awkward in each other's arms at first, but with increasing steadiness. Kor broke off his conversation with one of the council members and slid over to where Kaas stood. His first officer had not noticed the unusual pairing yet.

He was drinking and trying to avoid contact with any member of the *Enterprise* crew.

A few words were whispered, glances exchanged. Kaas waited until Kor had made his way across the floor and struck up a new conversation, this time with one of the Federation officers. Then he moved, starting out onto the dance floor, an angry, half-drunken glare dominating his expression.

A clutching hand, and McCoy found himself spun around to face the furious, weaving Kaas.

"Get away from her, human, this is my woman." Kali looked on quietly.

"Now just a minute," McCoy objected, his liquid amiability rapidly starting to fade. "All I did was ask her to dance. She didn't have to agree, and I certainly didn't . . ."

"She's my woman!" Kaas howled, not wanting to be distracted by facts. Most of his body weight was behind the wild swing he took at the doctor.

McCoy dodged the worst of it, still caught Kaas' fist in the side. He stumbled backward, over went a table laden with food and drink with a nerve-tingling crash. The taped music continued but now every eye in the room turned to them; every conversation ceased.

No one, not even the two security guards at the door, noticed the long-forgotten Kali slip out of the room through an open service hatch.

Gratified at the ease with which he had bowled over his unsuspecting opponent and not wanting to waste the opportunity, Kaas moved in quickly, hoping to get in a few damaging blows before they were separated.

He underestimated McCoy—a characteristic common to anyone who had ever fought the doctor hand to hand. McCoy had been knocked off balance, but he was more surprised by the sudden assault than hurt. And if his present condition was not analytical, it made him plenty combative.

He hit the first officer of the *Klothos* low, ramming his head into the other's midsection and knocking the wind out of him. Grappling wildly, the two officers rolled over and over on the floor.

McCoy flailed away with enough enthusiasm to keep the frustrated, furious Kaas from either doing any damage or getting free. One wild elbow even caught the Klingon officer under the bridge of his nose, an exceptionally painful jolt that started blood flowing.

It was Kirk who got his arms around McCoy's shoulders and dragged him off Kaas.

"Bones, stop it!" McCoy was still weaving on his feet. "What the blazes happened?"

Kaas climbed to his feet. That's when he first noticed the blood trailing from his nose. At the sight of that, he forgot what he was doing on the floor, forgot his position, forgot everything.

He went for his concealed disruptor pistol.

"Stop!" came a booming voice from the back of the room. Xerius' commanding tone. Kaas didn't hear him, just as he didn't hear Kor's frantic cry of *"Khaba dej'*, *Kaas!"* or the curse that followed. Roughly translated, it meant, "The idiot will ruin everything!"

Kor ran toward his first officer ... too late, he saw. The disruptor was already out and aimed at the two humans. Before anyone had a chance to reach Kaas, he fired.

The killing bolt faded into the air centimeters from McCoy's chest.

Kaas, startled not only by the failure of his pistol but by the sudden realization of what he had done, stared in confusion at the useless weapon. Before he could decide to fire, put the gun away, or do anything, Kor wrenched it from him. The first officer looked up slowly into his commander's eyes.

A milky gaze was fading rapidly from Kaas' corneas. He had been in a berserker frenzy. Kor struggled to control his own emotions. Not the first officer's fault, really, considering that the other had unexpectedly drawn blood.

But what a time to let a little blood intervene!

"Captain Kirk and Commander Kor, and these two,"

intoned Xerius solemnly, "will come to the council chamber in two minutes to face charges." There was a flash . . . several flashes. When Kirk and the others looked around, every member of the Elysian council had vanished.

The celebration had come to an end.

A low babble of conversation resumed in the room . . . low and concerned. All hint of the enforced pleasantries of moments ago was gone. Members of the two crews now had something real to talk about—a common threat of unknown dimension.

Kali did not participate, however. By then she had successfully made her way into the central computer room of the *Enterprise*, avoiding the depleted security forces.

Using a packet of compact tools taken from another pocket, she removed a certain panel buried far back in the main complex. The components visible beyond the panel pulsed with faint, miniature auroras, by-products of the energies flowing through them.

The tablet-sized machine slid neatly into place, well back among a maze of interlocking circuitry. The device would have been even better located in one of the engine rooms, but security was impenetrable. According to the schematics on board the *Klothos*, this was the closest she could get without being challenged.

Engineer Kanff had calculated it would be more than close enough.

No one saw her replace the panel or leave the room. A dozen or so technicians, some from the *Enterprise*, some from the *Klothos*, were passing through the nearest corridor, moving to a new work area. Kali blended in neatly with them.

When they reached the work section, she joined two of her shipmates and fell to assisting them as best she could. They eyed her strangely, but said nothing. It was not meet to question the actions of a superior officer. They went silently about their business.

She had successfully carried out the crucial part of

her mission. Now it remained only for her to wait and enjoy the spectacle to come.

There was no time to try and rig any kind of protective defensive field. It probably would not have been of much value. Previous experience had demonstrated that whatever transporter the Elysians possessed, it was perfectly capable of plucking any member of the crew off either the *Enterprise* or the *Klothos* any time the council wished.

So it was that once again Kirk and Kor, now accompanied by first officer Kaas and Dr. McCoy, found themselves standing in the cathedral-like council chamber before the assembled Elysians.

There was no attempt at explanation this time, no effort to make the visitors feel at ease. The enmity coming from the council was almost palpable. A feeling of decision that Kirk found frightening, hung in the air. There was to be no discussion or trial here. A decision of some sort had already been made.

In a place where there was an excess of only time, Xerius' speech was brief. "You have been informed. You have been warned. You have been instructed. And you know that any exercise of violence against another intelligent being is forbidden here." He glared at Kor.

"Your man began the fight and attempted to kill." Xerius looked around at his fellow council members. "I formally propose as penalty that we suspend the *Klothos* and its crew for a century of their time."

All his carefully constructed struts and buttresses supporting an intricately wrought plan had neatly been kicked out from under him when Kaas had lost his temper. Now Kor saw the foundation crumbling.

"My first officer was provoked," he protested, trying to project an air of outraged innocence. The excuse sounded lame. Xerius treated it with contempt.

"He attempted to kill—and would have, had we not prevented it at the final moment. There is no lesser penalty for such a crime."

"But I didn't know," Kaas objected. "I lost control of myself, saw only . . ."

"That will be enough," warned Xerius sharply. "You have spoken already . . . with your actions."

"May I say something, then?" Kirk asked.

"You may, Captain Kirk."

He took a step toward the dais, thinking rapidly. As a starship command flight officer he was required to know a fair amount of law, but that had never been one of his favorite subjects at the Academy, though he had done well in it. With his no-nonsense analytical approach, Spock had the better courtroom manner.

But Spock was not here. Kirk would have to argue his case as best he could, alone.

"Captain Kor and I—as you probably know—are going to try and break through the time-space barrier tomorrow. If you put the *Klothos* and its crew into suspension, you'll be punishing us as much as them. We can't leave as a single ship.

"I implore you to let our dual craft make this attempt as we've planned."

"This futile attempt at escape is so important to you?" Xerius was saying. "Despite what we have told you, that it is foredoomed to failure?"

"I repeat, we don't share your eternal pessimism. However you choose to see it . . . yes, it's that important to us."

"You *will* fail."

"We *must* try," Kirk pressed desperately. "Xerius," he went on, hoping the council leader didn't think he was being lectured, "in many respects, Elysia is a perfect society. It had endured a thousand years and proven that when given a chance, the most antagonistic peoples can live together in peace." And when given no other choice, he thought.

"But with all its virtues, it's not home. And with all its faults, we would prefer to return to our own continuum."

Far down the dais, Devna was heard to murmur, "As would many of us."

Xerius pretended not to hear.

"You insist on taking these would-be murderers with you?"

"I'd be lying if I didn't admit that Commander Kor and I regard each other with something less than brotherly affection," he admitted. Kor smiled toothily.

"But sometimes an injured man has to take medication that's not very pleasant, yet necessary to his survival. That's my situation regarding the *Klothos*."

Kirk's argument was simple and logically irrefutable. And so, after studying both men for several long moments, Xerius gave a reluctant nod.

"Very well. I release Commander Kor and First Officer Kaas into your custody, Captain Kirk." He looked sternly at both Klingons. "After your absurd escape attempt fails, the penalty will be carried out—should you survive."

Kor forced himself to fight down his triumphant smile and look nominally repentant. It wasn't too hard. If the Vulcan Spock's calculations proved inaccurate, the penalty might just as well be carried out. Better to sleep than be forced to endure an eternity of this repugnant civility—especially with humans and other Federation grass eaters!

"Lest you believe we think you ill fortune, I wish you good luck, Captain Kirk," the council leader finished.

"Preparations are completed," Kor announced.

Kirk looked up at the viewscreen. The image of Commander Kor stared back at him from his position on the bridge of the *Klothos*. A precision universal chronometer was mounted on one arm of the Klingon commander's chair and was synchronized to the one on the *Enterprise*. They had finished the conjoining work with several hours to spare.

"Ready here." Kirk turned his attention to the rising black band on the chair chronometer, watched it reach a preset numeral. At the instant it did so, there was a buzz from the helm. A preliminary check, successful.

Helm and navigation instrumentation on both ships were properly linked.

"Manual timing checks," Kirk reported.

Now nothing was left but to feed power to test Spock's theory.

Sulu was watching him, waiting.

"Prepare to accelerate to warp-six, Mr. Sulu."

"Standing by, sir."

"Ready to compute subordinate corrections if required, Captain," Arex said crisply.

"Communications standing by," Uhura added.

"Computer backup ready." Spock, relaxed, at ease.

Kirk glanced down at the chronometer set in his own chair-arm, silently counted off the seconds: three, two, one, accelerate.

A barely perceptible vibration ran through the deck as preset automatics took over and the linked ships suddenly leaped ahead, accelerating steadily.

Two members of the Elysian council stood in the otherwise deserted chamber and stared at the flowmetal screen which had appeared behind the council dais. Long-range monitors mounted on long-abandoned craft kept the *Enterprise-Klothos* in sight as it moved out of the ship cluster.

Devna and Xerius stared at the picture. As they watched, a third counselor entered, eyes going to the screen. Silver cataracts slid over Megan's eyes as her gaze reached outward.

"Escape," she mumbled. "All are concentrating on escape. Their ships move ever faster.

"Kirk of the *Enterprise* expresses confidence in the work of his technicians and engineers, in the ability of his first officer.

"Kor of the *Klothos,* too, exudes confidence in his personnel and in . . ."

Both hands went to her temples. She stumbled backward.

"No! The Klingons—have hidden an explosive device aboard the *Enterprise.* The picture is in Com-

mander Kor's mind. She will be destroyed. She will
..."

Xerius and Devna came out of shock simultaneously.
It was the council speaker who moved first, clutched at
the controls of the concealed microphone. Spoke frantically while staring at the screen.

"Intership emergency, intership emergency!"

"Power Control acknowledges, Speaker," a voice responded.

"Full broadcast to the fleeing starships, tight-beam
message to the *Enterprise*."

There was a pause, then ..., "Probing, Xerius. They
do not answer."

"Keep trying ... give me an open channel. *Enterprise*, this is Speaker Xerius. Respond, *Enterprise*! You
are in ..."

Descent into the Maelstrom, Kirk mused as the
whirlpool of light that delineated the space-time barrier
appeared on the screen. A wavering cyclone of force
they were rushing toward.

Unconsciously, both hands dug tighter into the arms
of the command chair. True, the *Klothos* had tried the
barrier, been rejected, and survived. But perhaps they
were moving so supremely fast that this time the barrier would reject them with less care. His grip didn't
relax.

"Warp-seven, Captain," Sulu reported.

"Everyone brace for resistance as we contact the barrier field," Kirk ordered unnecessarily.

"Sir!" Uhura's voice. "Xerius is trying to contact us.
The call is coming on an emergency frequency."

"Put it on the main speaker, Lieutenant." She
nudged a switch, and the speaker's voice immediately
sounded on the bridge.

"Captain Kirk, the Klingons have secreted an explosive device of small size but tremendous triggering
power in your ... in your computer chambers. Megan
reports it is located at ... a moment ... she is attempting to read ..."

The intercom went silent. Kirk's stomach was doing acrobatics.

"It is located," the speaker said, voice contact returning, "in the casement housing auxiliary power leads to the drive chamber. It will activate when you reach warp-eight. If it is not removed before then, it cannot be deactivated. It must then be removed carefully, according to Megan's reading of its internal structure, or ... (fizzle, sput) ... racinatio ..."

"Outer fringe of the barrier is disrupting communications, sir," Uhura reported.

"Stay with it, Lieutenant. Spock, Scotty." Both officers were already halfway to the elevator. Kirk punched a switch on his chair console.

"Computer room ... Captain speaking ... give me the tech in charge."

Brief pause, then, "Rodino here, Captain."

"Commander Spock and the chief are on their way back there to perform some surgery. Remove all access plates to the drive power leads, auxiliary casement. Don't touch anything else ... move, Rodino."

"Computer out," came the fast reply.

While the attention of the *Enterprise*'s command was otherwise engaged, their counterparts on the *Klothos* were intent on the main viewscreen. Their alert system had begun to sound, as it had once before only a few days ago.

"Approaching warp-eight, Exalted One," Kaas noted from his position at the science station.

A new sound began to penetrate the bridge, a sound Kor had listened to recently—just prior to being thrown into unconsciousness. A high, wailing roar generated by forces which existed in contempt of all natural law. A wild, thunderous moan which once heard was never to be forgotten. Not by Kor, nor by any member of the *Enterprise*'s crew, now subjected to the same buffeting.

"The barrier," the commander muttered, staring at the light storm ahead. They were close to it, now.

"He didn't specify *which* auxiliary leads it was be-

hind, damn it," Scott rumbled tightly. Shoving the startled Rodino aside, the chief engineer had gone through
the first such section. With blatant disregard for everything the manual said and for years of training, he rip-
ped at connections and leads, oblivious to the chances
of shock or to the damage he was doing.

The first panel he searched showed nothing, nor the
second. Delicate circuitry was shoved aside by the
small combination tool in his right hand. He started in
on the third, nudging aside a minor knot of microcir-
cuits, probably deactivating someone's favorite entertainment channel.

That could be fixed . . . later. Right now he wanted a
look a little deeper into the casement. Something
seemed to be reflecting a touch too much light back
there. Then he saw it. A small cylindrical section about
the size and shape of a large pill.

"There it is, Spock. I'll hold the lines aside."

Spock dropped to his knees as Scott moved slightly
aside. Spock moved his arm into the opening. Gently,
two fingers slid around the tablet, lifted, pulled it
slowly from its resting place by a double-fluid circuit.

He had it.

Seconds later, both men were standing, examining
the compact device. Spock imprinted its exterior design,
consistency, weight, color, shape in his mind for future
study. Then he moved to a boldly marked slot at the
far end of the chamber. A disposal niche.

There were three switches set in the wall beside it.
One labeled DISINTEGRATE, the second marked RE-
CYCLE and the third, was covered by a snapdown
protective top.

Spock flipped the red plastic up and placed the innoc-
uous-seeming tablet in the open niche. Then he
pressed the uncovered button. The red label alongside
it read: POWER EJECT.

Despite the coolness on the bridge, Kirk found he
was sweating. A vibration that did not come from the
engines now rattled the deck beneath them, shook the
arms of his chair where he gripped it. A teeth-

scratching screech screamed over the speakers and seemed to dig into his bones, despite Uhura's attempts to moderate it.

There was a sudden sharp jolt. Inside his skull a little voice chuckled, said, "Nice try, James T. . . . goodbye . . ."

Then without any warning, the vibration stopped, the high-pitched wail trailed off into a drifting sigh, and the view forward became awesomely normal—a vision of familiar stars and nebulae. The view was infinitely more glorious than the claustrophobic immortality they had left behind.

As prearranged, a single relay snapped over on board both ships. It begat a multitude of tiny clicks and snaps as beams, cables, and plates parted—sometimes softly, other times with the aid of tiny explosive bolts.

The *Enterprise-Klothos* fissioned, each half arching off in opposite directions.

Unrestrained cheering indicated the emotions on the *Klothos*' bridge. Anyone would have thought the crew had just won a major battle against overwhelming odds. In a sense, they had.

Her commander and first officer stared expectantly at the viewscreen in anticipation of further pyrotechnics. Long-range scanners struggled to hold the fast-moving dot that was the *Enterprise*.

For a moment, something seemed to have gone wrong. Then there was an impressive flowering of violet light. The cheering died quickly as the rest of the crew turned in surprise to gape at this new phenomenon. First one gaze, then another, and another, turned toward the command station.

"Exalted One," Kaas said formally, "this is a great moment for the Empire. May I have the honor of. . . ?"

"Not yet, not yet," Kor countered thoughtfully. "Give everyone time to think on it. Let them reach the proper conclusion by themselves. The result will be that much more pleasurable for them. We can confirm it at our leisure. I want to enjoy this as long as possible."

His predatory smile widened as he watched the angry flare fade from the screen ...

To see familiar stars again was a pleasure Kirk had not expected.

No, no ... that was not true. Inside, he had always really believed they would successfully escape the continuum trap—no matter how many times the Elysians had failed. There wasn't a barrier in the universe that Spock, Sulu, Arex and Scott couldn't break once they set their combined brainpower to searching for a solution.

That belief had wavered only once ... when the *Klothos* had tried the barrier and failed. Maybe he had felt so sure about it because they had never really been threatened. Kirk was used to facing down death—the promise of eternal life was something hard to feel terrified about.

Uhura interrupted his musings. He noted a calmness in her voice again that no promise of extended life could put there.

"Sir, I'm picking up a deep-space transmission at the extreme range of reception. It's from the *Klothos*." She paused. "Commander Kor is heading for his home station—there, they've just passed outside our effective communications limit."

"Don't keep us in suspense, Lieutenant," Kirk prompted. "What's the good commander done? Probably taken full credit for our escape from the time-space trap."

Uhura seemed to be having trouble controlling herself. "It's not ... that, Captain. They saw the device they planted aboard go off and apparently they felt it was still aboard.

"He thinks we've been destroyed—and he was trumpeting his triumph all the way back to Klingon Imperial Headquarters!"

"Commander Kor is exhibiting the typical egocentrism of ..." Spock stopped, observed that Kirk, Sulu and even Arex were now sharing in Uhura's laughter.

A steady high-pitched noise of a less ominous sort now permeated the bridge.

"I had thought that if such information inspired emotion in you," he said uncertainly, "it would have been of anger and not amusement."

"Don't you see, Spock?" Kirk turned to him, trying to retain his composure.

"See what, Captain?" The first officer was still confused.

"Consider what Kor is reporting, is claiming, Spock . . . and then try to visualize his face when the Empire's emissaries in the Federation send back word that we are still in excellent condition!"

Spock glanced around the usually efficient, smoothly running bridge. It had taken on the air of a carnival. He turned back to his console.

There was a certain problem in abstract mathematics he had been working on. He would return to a consideration of it now. But first he reviewed Kirk's explanation. The incongruity of the situation he perceived, of course. But he would not, if he lived to be a thousand, understand how it could produce in normally sensible human beings a state of transitory imbecility.

In response to his request, the computer laid the details of the problem before him once again. Bending his gaze to his hooded viewer, he found relief from the surrounding hysteria in the cool perfection of higher calculus. He was not, however, isolated in his reaction to the situation.

Had he known, it is quite likely that Commander Kor would not have been laughing, either . . .

PART III

MORE TRIBBLES, MORE TROUBLES

(Adapted from a script by David Gerrold)

XI

The call came in a few days later.

"Message from Starbase Twenty-three, Captain," Uhura announced. "Indication is priority signal, but not confidential."

"Put it on the main screen then, Lieutenant."

"Very good, sir."

Dim with distance, a face appeared ahead—a portrait of a young and rather harassed-looking communications officer. "Captain Kirk, my name is Massey. I'm with Emergency Interstellar Relief . . . Communications Section."

"So I see," Kirk replied.

From what Kirk had seen, members of the IRS wore expressions akin to this Massey's nearly constantly. The nature of their work, naturally. The young officer's gaze, however, seemed especially mournful.

"We've been trying to contact you for ages, Captain. Uh . . . how did your mission into the Delta Triangle go?"

Word certainly gets around in Starfleet, Kirk reflected.

"Standard exploration," he replied blandly, ignored a muffled choking sound from the region of the helm. "In this case, if it had taken us a day longer, you would have spent those ages trying to contact us."

169

The Sub-lieutenant looked uncertain, aware that Kirk was trying to tell him something and thoroughly unsure how to interpret it. A hand wiped wavy brown hair from his forehead.

"Glad to hear that, sir," he mumbled in response. "You're familiar with the operations of the Relief Service?"

This one was even younger than he looked, Kirk mused. Had he ever been that young? "I have some familiarity with the functions of Starfleet peripheral organizations," he deadpanned. "What can we do for you?"

Missing the sarcasm completely, the Sub-lieutenant turned crisply businesslike. "Do you know the location of Sherman's Planet?"

Kirk glanced over a shoulder. "Mr. Spock, could you ... ah, never mind. I remember." He looked back to the screen. "A newly settled world on the periphery of the Federation. Population is mixed human and Edoan." Arex nodded in confirmation. There were few worlds where the Edoans felt comfortable outside of their home system. Sherman's planet was one of them.

"I have a cousin in that colony, Captain."

That lent whatever difficulty Massey was about to delineate a touch of immediacy, as far as Kirk was concerned.

"I recall that Sherman's Planet is a fairly successful venture. Not a paradise world, maybe, but certainly a tame one."

"Quite true, Captain." The youngster was nodding vigorously. "It gave every promise of being a rich agricultural world, capable of exporting a wide variety of staples to the rest of the Federation. Records indicate that the initial seedings of the colonists would produce a first crop beyond anyone's expectations." His expression became more doleful.

"Unfortunately, it seems that the first survey team overlooked something. Occasionally, new worlds have surprises locked inside them that are not revealed at once. Sherman's Planet looks to be one of them.

"We're still not sure what the basic cause of the trouble is. A shifting deficiency in the soil, maybe the presence of a cyclic virus in the atmosphere. Whatever it is, it's deadly where mature grains are involved. As I say, we don't know yet. But the initial crop seems to be a complete failure.

"The soil chemists think they can solve the problem, develop a defense against it. But that will take a minimum of six standard months. The farmers on Sherman don't have six months. It's not a question of export now—it's a question of survival.

"What they do have is a double growing season, thanks to the planet's lushness and long summer. We've turned up a hybrid seed grain on the plains world of Kansastan. According to tests, it ought to be impervious to what's been hitting the Shermanites' crops.

"Two large cargo drones loaded with the hybrid seed are in parking orbit around KS. You are to proceed there, pick up the drones, and escort them to Sherman's Planet. At standard cruising speed you should get them there in plenty of time for the colonists to get the seed into the ground.

"If they don't get the seed, they'll face the coming winter without any crop at all. This is supposedly an established colony. They have only minor emergency supplies left. No crop and they'll face widespread famine. Predictions run as high as ten to eighteen percent fatalities. And the colony proper might never recover."

"The grain will get there. Don't worry, Massey. As you say, we've plenty of time." The best catastrophes, he reflected, were the ones that could be prevented.

"*Enterprise* out, Lieutenant Massey."

The Sub-lieutenant managed a weak grin—as much of a smile as the people in his business could mount—and signed off. Probably to turn his attention to some new disaster, Kirk mused. It took a special kind of person to stand up under the kind of anguished reports the IRS had to handle daily. Kirk did not envy the young man his job.

"Mr. Arex, Mr. Sulu . . . set a course for Kansastan."

"Aye, Captain," sounded the simultaneous acknowl-
edgment.

They had no difficulty in securing the drone grain
ships. Each was somewhat smaller than the *Enterprise*,
but nearly as powerful. High-speed, bulk carriers, their
sole purpose was to convey enormous loads across the
plenum in the shortest possible time.

The monitoring officer on the small space station or-
biting Kansastan was garrulous to the point of bore-
dom, so Kirk was glad when linkup was completed,
giving him a chance to depart.

Still, he couldn't help feeling sorry for the fellow. He
was assigned to a world whose people went about their
Federation business efficiently and with little fanfare.
They didn't get many visitors.

And that monitor might serve in that isolated post
until his retirement without a single promotion.

The journey to Sherman's Planet was passing
uneventfully. So uneventfully that when they were
three-quarters of the way to the outpost colony, Kirk
was considering beaming the nearest Starfleet base for
further orders.

Instead, he sighed, activated the recorder in the arm
of the command chair.

"Captain's Log, stardate 5526.2. Having been assigned to escort two robot grain ships to Sherman's Planet,
the *Enterprise* is now approximately . . ." He looked to
Arex. The navigator nodded, turned to his readouts
and recited a figure. Kirk repeated it into the recorder.

". . . from the colony. Upon completion of delivery
of the quinto-triticale seed, the *Enterprise* will proceed
to . . ."

"Captain? Captain." Sulu's tone was anxious.

Mildly irritated, Kirk put the Log on hold. "What is
it, Mr. Sulu? You know better to interrupt when I'm
making an official . . ."

"I'm sorry, sir, but I've just picked up some kind of
smaller vessel. A one-man scout or an independent
trader . . . can't be sure at this distance. It's running an

evasive course, sir, at top speed—with a Klingon battle cruiser in close pursuit."

Kirk thought rapidly, lifted his finger from the hold button. "Changing course to investigate the pursuit of a small ship of unknown origin by a Klingon ship of the line. Out." He looked to the front.

"Mr. Arex, alter course to put us on an intercept route with the smaller craft."

"Changing course, Captain," the navigator answered promptly.

Kirk drummed fingers on a chair arm, studied the screen impatiently. "Any confirmation of identity on either ship, Mr. Sulu?"

"Not yet, Captain." Sulu was bent over a gooseneck viewer.

"Captain?" Kirk looked around.

"Yes, Mr. Spock?"

The first officer looked over from the library computer console. "Among the information received by high-beam code transmission from Starfleet Science Center in the past several days was an item that it has not been necessary to mention until now. There are rumors from Federation agents that the Klingons have a new weapon, abilities unknown.

"Your timing is remarkable, as always, Mr. Spock," Kirk commented, straight faced. "The *Klothos* didn't have it."

"No, Captain. Had she, it seems certain Commander Kor would have employed it."

"Cruiser is closing rapidly on its target," Sulu announced, forestalling any further discussion of new Klingon potential. Spock turned to his sensor readouts.

"Initial scan indicates the smaller vessel is a one-man scout ship of common design. Federation manufacture and registry probable but not yet certain."

"I think I can get the other ship on a high-resolution scope, Captain," Sulu offered. He worked at his instrument board.

A second later the new picture appeared on the screen, showing the small scout with unusual sharpness, considering the range. A sudden burst of light flashed across the screen, disappeared, as if something had arced for a microsecond between the *Enterprise* and the fleeing scout.

Kirk already guessed the explanation. "Mr. Sulu, shift pickup, please."

Sulu figured it out only seconds later. His tone was one of puzzled amazement. "They're firing on him, Captain."

He adjusted another switch. A different scanner took over from the first. The new view showed the little craft's massive pursuer, clearly recognizable as a Klingon battle cruiser. As they watched, multiple ripples of light flared from the warship's prow as she let go with her secondary disruptor batteries.

Again Sulu changed views. This time the scout ship eclipsed the disruptor bolts and they passed on its far side. Kirk doubted the Klingon gunners would miss again. The scout vanished from the screen and from then on some instrumental calisthenics were required of Sulu to keep it on the screen.

The pilot was going all out to avoid being hit, Kirk noted. He was good, and his ship was mobile; but it couldn't dodge a warship's electronic predictors forever, couldn't continue to escape disruptor fire that could obliterate much larger prey.

A bigger question was the sanity of the Klingon's commander. His ship was so far within Federation space there was no possibility of navigational error. Unless he and his executive officers had gone completely mad, they knew exactly what they were doing and what chasing the scout ship this far implied. To risk such a blatant violation of Federation borders was a sign that someone desired to destroy that tiny ship very much, indeed.

Territorial intrusion took clear precedence over escort duty. "Ahead, warp-six."

Sulu and Arex coaxed response from the ship's engines. Kirk activated his chair intercom.

"Transporter room, report." A crackle of opening

channels, and then a familiar burr. "Transporter room ... Scott speakin'."

"Scotty?" Kirk's brow furrowed in mild surprise. "What are you doing there? Where's Chief Kyle?"

"On his second off-shift, Captain. I thought I'd take it for him. I've been goin' crazy tryin' to figure out how the Elysians picked you and Dr. McCoy off right through our defensive screens and ..."

"Never mind that now, Mr. Scott," Kirk interrupted quickly. "You haven't taken the console apart, I hope?"

"No, sir." Now it was Scott's turn to sound surprised. "I intend to eventually, but right now she's fully operational. Why? What's happenin'?"

"We've run into a Klingon battle cruiser chasing a solo scout and ..."

"A Klingon? This deep inside Federation ...?"

"I know, Scotty, I know. She's firing on the smaller ship. We're going to try and rescue its pilot."

"Aye, Captain!" There was a pause at the other end, then, "He's nothin' in the way of a screen, sir, but at this distance it'll take some time to scan the pattern of whoever's on board. I dinna want to bring him in in pieces."

"Get to work on it, Mr. Scott. When you lock in on him, don't hesitate. Bring him aboard."

"Aye, sir."

Kirk turned his attention back to the screen. Another set of light waves passed close by the scout. The cruiser was still firing. Someone muttered that the Klingons couldn't shoot worth a damn.

At the tail end of the mutter, a last bolt struck the ship a glancing blow. A tiny white cloud billowed from it as escaping atmosphere froze solid. The scout continued to move, but it was clearly disabled now.

Still no word from Scott. He spoke over his shoulder.

"Open general hailing frequencies, Lieutenant." Kirk waited a moment, giving Uhura time to comply, then spoke into the pickup once more.

"Klingon battle cruiser ... identify yourself. This is

Captain James Kirk commanding *USS Enterprise* speaking. You are violating Federation space. Identify yourself . . . halt firing on scout ship."

Sulu switched the forward scanner back again from the weaving scout to the cruiser. It did not take long to tell that the Klingons had no intention of altering their course or ceasing their attempts to destroy the fleeing scout. Several more disruptor bolts darted from the prow of the warship.

"Doesn't even bother to acknowledge," Kirk muttered. A certain amount of hesitation on the part of an interloper could be tolerated. Such outright contempt for a major treaty could not.

"Mr. Spock," he ordered, his voice lowering meaningfully, "you will note this violation and enter it officially in computer records. Mr. Sulu, arm all phasers. Deflector shields up. All hands to battle stations."

After Uhura activated the alarm, the *Enterprise* became a hive of instant activity. Dropping whatever they were doing when that klaxon sounded, each moved to his or her position of readiness.

"All stations report battle status, Captain," Uhura reported a few moments later.

"Phasers armed," Sulu announced. "Shields up." Several other switches were snapped over. "Ship is battle status." Kirk nodded, spoke to the mike in one last try.

"Klingon battle cruiser, this is your last chance. Identify yourself." Only the faint static of distant suns sounded back over the speakers. "Ahead, warp-eight . . . range, Mr. Sulu?"

"Closing, sir." Again the view foreward altered, back to the scout ship.

"The injured vessel is losing speed rapidly, Captain," informed Spock.

Kirk studied the image worriedly, spoke to the intercom. "Scotty, have you got that pilot yet? We're running out of time up here."

"Workin' on it, Captain," the chief engineer replied distractedly.

Another disruptor bolt flashed past the scout. A second. The third didn't miss. There was a brief flare of radiation from the superheated hull and the tiny vessel melted away like disintegrating butter, faster than a splinter of magnesium in a firestorm.

In the transporter room four lights all commenced blinking at once and several gauges did unnatural things. Lieutenant Commander Scott, after several abortive attempts to alter the reading above one particularly significant dial, launched into an impassioned diatribe concerning the Klingon's ancestry, origins, probable spiritual destination, morals and general lack of good taste. His outburst did nothing to improve the readouts, but it was decidedly therapeutic. Scott's only disappointment was that the Klingons could not listen in.

Actually, if they had been able to, it is doubtful Scott's aspersions could have made them any madder than they were already.

"They got him," Sulu muttered angrily.

"Maybe not." Kirk bent to the intercom. "Scotty? Scout's gone . . . disruptor bolt. The pilot?"

Scott's voice came back full of confusion. "I don't know, sir. That blast must have hit his ship at the crucial second. You should see some of these instrument readings, Captain. In college we once did an experiment which involved dropping an egg from a thousand meters up onto a concrete platform. That's kind of what the integration parameters look like now, sir.

"I *think* I got him out in one piece. The trick now's goin' to be puttin' him back that way."

"Scotty, you pro . . ."

"Captain!" Kirk turned at Sulu's warning shout. His gaze went to the screen. The Klingon cruiser was turning, turning in a wide arc and heading directly toward the *Enterprise*. It began to accelerate.

Spock raised an eyebrow. Kirk's eyes widened.

"They're confident of something," Spock theorized. There was a beep from his own console, and he glanced back to study a computer readout.

"Silhouette and class identification confirmed, Captain. Imperial battle cruiser *Devisor,* Captain Koloth commanding."

The Klingon warship continued to close the distance rapidly. But just before it entered effective phaser range, it sheered off, keeping the distance between them. A strange blue halo formed at the ship's bow, faint at first but growing steadily in size. It thickened until it had the consistency of blue smoke. There was a sharp flash, and the tenuous blob leaped away from the *Devisor* toward the *Enterprise.*

Arex stiffened in his seat as the screen was filled with expanding blue cloud.

"The new weapon, Mr. Spock?" Kirk asked.

"Some kind of solidified field effect, Captain." He was studying sensor readouts. "It will contact us in precisely four seconds." His hands tightened on the console edge. "It appears capable of producing a most remarkab . . ."

There was a lurch as the *Enterprise* rolled forty-five degrees on her port side. It swung upright again. All on-board lights had gone out momentarily. Now they flickered dimly on, operating on stored power.

". . . disruption," Spock concluded.

External hull scanners revealed that the *Enterprise* was now cloaked in the wavy blue field.

Disruption of another kind had affected the main transporter room. Both the instrumentation and Chief Engineer Scott were producing some startling effects.

Sulu was working controls hurriedly. His face wore an expression at least one part panic. "Captain, our engines are dead."

"We have been struck by some kind of projected stasis field," Spock reported evenly. "Our matter-antimatter generators are disabled. So are the impulse engines. We seem to be completely paralyzed. Most remarkable."

"I'm not feeling in an admiring mood," Kirk shot back. "All phasers . . . fire."

Sulu attempted to respond. His worried frown knotted tighter. "Phasers don't work either, sir."

"I might note that my admiration does not preclude a desire on my part for retaliation, Captain," Spock explained. "I must observe, however, that the photon torpedoes will probably not respond, either. It appears that this field is capable of neutralizing all high-order field and warp functions."

"We could always throw rocks," Uhura suggested.

"This new Klingon weapon must be one of surprising power if it can so thoroughly immobilize a large starship like the *Enterprise*," Spock continued, speaking to no one in particular. "The energy drain must be enormous. Almost insupportable, I should think." No one was listening closely.

Kirk was at the com. again. "Scotty, did you retrieve that pilot yet?"

"He's still in the beam, sir, but I can't integrate him. All transporter systems have been interrupted."

"You sure you've got him, though?"

The chief engineer glanced to the transporter alcove. A familiar shimmering of multicolored particles continued to hover there, outlining a rotund, vaguely humanoid form. And that was all it did, growing neither stronger nor weaker.

"Gauges indicate seventy-three percent solidification attained, Captain. But I need at least another eighteen percent to assure successful final integration. We're going to need more power for that, sir."

"Hang onto him, Scotty." For what? They were at the mercy of the Klingon ship, unable even to run. He hammered the arm of his chair once, twice.

"Captain," Uhura broke in, adjusting her earphone, "message coming in."

"Put it through, Lieutenant."

He forced himself to relax. Even managed a half smile . . . which lasted all of two seconds. But at least he was able to keep himself from shouting angrily as the image of the Klingon bridge formed on the screen. Most of it was blocked out by a single figure.

The Klingon commander turned from speaking to someone off-screen to smile ingratiatingly into the pickup. He was fighting natural instincts to achieve a patina of politeness.

"This is Captain Koloth of the battle cruiser *Devisor*. Have I the honor of addressing the renowned Captain James Kirk, who . . ."

"You're not calling to laud my reputation," Kirk interrupted him firmly. "Release my ship."

"Of course, Captain, of course. Gladly, happily." He positively oozed good fellowship. "There is only one small thing we require. You must turn over to me the pilot of the little ship we were escorting."

"Didn't look like you wanted to escort him very far," Kirk observed. "In any case, I haven't got anybody to give you. Your last bolt dissolved him along with his ship."

Koloth assumed a sad smile. "I beg to differ with you, Captain Kirk, but our sensors distinctly recorded certain powerful energies at work on board the small ship at the moment of disruption. Computer analysis identifies same as a transporter beam of a type well known to be mounted on your class cruiser.

"As there are no other ships of your class in this immediate area save yourself, I must therefore assume the beam came from your ship. This in itself is not an arguable thing, but sensors further indicate a probability of better than half that the pilot of the scout was successfully removed before his vessel unfortunately self-destructed."

"You lie about as well as you navigate, Captain Koloth," Kirk countered. "In any case that ship was of Federation registry, operating well inside Federation boundaries—something you might also take notice of. The pilot is under our protection."

Koloth's face turned the color of a bad apple. He appeared to be trembling slightly. Somehow the captain was maintaining an iron control over his emotions. Something vital was necessary to force such restrictions on him.

It was.

"Captain, this person has committed ecological sabotage against the Imperium. If I have to take him by force I will."

"Temper, temper, Koloth. The first Klingon to step aboard this ship uninvited will be the last Klingon. Mr. Spock, full internal security alert."

For some reason, Kirk's final refusal seemed to calm Koloth. Even to widen his smile. "I'm afraid, Captain Kirk, that you'll find your hand weapons do not operate any better than your major armament."

Uhura had noticed something on her board and leaned over to whisper it to Spock. "Mr. Spock, I'm losing contact with our robot grain ships. They are not held by the stasis field and so they are continuing on course."

"What was that?" Kirk asked, looking over at the science station.

"I repeat, Captain," Koloth continued, "you must turn over to us the . . ."

"A moment, Captain. This situation calls for consultation with my officers."

Koloth looked disgusted.

"Ah, your archaic democratic principles? You have a few minutes, Captain, no longer. My patience is growing thin. If by that time you have not beamed the pilot over to us we will destroy your ship piecemeal as it sits helpless within our field."

"All right, Koloth, all right. You've made your point. Just give me a few minutes to talk this out." He rose from the chair, turned to Uhura.

"Lieutenant, cut off reception."

"Yes, sir." She complied as Kirk walked over to stare at the readouts above her.

"As you can see, sir," she commented, gesturing at the monitoring gauges, "they're moving off."

"Then they still have power. Can we control the robot ships, Sulu, in our present state?"

"Affirmative, sir," the helmsman replied a moment later. "Our remote guidance system is a low-order field effect and not affected by the Klingon stasis."

"Koloth made no mention of them. There's a chance

he's so concerned with us he has forgotten about them. Bring them back, Mr. Sulu—and have them ram the Klingon ship."

"Captain . . ."

Kirk looked over at his first officer.

"You cannot afford to lose that grain," Spock insisted. "The situation on Sherman's Planet . . ."

Kirk cut him off. "I can afford even less to lose the *Enterprise*, Mr. Spock. Once he gets what he wants, do you think Koloth will let us go to report this serious violation of Federation territory? Why should he, considering where he's got us?"

Sulu was working furiously at his instruments as Kirk took his seat again. "Open the hailing frequency again, Lieutenant Uhura." The screen cleared quickly. "Captain Koloth? We've reached a decision." He paused a moment for effect and to give the robot ships a few seconds more to gain on the *Devisor*.

"I'm going to give you one last chance to release the *Enterprise*."

Koloth assumed an expression of incredulity. "*You're* going to give *me* one more chance?" His voice dissolved in Klingon laughter—hacking, unmelodious, unamusing. Apparently someone off-screen said something equally unamusing, because Koloth abruptly was listening hard and looking to his left. He was frowning when he turned back to Kirk.

"It won't work, Captain."

Koloth's face disappeared and the screen went blank. Kirk was not sorry to see him go. He smiled slightly himself. The threat was working, otherwise Koloth would still be there, gloating.

Their counterattack was crude and primitive and would have appalled the men who had designed the *Enterprise*'s offensive weaponry. This didn't change the fact that it was working. Either of the robot ships could make a very thorough mess of the *Devisor*.

Sulu expanded their field of vision. At the same time, two new azure bubbles began to form at the *Devisor*'s bow. They grew rapidly in size. Again the brief flare splitting them off from the mother ship and then they were moving away in opposite directions, toward the onrushing robots.

"Incredible," Spock was murmuring, "utterly incredible . . . the amount of energy that must be required to maintain those fields."

' Sulu switched to a deeper pickup to follow one of the blue fogs as it headed toward an approaching grain carrier. As they watched, it suddenly seemed to flutter, uncertain as an albatross coming in for a landing. Fluttered, wavered . . . thinned . . . dissolved.

So did its companion cloud. So did the major field surrounding the *Enterprise*. The starship gave a little shudder as it was released from paralysis.

"I thought so," commented Spock with barely a hint of satisfaction in his voice. "They couldn't maintain it. They didn't have enough power. Even a ship twice the size of the *Devisor* . . ."

Kirk wasn't really listening. "Keep phasers locked on target, Mr. Sulu. But hold your fire until they fire first. Give them a chance to back off."

"Aye, sir." The helmsman kept his face turned away so his Captain wouldn't see the undiplomatic, predatory gleam in his eyes.

Flashes of a deeper blue erupted from the *Devisor*'s prow . . . her main disruptor batteries this time. The first barrage destroyed the propulsion units of one of the robots, missing the huge cargo module. A second attack missed the other carrier, badly.

"Apparently their battle capacity is way down," Spock observed. "They only damaged one ship. Missing two unscreened drones at this range indicates a definite lack of offensive power—for the moment, at least."

As if in confirmation, the *Devisor* turned away from the *Enterprise* in a sweeping curve, away from the remaining charging drone.

"Veering off," Sulu noted formally, locked to his console.

Spock was bent over his hooded viewer. "Sensors indicate their power cells are almost exhausted. I doubt they possess more than minimal deflector capability. We could destroy them at will."

Kirk nodded. "Yes, and I bet Koloth knew exactly what he was asking of his ship. He took a tremendous gamble, and he lost.

"Right now I'm more curious in finding out just what he felt was worth the loss of his ship and an interstellar incident bordering on an act of war. Something has made them awfully angry. They *really* wanted that pilot." He relaxed as the *Devisor* passed out of disruptor range and turned to the com.

"Mr. Scott . . . can you integrate that pilot now?"

"It will still take a few minutes, Captain," came the tired reply. "He was scattered to hell and gone, but he's locked in solid. I just need a little time to double-check integration."

"We'll be right there, Scotty. Kirk out." He rose from the chair. "Lieutenant Uhura, call Dr. McCoy to the transporter room. In addition to anything incurred in delayed transport, we don't know what injuries this person may have suffered before we took him off his ship."

"Very well, Captain." She turned to contact Sick Bay.

"Mr. Spock . . . ?"

XII

Both men were silent as the elevator took them toward the transporter room. But their thoughts were similar. Each wondered what had made the Empire send a warship so far into Federation territory. True, the Klingons placed a great deal of importance on re-venge. But that hardly seemed a sufficient explanation. Though for a moment, Captain Koloth had been as an-gry as any Klingon officer Kirk had ever seen.

Ecological sabotage, he had said. Well, to a Klingon that might mean any number of offenses which did not really merit destruction. They would find out exactly what was going on in a very few seconds—from the object of the Klingon's wrath.

McCoy was waiting for them as they entered. Kirk's attention was drawn immediately to the transporter al-cove. A sharp silhouette there still shimmered with color.

"Haven't got him yet, Mr. Scott?"

"Just finalizing him now, sir. I've been integrating very slowly. No tellin' what a long delay in transport will do. It's almost fail-safe, sir, but there are still histo-ries of peculiar aberrations bein' produced when such delayed folks were rushed back."

Kirk held his impatience and stared into the cham-ber. The vibrant glow began to fade and a human shape to emerge. Or . . . was it? There seemed to be a multiple form. No . . . one human, all right. Very stout, round. One human—surrounded by lots of little round stout things, very unhuman. Quite a number of little round stout shapes.

The last of the transporter hue started to fade out and the pilot became recognizable—along with the other beings.

Spock raised an eyebrow uncertainly. "It would ap-pear to be . . ."

Kirk recognized it . . . them, too. Wished fer-vently—oh, how fervently he did not. His words were measured, reluctant. "I think we know that man."

McCoy broke in.

"I don't want to think about it!" The doctor be-stowed an anguished look on the chief engineer. "Scotty, what you said about delays in transport pro-ducing aberrations—I didn't think you meant anything quite this hideous."

Scott had also recognized the figure and was undergoing mild shock himself. "Not again!" he finally howled.

"Cyrano Jones." Kirk finally said it out, making the name sound like a curse. And in a sense that pudgy, falsely Falstaffian figure surely was.

Cyrano Jones smiled at them. He beamed. He expanded, fairly radiating good humor, hands relaxed on hips. Faint mewing sounds issued from the region of his ankles.

"And he's got tribbles with him," Scotty groaned.

When the cylindrical transporter effect had ceased, the tribbles Jones had clustered around him immediately spilled across the alcove floor. Kirk and Spock glanced at each other, exchanged telepathic sighs.

Kirk moved to the subsidiary console and punched the switch that would tie him in with the log. He needed a couple of minutes of enforced order before he could begin to deal rationally with this situation. As if anyone could deal rationally with tribbles. However . . .

"Captain's Log, supplemental. Our rescue of the pilot of the one-man ship being pursued by the Klingon cruiser *Devisor* has given us important knowledge of a new Klingon weapon—as yet unperfected.

"It has also inflicted on us—for as short a time as possible—the presence of Cyrano Jones, interstellar trader and general nuisance."

"General trader and interstellar nuisance," Scott corrected grimly.

Nudging tribbles out of his path, Jones made his way toward Kirk. "Ah, Captain Kirk. My old friend, Captain Kirk!" He extended his arms to clasp the captain in a fraternal embrace. Fortunately, Kirk had the transporter console between him and Jones.

Kirk turned to the goggle-eyed ensign who had been assisting Scott at the transporter's backup instrumentation. "Seal off this area, Mister, and I mean tight."

"Aye, sir," the man acknowledged, moving to comply.

Kirk's feet suddenly felt unnaturally warm. He looked down and the reason became apparent. Two large tribbles had sandwiched his right ankle. They were rubbing against him from both sides, cooing and purring.

He took an angry step to the side. Both tribbles fumbled to follow him, distracting his attention from the mewing horde which had quickly spread throughout the room from their landing place in the transporter alcove.

Kirk moved up close to confront their owner. His indignation would have been helped greatly if Jones had possessed a face and disposition more like Koloth's and less like that of a beardless St. Nick. Even so, Kirk managed to work up a good dose of righteous anger.

"You know the law about transporting species proven harmful, Jones."

"Harmful, Captain?" The trader was a fount of innocence. Kirk made an angry gesture to encompass the room.

"Well then, what would you call these?"

"Tribbles, Captain."

That was the last straw . . . or hair, in this case. Kirk had just endured the trauma of saving his ship from a previously unknown and nearly fatal weapon to save someone whom he almost wished he had never met in the first place.

"Don't get smart with me, Jones. Believe me, I'm not in the mood."

"Captain, really, I assure you. I wasn't being smart at your expense." Kirk eyed him warningly. "These aren't harmful. These are safe tribbles."

McCoy stood nearby, watching and listening. He had knelt and scooped up a straw-colored, furry ball. It immediately tried to crawl up his arm, rubbing and purring. He used his other hand to pluck it off, shook it threateningly at Jones. The abused tribble purred indignantly.

"As you are well aware, Jones, there is no such thing as a safe tribble."

"A safe tribble," Spock amplified, in his best professional tone, "is a contradiction in terms. I am surprised, Mr. Jones, that you would attempt to fool us with so obvious a lie—particularly us, to whom tribbles are well remembered for their dangerous reproductive proclivities."

"And they breed fast, too," Jones admitted. "Don't you see? Gentlemen, that's why these tribbles are safe." He was pleading with them. "They don't reproduce."

Four stunned faces stared back at him. McCoy was the first to voice the skepticism all felt. "Don't reproduce? Who ever heard of a tribble that didn't ..."

"I've had them genetically engineered for compatability with humanoid ecologies," the trader added quickly. "A simple gene manipulation coupled with some selective breeding. See how friendly and lovable they are?"

Of course they were friendly and lovable. Tribbles were as well known for being friendly and lovable as they were for reproducing at astronomical rates. And this bunch was every bit as affectionate as any Kirk had seen before. They rubbed and purred and mewed and cuddled with boundless enthusiasm. And as he looked around the room, he had to admit he didn't see a hint of tribbles reproducing.

Not that there was anything for them to reproduce on, but he had seen tribbles seemingly multiply out of thin air. There did not appear to be any more now than when they first materialized.

"Not a baby in the bunch," Jones pointed out proudly. "You know what great pets they make, Captain. Profitable, too."

Something had been nagging at the back of Kirk's mind while Jones had been spouting his smooth sales spiel. Now he had it.

"Jones, how did you get away from Space Station K-Seven in the first place. You were supposed to take care of all the tribbles there. Regardless of what genetic engineering you claim to have done on these, the tribbles on K-Seven were definitely not altered for non-reproduction. You couldn't have cleaned them off in such a short time."

Jones was fumbling at his copious pockets. "Quite so, Captain. But I managed a short parole and found myself some help. Ecologically sound, efficient, unoffensive help."

The thing he took from his pocket was red, had numerous arms or legs or both, and looked decidedly unfriendly.

"This, Captain, is a tribble predator. It's called a glommer."

"Interesting, if true," commented Spock, studying the creature and reserving judgment. "Is the name derivative or descriptive?"

"See for yourself," Jones said, winking.

He put the glommer on the floor. Making rumbling sounds like a toy volcano, it hesitated, orienting itself. It froze stiffly, then started creeping toward the nearest tribble. Pausing a short distance from a moderate-sized specimen, it tensed. Kirk thought he could see the thick hairs on the creature's appendages stiffen slightly. Without a sound and with surprising suddenness, it sprang at its prey like a wolf spider. The tribble never had a chance as the glommer landed on it.

It spread its body surface wide, engulfing the tribble completely. There was a harried series of barely audible slurping sounds accompanied by a violent quivering. Then the predator relaxed.

But only for a moment. In addition to being efficient, it was also apparently ravenous. Its metabolism seemed geared to continual consumption. Bottom hairs tensing, it stalked off after another tribble. Not even a hair was left of the first.

McCoy was impressed. "Neat, too."

But Kirk, having satisfied himself that Jones apparently was not a fugitive from K-seven, was interested in something much more important than glommer hygiene. Even McCoy looked away from the interesting glommer-versus-tribble drama to listen to Jones' answer.

"Jones, just why *were* the Klingons chasing you?" The trader looked at the walls, the ceiling, his tribbles—anywhere to avoid meeting Kirk's waiting gaze.

"Well," the Captain prompted, "are you going to tell me you don't know?" Given any possible out, Jones leaped at it, nodding vigorously.

"That's it exactly, Captain! I don't. The Klingons have notoriously bad tempers, you know."

"While it must be admitted that the Klingon mental state tends toward the bellicose," Spock observed, "they still retain a sense of proportion when exercising their animosities. I do not see a Klingon cruiser captain entering Federation space to attack a Federation vessel in a fit of pique. Nor for mere recreation, or because his liver was bothering him."

"You're right about their temper, though," Kirk added. "Captain Koloth seemed oddly upset over something he called ecological sabotage."

Jones' eyes took on a rotundity that matched his belly. "Me? A saboteur? I ask you now, Captain, do *I* look like a saboteur?" He assumed an air of outraged dignity.

"Captain Koloth was pretty emphatic about it," Kirk continued, watching the trader carefully.

"I'm not responsible for Captain Koloth's perverse imagination," Jones insisted.

"If it was imagination." Kirk's tone turned coaxing. "Are you sure, Cyrano, that you didn't . . . ," and he held up a hand with thumb and forefinger squeezing a centimeter of air, ". . . maybe accidentally perhaps possibly perform some teensy weensy little act that might have caused the Klingons to overreact like this?"

Jones glanced reluctantly at Spock, then at McCoy and saw no relief from that quarter. He looked at the floor.

"Actually, it was such a little thing. I can't understand why they got so upset. You understand, don't you, Captain?"

Kirk's tone indicated there was an outside chance he did not:

"What did you do?"

Jones tried to look nonchalant, even managed a slight laugh. "Nothing at all, really. I only sold ... them ... some ... uh ... tribbles ..."

Kirk's voice dropped dangerously. "You sold tribbles on a Klingon planet?"

"Well," the trader protested lamely, "I didn't *know* it was a Klingon planet."

"What species were the inhabitants," Kirk pressed relentlessly.

"Oh, mixed. You know, a mongrel world. Tellerites, Sironians, a few Romulans—Klingons, too."

"How about *outside* the customs port." This from Spock. Jones pretended not to hear.

"I beg your pardon, Mr. Spock?"

"I believe you heard me correctly, Mr. Jones. The population *outside* the free customs and reception station. What did it consist of?"

Jones watched the glommer continue to devour tribbles at an astonishing rate. "Uh ... Klingons ... mostly."

"What was that? Speak up," Kirk ordered.

"Klingons ... they were all Klingons!" Jones exploded. "But where I set down it was a mixed populace, Captain. So how could I tell for certain it was a Klingon planet?"

Kirk had had enough. "Jones," he began, as though he were lecturing a five-year-old, "tribbles don't like Klingons. You *know* tribbles don't like Klingons. Didn't you think they might object to your selling tribbles to visitors at their landing station?"

"Ah well, Klingons like tribbles even less," Jones confessed, ignoring Kirk's question. "It was lucky you came along and saved me when you did, friend Kirk. I couldn't have outrun them much longer."

"I'd estimate about another two seconds," Kirk theorized, wistfully. Jones nodded in somber agreement.

"You snatched me from the jaws of death at the moment of judgment, Captain. I should have known that in a desperate situation, our life-long friendship, the high regard in which you hold me, your unrelenting desire to see justice done . . ."

Trying to control his stomach, Kirk switched to less emotionally charged subject matter. "I am sure, Jones, that a quick scan of our files will show that you stand in violation of three Federation mandates and forty-seven local laws plus various attendant paragraphs thereunto appended. I am formally placing you under arrest."

That pronouncment was sufficiently impressive to draw from Jones a stunned gasp. Although anything was preferable to being either obliterated by or turned over to the tender mercies of the Klingons, Jones was not enamored of Federation mind-wipe techniques. Federation criminal psycho-engineers were an especially dull lot. They tended to remove one's most interesting memories.

"You're confined to quarters until we complete our current mission. Then we'll proceed to the nearest Starfleet base and turn you over to the proper authorities."

Jones was thinking furiously. "Captain, couldn't we talk this over?"

Kirk's reply was a look of such overpowering silent fury that even the trader was cowed.

"I didn't think so," the trader mumbled.

Kirk turned to the ensign at the door. "Mr. Hacker, keep an eye on our visitor. Call security and have them prepare suitable accommodations for him." He nodded in Jones' direction.

The ensign moved to the com. to comply.

"Bones, let's take a couple of these so-called altered tribbles down to your lab and check out Jones' claims. If there's any truth to them, it'll be a first."

"All right, Jim." McCoy busied himself gathering up suitable specimens.

They headed for the elevator. Kirk looked back to Jones. "If these turn out to be normal tribbles, Jones, I'm personally going to order you placed in solitary with tribble mewing played round the clock into your cell at a dozen times normal volume."

"Really, Captain, do you think I would lie to you about something as important, as vital, as incriminating as this?"

"Yes," Kirk replied without hesitation. "Let's go, gentlemen." He paused as the elevator doors opened, had a last thought. "Oh, Mr. Hacker?"

The ensign looked back. "Sir?"

Kirk spoke as he nudged a tribble out of the elevator with his foot. "Don't listen to anything he says. And above all . . . don't let him sell you anything."

"Yes, sir."

At McCoy's request, they all met in the main briefing room an hour later. The doctor had spent much of that time putting the sample tribbles through every test he could thing of. He had also spent much of the time going *hmmmm* a lot.

Tribbles were the most interesting things to study. And these tribbles offered some surprises. He picked up one specimen—an unusually large tribble, Kirk thought—and gestured with it as he spoke.

"I'm afraid Cyrano Jones was right, Jim. These tribbles don't reproduce. They just get fat."

"Are you sure, Bones?"

"Absolutely. Any excess food turns into flesh instead of stimulating reproduction." He put the corpulent tribble on the floor. It immediately crept over to Kirk and crawled up and down one boot, rubbing and purring.

"So I don't think we have anything to worry about."

"Not as far as the tribbles are concerned, anyway," Kirk agreed. "This new Klingon weapon is another matter. Koloth was adamant about getting his hands on Jones. We may not have seen the last of them." He reached down and pulled the tribble off his boot, tossed it into a far corner—as gently as possible, it seemed to Scott.

"It is an energy-sapping field of great strength, Captain," Spock commented. "It totally immobilizes a ship and its weapons capacity. But it appears that when extended to its ultimate limits, it also immobilizes the attacker as well."

"Aye," agreed Scott. "If that's true then it's a weapon that leaves them as helpless as it leaves us."

"I believe I just said that, Mr. Scott," observed Spock.

There was a pause while everyone present considered this information.

"The practical advantages of such a weapon would seem to be limited," Kirk concluded.

"Limited, perhaps," put in Spock. "But that does not obviate its initial, overwhelming effect." He considered another moment, then went on. "The key question is, how long does it take them to recharge? They'll probably attack us again as soon as they're back up to full power.

"If Captain Koloth has any ability in tactics, he will undoubtedly begin by destroying the remaining robot ships to prevent us from using the same trick again. That would put us in a difficult position, indeed." He looked unusually somber. "They must want Cyrano Jones very badly indeed."

"He really doesn't seem the saboteur type, Jim," McCoy commented.

Kirk stared at the fine grain in the wood table-top and wished his thoughts were as straight. "Yes . . . yes. And yet, I get the impression there's something he's not telling us. He is still holding something back." He took a deep breath, looked up. "That will be discovered in due time. Mr. Scott, let's see a status report on the damaged grain ship."

Scott hit the necessary switch, and the triple table-screen popped up in front of them. Further manipulation of controls produced pictures which illustrated his commentary.

"Well, sir, in the past hour we've managed to transfer all the seed grain aboard. And mind, Captain, it wasn't easy finding room to store it all. We filled the shuttle-craft hangars, all our extra holds, and we've even got containers of that quinto-triticale in the less frequently used corridors of the ship.

"Fortunately, it was modular instead of bulk packed. Otherwise we would have had to repack every grain in smaller containers to fit on board. As it is, not only does the grain hamper movement throughout the ship, but there are a number of activities that will have to be limited, or even curtailed, until we deliver it to Sherman's Planet. For example, we can't use the Shuttle Bay at all."

"What about the possibility of repairing the damaged grain carrier?"

"Not a chance in a million, sir," Scott replied, shaking his head firmly. "Her engines were ninety-percent destroyed. She needs to be rebuilt, not repaired." He sighed deeply. "And we've still got that other robot ship to escort, too. I don't like it at all, sir."

"Nor do I, Mr. Scott. But we'll have to manage with the grain on board, somehow. Sherman's Planet needs it desperately."

"Aye, sir, aye . . . I know." The chief engineer sounded resigned. "It's just that everything seems to happen at once sometimes, sir. Tribbles on the ship, quinto-triticale in the corridors, Klingons in the quadrant. . ."
He shook his head at the injustice of it all. "Why, sir, it's enough to ruin your whole day."

"Let's hope the worst is over, Scotty." Kirk rose. "This meeting is adjourned, gentlemen." He reached under the table to deactivate the triple viewer. What he got for a response was a loud mew.

"They appear to be fond of you, Captain," Spock observed with a straight face.

"I'm not flattered." Kirk disgustedly removed the curious tribble from the control panel and hit the proper switch.

For a little while it seemed as if Kirk's wish might come true—the worst of their difficulties might be past. Nothing happened in the next several hours that approached crisis proportions.

That did not mean, however, the *Enterprise* was without interesting activity. Down in a dimly lit corridor the glommer—forgotten by an introspective Jones—was stalking another tribble.

The glommer got within range, tensed, leaped—and was bucked off. Growling in surprise, it hopped after the retreating tribble. Quickly overtaking the tribble, it proceeded to ingest—the effort producing rather more commotion than ever before because the tribble it had pounced on was larger than a man's head. That tribble was almost more than the glommer could handle—almost.

The glommer paused a moment, belched, and sat recovering its strength. Discharging another deposit of converted tribble it promptly stalked off in search of further prey, now wobbling a little unsteadily from side to side.

The calm on the bridge did not last nearly as long as Kirk had hoped. He had hoped for five days of it, time enough in which to reach Sherman's Planet.

Instead, he had had only the few hours following McCoy's briefing before Spock broke the stillness. "Captain, sensors are picking up an approaching Klingon cruiser." A brief, hopeful pause, then, "It appears to be the *Devisor*."

Kirk had been standing talking to Sulu, now moved quickly to the Science Station for a personal check of the sensor readouts. Damn! Damn Cyrano Jones and damn tribbles and damn the Klingon's persistence! He strode back to his seat, shoved the twenty-kilogram tribble off.

"Deflector shields up—stand by all phasers."

A sudden thought struck him and he eyed the tribble carefully. Wait a minute—a twenty-kilo tribble?

"How fat do these things get, anyway?" He hadn't noticed any this size when Jones had first come on board. Anyway, McCoy was not around to answer, and Spock was occupied. A second later Sulu removed all thoughts of tribbles.

"Klingon cruiser approaching rapidly, sir, on interception course. Phaser range in thirty seconds."

"Coming in fast," Spock commented with his usual objective detachment. "Obviously they can recharge their power cells in a matter of hours. Interesting, if true." He did not explain his cryptic final comment, and Kirk was too busy to ask about it.

"Mr. Arex, Mr. Sulu . . . use the robot ship as a decoy. Have it change course and move off due west, up seventy degrees. We can use it to give the Klingons more trouble, since they can't paralyze more than one ship at a time with their field."

The *Devisor* continued to approach confidently as the remaining robot grain carrier peeled off on a new course. As soon as she was far enough off, Sulu activated the helm and the *Enterprise* also changed course.

"Commencing evasive tactics," he reported crisply.

Governed now in part by her battle computer, the *Enterprise* began an erratic weave designed to leave the Klingons with the minimum possible target. The Klingon ship adjusted its path correspondingly, but not to pursue.

"*Devisor* is veering away," Spock observed.

The battle cruiser fired a single powerful disruptor bolt—not at the starship, but at the remaining drone. The bolt neatly severed the clumsy cargo module from the dual propulsion units.

"My error, Captain," Spock corrected. "They were not veering away. They were moving to attack the grain ship."

Sulu checked his gooseneck viewer. "But they didn't destroy it, sir." Kirk relaxed a hair. "They only wrecked the propulsion units. The cargo pod is intact." He looked up from the viewer. "Maybe we should modify our opinion of Captain Koloth's marksmen."

"It appears they are quite accurate," Spock concurred, "when firing on undefended cargo drones."

"They've changed course again," Sulu reported. "They're coming in after us."

"Stand by phasers," Kirk warned.

"Phasers armed and ready, sir." Sulu's hand hovered over the firing switch. Arex shifted their position so that the main batteries would have an unobstructed line of fire on the *Devisor*. On the viewscreen, brilliant blue flares erupted from the cruiser's nose.

"Disruptors," Spock announced calmly.

A second later the bolts impacted on the *Enterprise*—only to sputter harmlessly on their shields. They felt a mild lurch as the ship reeled with the absorbtion of the tremendous destructive energy, but no one was knocked from their seat.

"Damage report, Mr. Sulu."

"No damage reported, sir," said the helmsman quickly. "Shields holding firm."

"Fire at will, Mr. Sulu."

"Firing, sir."

The battle continued for several minutes—long by intership standards—as the *Enterprise* and *Devisor* wheeled about a common center which shifted every second. Disruptor bolts alternated with phasers, probing for a weakness in the absorbing screens. Multiple barrages glanced off, were handled by opposing defenses.

The repetitive rattling caused only minor damage on the two cruisers. The *Enterprise* suffered slightly more than the *Devisor* because the temporary cargo she was carrying in her corridors and holds was not secured for battle running.

Succeeding jolts broke open one grain container after another. Of itself, the damage was minor. The containers could be easily repaired, the grain recollected.

Except in a couple of corridors, corridors no one was watching because all were at battle stations—corridors where a concerted mewing and cooing suddenly rose appreciably in volume.

Like a fuzzy glacier, clumps of tribbles started creeping rapidly toward the protein-rich kernels of quinto-triticale.

Some of the tribbles were no longer very small . . .

XIII

Now was the time, Kirk decided, to see if his strategy had paid off. By this time, Captain Koloth was hopefully convinced that the *Enterprise* was armed only with phasers and he had adjusted his defenses accordingly. They had one chance to catch him napping.

"Photon torpedoes, Mr. Sulu. Fire."

"Torpedoes away, sir."

All eyes moved to the screen, where computer-guided deep-space scanners held the *Devisor* fixed on the screen like a bug under chloroform.

"Three, two, one . . . impact," Sulu counted down. Then, "Torpedo miss."

But the image of the *Devisor* was starting to shrink. Spock checked his sensors, frowned. "They appear to be running away, Captain. Most odd. They did not use their stasis weapon at all."

"Maybe you were right, Mr. Spock, and they could only partly recharge their power cells, only enough to manage a conventional attack."

"Then why break off the engagement?" Spock wondered aloud. "I detect no sign of serious damage. Unless their attack achieved some unimaginable purpose."

"They disabled the robot carrier, " Sulu noted.

"Before they engaged us," mused Kirk. "No, Spock's right. It doesn't make sense. Koloth knew his battle capabilities before he attacked." He shook his head, feeling they were missing something.

"Well, put a tractor beam on the disabled drone. We'll have to try and take it in tow."

"Now that could be their intention exactly, Captain,"

Spock suggested. "Towing the drone will be a drag both on our available power and maneuverability. We're already carrying the extra mass of the first carrier's cargo. Captain Koloth's engineers have undoubtedly calculated how much energy this will sap from our battle capacity."

"We can't do anything about the extra mass on board, Mr. Spock, but we could break the tow instantly in the event of another attack."

"That is true, Captain. But the *Devisor* could attack and run, attack and run. If Koloth is aware of the situation on Sherman's Planet he knows we are operating within certain time restrictions. Eventually his chances of catching us with the second drone under tow will increase."

"That seems logical," Kirk admitted.

"Thank you, Captain."

"Well, Mr. Spock?" he said, after a short pause.

"Well what, Captain?"

"You've already correctly analyzed the situation. We cannot tow the damaged robot ship indefinitely, nor can we abandon it. And there is no room for more quinto-triticale on board. I assume you have some suggestions as to what we can do."

Spock paused in thought, Vulcan gears turning at top speed. "Yes, Captain, we can throw tribbles at them."

Kirk's expression underwent a succession of variations. Arex's reaction was mostly internal, but much the same.

"I thought Vulcans didn't have a sense of humor," he finally ventured.

"We do not, Captain. Allow me to think this out."

Kirk regarded his first officer with a gaze of honest confusion.

Down in one of the lower storage holds a door had burst, flooding the deck with quinto-triticale. Instantly the hillock of golden-brown seeds was inundated by a horde of tribbles of impressive bulk.

At the base of the broken door the glommer was

struggling with one of the tribbles. This particular one had the dimensions of a large, furry hassock. It ignored the furious, frustrated glommer on its topside and continued to munch contentedly on the sudden nutritious bonanza.

As Scott was returning to the bridge, he made a quick trip back to Engineering Central for a first-hand check on the amount of power the cargo drone tow was drawing. A harried security sergeant confronted him in a corridor, tried to babble an explanation of what he had seen. His story was enough to detour Scott temporarily from the bridge.

He was still talking when the elevator doors opened to the low deck. Scott needed less than two minutes to evaluate the situation and head for the bridge at top speed.

"Captain," he said, walking directly to the command chair, "we've got broken cargo pods in all the corridors, and some of the storage holds themselves have burst. The tribbles have gotten into the grain. No need to tell you what they're doing." He paused to catch his breath.

"Eating, I should suppose," observed Spock blandly. He glanced at the base of the navigation console significantly, where a fifty-kilo tribble had appeared. The enormous fur ball was rubbing at the legs of an irritated Sulu. Then Spock began making some quick computations at his console.

"Given the exceptional nutritive value of the hybrid grain, I should say that at their estimated rate of conversion these altered tribbles will ..."

"Altered!" Kirk stopped listening to Spock. "Get Cyrano Jones up here on the double, Scotty."

"Aye, sir." He headed for the elevator again while Uhura notified the brig.

Kirk rose and walked to the helm-navigation console, nearly tripping over an elongated tribble in the process. Glancing up occasionally at the main viewscreen for signs of the *Devisor*, he examined certain readouts.

"Any sign of Captain Koloth's ship?"

"Nothing yet, sir," Sulu reported.

"Keep scanning. They'll probably come at us from a different quadrant this time."

It wasn't long before Scott reappeared, pushing a puzzled Cyrano Jones urgently before him.

"Ah, Captain Kirk. What can I do for you? From the attitude displayed by your chief engineer," and he looked reprovingly at Scott, who returned the favor with a glance suggesting that he would have liked to display Jones in the nearest converter, "I gather that it is a matter of some gravity."

"Not gravity—grain," Kirk corrected him furiously. "Your shribbles are all over my trip . . . your tribbles are all over my ship." *Easy, James T., easy.* "My security personnel can't find them all, despite the fact," and he kicked at a hundred-kilo tribble where an eighty-kilo tribble had been only moments before, "that they're hardly inconspicuous anymore."

The tribble cooed, tried to rub against his ankle.

Jones shrugged. "You need better security men then, Captain. As you say, they shouldn't be hard to find." He looked interestedly at the apparition Kirk had just kicked.

With enormous effort, Kirk held his emotions in check. "Mr. Jones, you are in enough trouble already. Feeble attempts at humor will only exacerbate your situation." He returned to his station.

"Oh, Captain," Jones protested, "a harmless little tribble. What can they hurt?"

Kirk put his shoulder to the hundred-kilo tribble sitting in the command chair and shoved it out. "Harmless? Maybe. But little? In any case, the main problem is that they're eating the quinto-triticale."

"The what?" Jones looked confused.

"The grain."

The trader looked troubled for the first time. "Captain, you have grain on this ship?"

"What?" Kirk was staring at the screen. Naturally the *Devisor* would show up any second. "Yes . . . grain.

Seed grain, to prevent a serious famine on Sherman's Planet. It won't be prevented if your tribbles continue eating at the rate they are."

"But they're hungry, Captain," Jones protested, spreading his hands in a gesture of helplessness.

"So are the people on Sherman's Planet!" Kirk countered tightly. His shout echoed across the bridge. The gigantic purple tribble he had just pushed out of his seat mewed uncomfortably and edged away a little.

"A little tribble, Jones, doesn't eat much. A big tribble does. And these are getting bigger."

That's when it came to him,

"Jones, is this the ecological sabotage the Klingons are so mad about? Is this why Captain Koloth is willing to risk his ship to get you back? The Klingons have a lot of pride, Jones. No wonder they want you."

The trader started to object, but a sudden shout from Sulu's station shattered the conversation.

"Captain, the *Devisor* is coming back."

There, he knew it was too much to hope for. Now he understood why the Klingons wouldn't break off the engagement.

McCoy chose that moment to enter the bridge. Both hands were full of tribble. "Jim, there's something about these tribbles . . ."

"Later, Bones," Kirk interrupted tiredly. He started to sit down, paused. The tribble in it weighed at least one hundred and forty but otherwise it was just like the one he'd shoved out a minute before.

Which raised another interesting question. How fat did the tribbles grow . . . and how fast?

One crisis at a time. Panting, he shoved the tribble out of his seat once more, sat down.

"Mr. Sulu, release the tow on the robot carrier. All deflector shields on full. Stand by phasers and photon torpedoes." He paused and looked first at Jones and then McCoy. "And all non-combatants off the bridge."

McCoy nodded, took charge of Jones. But first he dumped the overflowing tribble he had been holding.

Everyone's attention was fixed on the screen, which

now showed the approaching *Devisor* once again. Kirk diverted his attention long enough to thumb a certain switch under his right hand.

"Captain's Log, supplemental," he recited in a soft voice. "The Klingon battle cruiser *Devisor*, under command of Captain Koloth, appears about to force us into another battle for custody of the trader Cyrano Jones." He cut off. Elaboration would have to wait for leisure time.

On screen, the *Devisor* continued its relentless approach with little recourse to subtlety. Apparently this was to be another head-on attack like the first.

"Contact in thirty seconds," announced Spock.

"Ready photon torpedoes, Mr. Sulu."

The *Devisor* now filled the screen. An ominous cloud of fluttering azure began to form at its prow. Apparently the stasis projector was back in operation. And this time they had no robot ships to throw at it.

"Fire one, fire two."

"One and two away," Sulu announced. "Three, two, one ... impact." Seconds pause, then, "Minus one, minus two ... something's wrong, Captain. I show impact but no reaction."

"Are you positive, Mr. Sulu?"

"Absolutely, sir. We show definite ..."

"I think I know what has happened, Captain," said Spock. "Both torpedoes impinged on the stasis field the *Devisor* is building. Considering the known power of such a field, I have no doubt that the drive and detonation mechanisms of the torpedoes were paralyzed when they reached it."

"Evasive emergency maneuvers, Mr. Sulu," was all Kirk could say.

"Aye, Captain."

Too late—the field enveloped the *Enterprise* even as Sulu directed a convoluted course across the starfield. Enveloped them in a rippling miasma of brilliant blue.

The *Enterprise* gave a sickening lurch. Kirk groaned inwardly. That had not done the weakened grain containers below any good. Little could be done to repair them while the ship remained on battle status.

And so in numerous corridors and holds, the tribble orgy continued unabated.

"That's done it," cursed Scott, looking up from his engineering console in anger and alarm. "We're caught again."

"Message coming in, Captain, over ship-to-ship hailing frequency," Uhura announced. Kirk sighed. He already had a fair idea of what the message would contain.

"Put it through, Lieutenant."

"Yes, sir." Moments later a picture of Captain Koloth—a broadly grinning, self-satisfied Captain Koloth—appeared once more on the main viewscreen. Kirk noted the clarity of the image though he would not have objected to some distortion blotting out some of his smile.

Visual and aural communications were low-order field functions, of course, and thus were not affected by the stasis field, as were . . .

Something was trying to fuse in the back of his head. He could not spare the time to study it. Koloth wouldn't give it to him.

"Captain Kirk. I am so glad to see that you have not suffered any injury yet, nor," he looked to left and right, "have any of your crew. This pleases me. We will take control of your vessel intact, it appears."

"Not if I can help it," Kirk said grimly. Koloth's smile disappeared and barely controlled fury colored his cheeks.

"You cannot help it and *I want your prisoner, Captain.*"

"Control yourself, Koloth, or you'll burst a blood vessel. Much as it pains me to admit to it, Cyrano Jones is a citizen of the Federation, and therefore is entitled to Federation protection. I am afraid I must refuse your request." He thought, added, "You have no idea how much it pains me to refuse your request."

"I regret any emotional upset it has caused you,"

Koloth continued with biting sarcasm. "If it will alleviate your agony any, Captain Kirk, let me assure you this is not a 'request.'" For an unguarded moment he sounded almost regretful—for a Klingon.

"Don't force me to take steps we will both regret."

"Not a chance," Kirk snarled. Stasis field or no, he had taken about all he could handle of Koloth.

"Close channel, Lieutenant," Kirk ordered, pacing near Sulu.

"With pleasure, sir." She hit a switch and Koloth's image abruptly faded from the screen.

Kirk started back to his seat . . . and stopped, his lower jar descending slightly. Even a friend would have been hard put to interpret his expression.

A contentedly mewing tribble occupied the command chair. It weighed two hundred and fifty kilos if it weighed a gram. Folding his arms, Kirk turned to stare at the viewscreen again.

"Aren't you going to sit down, Captain?" Spock inquired.

"I think I'll stand for now, Mr. Spock—haven't you got some important computations to do?"

Spock hesitated, started to say something and thought better of it, turning back to his console.

Meanwhile, Captain Koloth and his first officer were deep in a strategy conference. The next move was theirs. Koloth finally muttered to Korax, "Initiate boarding plan C." The first officer's eyes lit and he replied enthusiastically.

"Yes, Exalted One!"

Kirk was still eyeing the behemoth tribble purring noisily in his chair when everything that had been floating loose in his head suddenly got together. He walked over to Scott, who was monitoring the engineering console and looking distraught.

"Mr. Scott," he instructed, a slightly dreamy, thoughtful expression on his face, "we are going to implement Emergency Defense Plan B."

"Yes, sir," Scott answered snappily. "Emergency Defense Plan B." A look of uncertainty came over him and he asked hesitantly, "Ah, Captain ... I don't believe I'm familiar with Emergency Defense Plan B."

"That's because it's only used in extremely unusual circumstances, Mr. Scott."

"Oh," the chief engineer commented.

"And also," he added, turning away, "because I've just made it up—thanks to a suggestion by Mr. Spock. Stand by."

"Standin' by, sir," Scott said, still puzzled but ready for orders.

Odd, Scott mused. The ship's engines and all of their weaponry were frozen; the Klingons were threatening to take over the ship; they were suffering under the combined appetites of an influx of Fafnirian tribbles—and yet it had seemed as if Kirk had a smile on his face ...

Korax studied his personal timer. Twenty-two *kuvits* had passed since the final warning had been given to Captain Kirk of the *Enterprise*. It had taken that long to assemble the forces necessary to implement the assault plan. Kirk would never be able to claim he had not been given sufficient time to think over the surrender terms.

Now it was too late. He stood by the chief transporter officer of the *Devisor* and watched the first platoon of Klingon marines assemble in the transporter chamber.

The sudden appearance of a large, well coordinated boarding party on board might not be a total surprise to the Federation crew ... but it should have no trouble overwhelming any resistance. The supposedly peaceful Federation starships carried no such trained attack groups.

He nodded to the officer in charge, who started to advance his men to positions within the transporter alcove. The officer took a step forward—and froze, gaping.

Something was materializing, not only in the alcove

itself but in the room. Several marines moved aside, hands edging nervously toward their disruptor pistols. Had Kirk decided on the same course of action as Captain Koloth? It seemed wholly out of character, and yet . . .

The transporter effect intensified. Faint, huge silhouettes began to form. Abruptly, the effect faded—and every Klingon in the chamber recoiled in horror.

Suddenly, the room was filled with giant emotionally disturbed tribbles.

And in the corridors, in storage holds, in private rooms startled crew members were treated to the most unwelcome sight of tribbles abruptly materializing in front of them, behind them, and, in the case of one nearly suffocated dozer, on top of them.

Scott kept a close watch on his console and a ready ear to the com. linkup with the transporters. Moving the tribbles to the *Enterprise*'s transporters at first had looked like an impossible task, until someone had suggested a method almost too simple.

All they had to do was have any human crew member demonstrate affection toward one of the furry goliaths. Whereupon, cooing and mewing like any healthy tribble, it would follow the coaxing human to any point in the ship.

Scott's smile widened. The Klingons, of course, would be utterly unable to duplicate this maneuver. No self-respecting tribble would have anything to do with a Klingon. He didn't envy any member of the *Devisor*'s crew who tried.

Chief Kyle concluded this report at the other end of the com. Several stats were relayed to Scott, who surveyed them briefly, then looked over to the waiting Kirk.

"Emergency Plan B complete, sir. Chief Kyle reports all transporting has been carried out as directed."

"Open hailing frequencies, Lieutenant."

Uhura acknowledged and seconds later the portrait of an as yet unruffled Captain Koloth appeared on the screen.

"Captain Koloth, are you prepared to release my ship yet?"

Koloth stared back incredulously. "Release your ship? Kirk, you are monotonous. Your ship's armament is completely inoperative and in a few minutes you will not even have the option of surrender."

"That's not an option I require, Koloth," Kirk countered. "You don't know yet then, do you?"

"Know," said Koloth irritably. "Know what?"

"That we have immobilized your ship worse than you have immobilized ours."

"I doubt that. Our instruments report nothing except some fragmentary transporter activity and . . ." He paused and a thoughtful expression came over his face. "You could not transport any weapons aboard, of course, and you wouldn't attempt an assault with armed personnel, but . . ." A longer pause now.

"Kirk?"

"Yes, Captain? What seems to be the matter? Are you feeling all right? If not, I'd suggest . . ."

"Tribbles, Kirk?"

The Captain's grin grew even wider. "Tribbles."

Koloth started to say something, was interrupted as a Klingon junior officer entered the picture. The two conversed below range of the aural pickup for several moments. The junior officer spoke rapidly, punctuating his words with many erratic gestures. Koloth's face went through a repertoire of expressions suprising even for a Klingon. When the junior officer had left the picture, the *Devisor*'s commander turned slowly back to face the screen.

"Kirk, I am compelled by circumstances to reveal an Imperial scientific secret. When the full report of this incident is known, I shall probably be chastized for it. I may be broken. But under the circumstances I see no alternative.

"Cyrano Jones stole a Klingon genetic construct—an artificially produced creature—from one of our worlds. It was designed to be a tribble predator. It is the prototype, and the only one to survive many hundreds of attempts at cross-breeding.

"We *must* have it back. I am authorized to use any means to secure its return. I hope that includes imparting this sensitive information to you. The Imperium is willing to chance war to gain its return."

"Surely you don't expect me to believe you can't produce others?"

"That is precisely the situation, Kirk." A hint of desperation had crept into Koloth's voice. No talk of surrender now. "I am told that the production of this first success cannot be duplicated. Apparently its creation was as much the result of chance as careful planning.

"This specimen can, however, reproduce by asexual division. We must have it in order to produce others from it. And we need those to get rid of the tribbles Jones disposed of before they completely overrun the world on which he left them."

"And that's all you want—the predator?" Kirk asked.

Koloth gathered himself. "I am prepared to forgo my demand for the return of Jones. But we must have the glommer."

"Oh well," Kirk replied easily, "if that's all." He glanced back. "Mr. Scott, instruct Chief Kyle to transport the glommer over to the *Devisor*. We do have the glommer?"

"Aye, sir. Mr. Jones recovered it himself as we were drivin' the tribbles to the transporters."

Two security guards hustled Jones along between them some minutes later. He seemed somewhat reluctant to part with "his" glommer. It nestled under one of his arms. He was looking around wildly. His gaze finally settled on Scott, who had come down to join Kyle for the crucial transfer.

"You can't do this to me! Under space salvage laws it's mine." He stroked the glommer possessively and it growled softly once.

Scott sounded tried. "As you well know, a planetary surface is not exactly covered by free-space salvage statutes. But if it's a matter of sentimental attachment, that might put a different light on things, Jones."

The trader looked hopeful.

"If you're that attached to the little beastie, I wouldn't dream of separatin' the two of you."

Jones looked wary, but still hopeful. "And that is the case, Mr. Scott." He stroked it again, made babying noises at it. "I couldn't bear to be parted from my little glommer, after all we've gone through together. It's almost like a child to me, a part of my own self!"

"I understand," Scott confessed. "So . . . we'll transport you over with it."

"Given the current situation and in the interests of interstellar cooperation," Jones said at breakneck speed, "I withdraw my claim."

Without shedding so much as a tear, Jones put the glommer in the transporter, backed out. Scott nodded to Kyle, who engaged the transporter.

On the bridge, Kirk noted the subsidence of the stasis field concurrent with the glommer's transporting. Resumption of full power was suitably detailed by Sulu and Arex. Almost immediately thereafter, the *Devisor* was seen moving away at high speed.

Kirk watched it go, feeling better than he had in some time. "At least we can submit a detailed report on the stasis weapon . . . and although something will have to be found as a defense against it, it's far from being a superweapon. The power drain makes it vulnerable to a second ship. It's main value is in convincing us of its omnipotence, and we've exploded that possibility."

"Quite so, Captain," commented Spock thoughtfully. "Tribbles appear to be a much more effective weapon."

There was a buzz from his chair com. and he acknowledged. "Yes?"

McCoy here, Jim. I'd like you and Spock to come down to the lab. I've made an interesting discovery."

After assuring himself that the *Devisor* was too far away to catch them even at top pursuit speed, Kirk took Spock and made his way down to Sick Bay.

Moments later they found themselves examining the

single giant tribble Bones had saved for experimental purposes. It sat behind a glass wall and munched happily on leftovers from the third shift's lunch.

"You see, Jim, Jones' genetic engineering was very slipshod. He fooled us at first but it's doubtful he could have hidden the truth forever. These tribbles don't reproduce, just as he claimed . . . when *they're normal sized.*

"But because he didn't slow their metabolism permanently, his secret would reveal itself eventually. These aren't giant tribbles . . . they're cooperative colonies. Like our coral, for example, only softer."

"Then that means . . . ," Kirk began, staring at the hulking yellow tribble, "that . . ."

McCoy nodded silently.

Both of Spock's eyebrows went up.

On board the *Devisor*, Koloth was heading for the engine room. He was holding the glommer and stroking it gently. Since glommers shared their disposition, they didn't dislike Klingons. A frantic, excited Korax met him in the passageway.

"Captain, report from Chief Engineer Kurr. His people have had to evacuate the engine room and operate the ship on automatic because the main engine chamber is filled with tribbles."

"I know," Koloth replied with a vicious smile. "We can finally do something about that. Then we're going back after the *Enterprise*."

"But sir . . ." Korax was desperately trying to add something, but Koloth waved him off.

"You'll see, Korax."

Together, they approached the access door to the main engine room. While Korax stood back doubtfully, Koloth put the glommer on the deck opposite the door. Stepping back, he activated the door and focused his attention on the poised glommer.

In fact, his attention was so focused on the glommer that he did not notice the sudden alteration of his first officer's expression, nor what had caused it.

He spoke directly to the glommer. "Attack!"

The glommer seemed to lean back. And back . . . and back. It gave a funny little shake, turned and rocketed off down the corridor in a series of olympian hops, making a sound like a dog with empty tin cans tied to its tail.

Koloth abruptly grew aware of another sound, a low, rhythmic rumbling which a Terran would have likened to an idling locomotive. To Koloth it sounded like approaching thunder.

The captain turned quickly, backed away from the source of that deep-throated pulsing. It was horrible, it was ghastly . . .

It was the angry mewing of a two-ton tribble that filled the *Devisor*'s engine room from floor to ceiling.

"He did it again," he swore. "That plated, overbearing excuse for a starship captain did it to us again!" He jabbed a finger at the growling colossus.

In such an emotional moment, even an Imperial board of inquiry would find reasons for absolving Koloth for an instinctive reaction.

Korax didn't stop to think, either. Instead, he whipped out his disruptor pistol and fired with admirable speed. The miniature bolts from the powerful hand weapon contacted the furry yellow wall. A bright flash temporarily blinded both officers.

Koloth felt the new pressure at his legs and waist even before vision returned. He tried to move . . . first to his right, then left, forward and back. No luck. He was thoroughly pinned in place by . . . something.

Another blink cleared his eyes and revealed the reason.

The entire corridor—all the way from the nearest bend to the depths of the engine room—was now hip deep in tribbles. Not giant tribbles but large normal tribbles. Very large normal tribbles.

Tribbles didn't like Klingons.

"Let us not panic, Korax," instructed Koloth. He was calm, he told himself. Quite calm. "Let us try to move one step at a time toward the nearest exit."

Both men tried to move, found that even the slightest attempt produced a frightening rise in the volume of mewing around them.

"I don't seem to be making any progress, Exalted One. Should I. . . ?" He held up his disruptor pistol.

"Put that away, you idiot!" Koloth cursed . . . but softly, softly. "Don't ever do that again. I'll break you to sanitation engineer . . . twelfth class."

"Yes, sir," said an abashed Korax, suddenly aware of what he had been about to do. He put the pistol away slowly. Both officers stood in the sea of nervous tribbles and stared at each other.

After several long minutes, Korax ventured to ask, "What now, Exalted One?"

"Now, Korax? We wait till we are rescued, of course. I don't know what else to do. Have you any brilliant suggestions, perhaps?"

"No, sir. There's just one thing."

"Well, what is it?"

The first officer of the *Devisor* looked down.

"Either we're shrinking, sir, or these tribbles are getting bigger."

Koloth made a strangled sound . . .

Kirk, Spock, Scott and Jones stood in the lab and watched the giant tribble shiver while McCoy explained what was happening.

"A simple shot of neo-ethylene fixes everything, gentlemen. The catalyst drug induces the tribble colony to break down into its individual smaller units . . . but also enables them to retain their engineered metabolic stability. These really *will* be safe tribbles."

Even as he spoke, the oversized tribble was rapidly collapsing into dozens of little, normal tribbles . . . like a big fuzzy ice cube melting into chunks.

"What about the Klingons?" asked Jones.

McCoy thought a moment, spoke slowly. "Unless they discover how to treat their tribbles—and do so soon—the *Devisor* isn't going to be big enough for all

of them. Even if they do so, of course, the smaller tribbles will still retain their dislike of Klingons."

Kirk turned to leave, stopped as he spotted something up near a Jeffries tube. "Say, here's one you
didn't get, Bones."

McCoy came over, glanced up the tube also. "Yes, I
did, Jim." He turned to inspect one of the small tribbles, let it crawl up his arm, purring.

"But it hasn't . . . ," Kirk began. He was drowned out
by a loud, muffled *flumpppp!* as the hidden giant colony suddenly dissolved into hundreds of component
tribbles.

Kirk dug himself out of the mound of cooing, pulsing balls, spat out a mouthful of tribble fur and gazing
imploringly heavenward.

"Someday I'll learn," he murmured solemnly.

"Aye, Captain," agreed Scotty, standing nearby and
observing the talus of the hirsute avalanche. "But
you've got to admit, if we have to have tribbles, it's
best if all our tribbles are little ones . . ."

The orange tribble that Kirk threw mewed indignantly as it bounced off the chief engineer's retreating
back . . .